# THE CAT WHO
# TAILED
# A THIEF

G·K
Hall
&C⁰

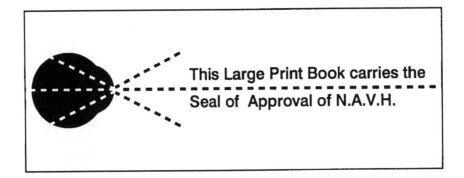

# THE CAT WHO TAILED A THIEF

## LILIAN JACKSON BRAUN

**G.K. Hall & Co.**
**Thorndike, Maine**

Published in 1997 by arrangement with G.P. Putnam's Sons.

G.K. Hall Large Print Core Collection.

The text of this Large Print edition is unabridged.
Other aspects of the book may vary from the original edition.

Set in 16 pt. Plantin by Al Chase.

Printed in the United States on permanent paper.

---

**Library of Congress Cataloging in Publication Data**

Braun, Lilian Jackson.
   The Cat who tailed a thief / Lillian [i.e. Lilian] Jackson Braun.
      p.  cm.
   ISBN 0-7838-8046-4 (lg. print : hc)
   ISBN 0-7838-8047-2 (lg. print : sc)
   1. Large type books. 2. Qwilleran, Jim (Fictitious character) —
Fiction. 3. Journalists — United States — Fiction. 4. Siamese
cat — United States — Fiction 5. Cats — United States —
Fiction. I. Title.
   [PS3552.R354C365  1997b]
   813'.54—dc21                                              96-39481

Dedicated to Earl Bettinger,
The Husband Who. . . .

It was a strange winter in Moose County, 400 miles north of everywhere. First, there was disagreement about the long-range weather forecast. The weatherman at the local radio station predicted a winter of zero temperature, daily snow, minus-sixty windchill, and paralyzing blizzards — in other words: normal. On the other hand, farmers and woodsmen who observed the behavior of the fuzzy caterpillars insisted the winter would be mild. Bad news!

No one wanted a mild winter. Merchants had invested in large inventories of snowblowers, antifreeze, snowshoes, and long johns. The farmers themselves needed a heavy snow cover to ensure a good summer crop. Dogsledders and icefishermen stood to lose a whole season of wholesome outdoor sport. As for the First Annual Ice Festival, it was doomed. All that — plus the unthinkable possibility of a green Christmas!

Throughout November, traditionally a month of natural disasters, the weather was disappointingly good, and the natives cursed the fuzzy caterpillars. Then . . . suddenly, in mid-December, temperatures plummeted and a few inches of no-melt snow started to fall every day. In downtown Pickax, the county seat, the Department of Public Works plows threw up the usual eight-foot walls of snow along curbs and around parking lots. Young people did their Christmas shopping on cross-country skis, and sleigh bells could be heard on Main Street. Best of all, the schools closed twice during the month because of blizzard conditions.

The weather was only the first strange happening of the winter, however. In late December, an outbreak of petty larceny dampened the holiday spirit in Pickax. Trivial items began to disappear from cars and public places, prompting the local newspaper to run an editorial:

Play Safe! Lock Up! Be Alert!

You leave a video on the seat of your car while paying for self-serve gas. You never see it again.

You forget your gloves in the post office. Minutes later, they're gone.

You hang your sun-glare glasses on a supermarket cart while you select oranges. The glasses disappear.

Who is to blame? Mischievous kids? Gremlins? Your failing memory? The time has come to stop searching for excuses and start playing safe. In Moose County we're foolishly lax about security. We must learn to lock our cars . . . put valuables in the trunk . . . keep an eye on belongings . . . stay alert!

Some say the incidents are minor, and the

pilfering is a temporary nuisance like Mosquito Week in spring. If that's what you think, listen to our police chief, Andrew Brodie, who says, "A community that tolerates minor violations leaves the door open for major crimes."

Natives of Moose County were a stubborn, independent breed descended from early pioneers, and it would take more than an editorial in the *Moose County Something* to change their ways. Yet, there was one prominent citizen who applauded the police chief's maxim.

Jim Qwilleran was not a native but a transplant from Down Below, as the locals called the metropolitan cities to the south. Surprising circumstances had brought him to Pickax (population 3,000), and he was surprisingly content with small-town life.

Qwilleran was a tall, well-built, middle-aged man with a luxuriant pepper-and-salt moustache and hair graying at the temples. If asked, he would say that he perceived himself as:

A journalist, semi-retired.

A former crime reporter and author of a book on urban crime.

Writer of a twice-weekly column for the *Something*.

Devoted friend of Polly Duncan, head of the Pickax Public Library.

Protector and slave of two Siamese cats.

Fairly agreeable person blessed with many

friends. All of that would be true . . . He would not perceive himself, however, as the richest man in the northeast central United States, but that, too, would be true.

An enormous inheritance, the Klingenschoen fortune, had brought Qwilleran to this remote region. Yet, he was uncomfortable with money — its trappings as well as its responsibilities — and he immediately consigned his billions to philanthropic purposes. For several years, the Klingenschoen Foundation had been managed by a Chicago think tank, with little or no attention from James Mackintosh Qwilleran.

It was not only this generous gesture that caused him to be esteemed in Moose County. Admirers cited his entertaining column, "Straight from the Qwill Pen" . . . his amiable disposition and sense of humor . . . his lack of pretension . . . his sympathetic way of listening . . . and, of course, his magnificent moustache. Its drooping contours, together with his brooding eyes, gave him a look of melancholy that made people wonder about his past. Actually, there was more to that moustache than met the eye.

On the morning of December 23, Qwilleran said good-bye to the Siamese and gave instructions for their deportment in his absence. The more intelligently one talks to cats, he believed, the smarter they become. Their deep blue eyes gazed at him soberly. Did they know what he was saying? Or were they waiting patiently for him to leave so they could start their morning nap?

He was setting out to do his Christmas shopping, but first he had to hand in his copy at the newspaper office: a thousand words on Santa Claus for the "Qwill Pen." It was hardly a newsworthy topic, but he had a columnist's knack of making it sound fresh.

The premises of the *Moose County Something* were always devoid of seasonal decorations, leaving such frivolities to stores and restaurants. Qwilleran was surprised, therefore, to see a small decorated tree on a file cabinet in the publisher's office. Arch Riker, his lifelong friend and fellow journalist, had followed him to Pickax to be publisher and editor-in-chief of the new backwoods paper. A paunchy, ruddy-faced man with thinning hair, he sat in a high-backed executive chair and looked happy. Not only had he realized his dream of running his own newspaper; he had married the plump and congenial woman who wrote the food page.

"Mildred and I are expecting you and Polly to have Christmas dinner with us," he reminded Qwilleran.

"Turkey, I hope," he replied, thinking of leftovers for his housemates. "What's that tree on your file cabinet?"

"It was Wilfred's idea," Riker said almost apologetically. "He made the ornaments with newsprint and gold spray."

Wilfred Sugbury was secretary to the executives — a quiet, hardworking young man who

11

had not only amazed the staff by winning a seventy-mile bike race but was now taking an origami course at the community college. Qwilleran, on his way out, complimented Wilfred on his handiwork.

"I'd be glad to make one for you, Mr. Q," he said.

"It wouldn't last five minutes, Wilfred. The cats would reduce it to confetti. They have no appreciation of art. Thanks just the same."

To fortify himself for the task of gift-shopping, Qwilleran drove to Lois's Luncheonette, a primitive side-street hole-in-the-wall that had been serving comfort food to downtown workers and shoppers for thirty years. Lois Inchpot was an imposing woman, who dispensed pancakes and opinions with the authority of a celebrity. Indeed, the city had recently celebrated Lois Inchpot Day, by mayoral proclamation.

When Qwilleran entered, she was banging the old-fashioned cash register and holding forth in a throaty voice: "If we have a mild winter, like the caterpillars said, we'll be swamped with bugs next summer! . . . Hi, Mr. Q! Come on in! Sit anywhere that ain't sticky. My customers got bad aim with the syrup bottle."

"How's Lenny?" Qwilleran asked. Her son had been hurt in an explosion.

"That boy of mine!" she said proudly. "Nothin' stops him! He has mornin' classes at the college, and then he's found himself a swell part-time job, managin' the clubhouse at Indian Village. He gave you as a reference, Mr. Q. Hope you don't mind."

"He's going to be a workaholic like his mother."

"Better'n takin' after his father! . . . Done your Christmas shoppin', Mr. Q?"

"Don't rush me, Lois. It's only the twenty-third."

The first gift he purchased was a bottle of Scotch. He carried it in a brown paper bag under his folded jacket when he climbed the stairs to police headquarters at city hall. He was a frequent visitor, and the sergeant at the desk jerked his head toward the inner office, saying, "He's in." The chief was visible through a glass partition, hunched over the computer that he earnestly hated.

Brodie was a tough cop who resented civilian interference, and yet he had learned to appreciate the newsman's tips and opinions that sometimes helped crack a case. On the job he had old-fash-ioned ideas of law and order and a gruff manner to match. Off duty, he was a genial Scot who played the bagpipe and strutted in a kilt at civic functions.

Qwilleran, placing his jacket carefully on a chairseat and sliding into another, said, "I see you got your name in the paper again, Andy. Who's your press agent? Planning to run for mayor? I'll campaign for you."

With a fierce scowl usually reserved for the

computer, Brodie shot back, "If I had an over-grown moustache like yours, I'd get my picture in the paper, too. What's on your mind?"

"I want to know if you believe what you said in the paper."

"It's a known fact! Let the hoods urinate in public and — next thing you know — they're spray-painting the courthouse, and after that they're pushing drugs, and then robbing banks, and then killing cops."

"Any suspects in the pilfering?"

The chief leaned back in his chair and folded his arms. "Could be punks from Chipmunk. Could be a roving gang from Lockmaster. Could be the kids that hang around George Breze's dump. We're investigating."

"Do you see any pattern developing? There should be a pattern by now."

"Well, for one thing, there's a pattern in what they don't do. They don't steal Social Security checks from mailboxes, or rip out car radios, or break into doctors' offices. It's all piddlin' stuff, so far. Another thing: There's no two incidents alike, and locations are scattered. It always happens after dark, too. They avoid shoplifting in stores with bright lights and wide-awake clerks."

Qwilleran said, "I've been thinking it could be a game, like a treasure hunt — perhaps initiation rites for a juvenile cult."

"We've talked to school principals and Dr. Prelligate at the college. They say there's no sign of suspicious activity."

"They'd be the last to know," Qwilleran muttered.

"There's another possibility. I predicted something like this after the financial bust in Sawdust City. The town's had a lot of hardship cases this winter, and it's rough to be hard-up at Christmastime, especially if you've got kids."

"But the organized charities have raised record sums for the Christmas Fund, and the K Foundation is matching their efforts, dollar for dollar."

"I know, but some cases always fall through the cracks, or they panic and try to take things in their own hands." He indulged in a bitter chuckle. "Perhaps they hit on the secret: How to do Christmas shopping without money and without crowds."

Qwilleran said, "If the thefts are scattered, as you say, someone's buying a lot of gas to drive around and swipe trivial items. It must be a group effort."

Brodie threw up his hands. "The whole thing's crazy!"

"Okay, let me add an incident to your list. This is the reason I'm here." Qwilleran paused until he had the man's curiosity aroused. "We all know the Old Stone Church is collecting warm clothing for needy families. There's a drop-off box behind the building. Every Wednesday the volunteers show up for sorting and mending. I told them I'd drop off a bundle Tuesday night — which I did — a plastic bag

15

full of things in good condition: jackets, sweaters, gloves, etc. But when they opened the box the next morning, it wasn't there. They phoned me to see if I'd forgotten."

The chief grunted. "No lock on the box?"

"Who thinks about locks in this neck of the woods? That was the thrust of our editorial! We nagged our readers into buckling up; now we'll nag them into locking up."

Brodie chuckled again. "If you spot a guy walking around town in your rags, follow him and take his picture."

"Sure. And ask for his name and address."

"My old grandmother in Scotland could tail a thief with scissors, a piece of string, and a witch's chant. Too bad she died before I got into law enforcement." Then he grinned. "Why don't you assign your smart cat to the case?" The chief was the only person in the north country who knew about the remarkable talents of Qwilleran's male Siamese. The cat did indeed have gifts that set him apart, and Qwilleran tried to conceal the fact, for various reasons. Yet it had leaked to Brodie from a source Down Below, and now the two men bantered about "that smart cat" whose highly developed senses gave him an edge over most humans.

"Koko doesn't accept assignments," Qwilleran said with a straight face. "He conducts his own investigations. Right now he has a gang of wild rabbits under surveillance." Then he added in a serious tone, "But last night, Andy, he jumped

16

on my bookshelf and knocked down a Russian novel titled *The Thief.* Was that a coincidence, or what?"

"Does he read Russian?" Brodie asked, only half in jest.

"Mine is an English translation."

The chief grunted ambiguously and changed the subject. "I hear you and your smart cat aren't living in the barn this winter. How come?" There was disappointment in the question. He often visited the converted apple barn after hours, dropping in for a nightcap and some shoptalk. Qwilleran, though not a drinker himself, stocked the best brands for his guests.

"It's like this, Andy," he explained. "With four stories of wide-open space, it's impossible to heat evenly. The top balcony is like a sauna while the main floor is chilly. The cats used to go to the top level to get warm, and they'd end up half-cooked. They were so groggy from the heat, they couldn't walk straight. So I bought a condo in Indian Village for the cold months. I can rent it to vacationers in summer. It's nowhere near the size of the barn, of course, but it's adequate, and the county snowplows keep the access road open, for the simple reason that so many politicos live out there . . . By the way, I had my condo furnished by your talented daughter."

The chief nodded a grudging acknowledgment of the family compliment. In spite of Fran Brodie's success as an interior designer, her father considered it a frivolous choice of career.

Standing up and presenting the brown paper bag, Qwilleran said, "Here's a wee dram of Christmas cheer, Andy. See you after the holidays."

In earlier days Qwilleran had been frugal by nature and by necessity — while growing up with a single parent, earning his way through college, and working as an underpaid reporter Down Below. His new financial status had introduced him to the luxury of largesse, however. He still practiced certain economies, such as buying used cars for himself, but he enjoyed giving presents, buying drinks, sending flowers, treating companions to dinner, and tipping generously.

When he finally tackled his Christmas shopping on December 23, his list was a long one. Fortunately, he was a speedy shopper who made quick decisions and never had to ask prices. For his shopping spree he left his car in the municipal parking lot, then zipped up his padded jacket, yanked down his wool earflaps, pulled on his lined gloves, and trudged around downtown in snowboots.

Main Street was thronged with shoppers weaving merrily between head-high walls of snow. There was a wintry sun, just bright enough to make the flecks of mica sparkle in the stone facades of store and office buildings, and garlands of greens festooned from rooftops and looped across the street between lightpoles. The babble of voices and rumble of slow-moving vehicles were hushed by the tons of snow piled everywhere and packed hard between the curbs. (Roadways were not salted in Moose County.) Yet, strangely, the acoustical phenomenon emphasized the bursts of Christmas music, the occasional jingle of sleigh bells, and the brassy clang of Santa's handbell on the street corner.

First Qwilleran went to Lanspeaks' Department Store to buy something for Polly Duncan, the main name on his gift list. Carol Lanspeak herself waited on him. She and her husband were an admirable pair: good business heads, civic leaders, and major talents in the Pickax Theatre Club. If they had not come home to Pickax to run the family business, Qwilleran believed, Larry and Carol could have been another Cronyn and Tandy, or Lunt and Fontanne.

Carol said to him with a touch of fond rebuke, "I knew you'd pop in at the last minute, so I set aside a suit in Polly's size, a lovely suede in terracotta. She's down to a size fourteen since her surgery. What did those cardiovascular people *do to her?*"

"They convinced her to go for two-mile walks and give up all my favorite foods."

"Well, she looks wonderful! And she's drifting away from those dreary grays and blues."

Qwilleran gave the suit a single glance and said, "I'll take it."

"There's also a silk blouse with a lot of zing that'll —"

"I'll take that, too." The blouse was patterned

19

in an overscaled houndstooth check in terra-cotta and British white.

"Polly will swoon over it!" Carol promised.

"Polly doesn't swoon easily," he said. She was a charming woman of his own age, with a soft and musical voice, but there was an iron hand in the velvet glove that ran the public library.

"Where are you two spending Christmas day, Qwill?"

"With the Rikers. Do you and Larry have big plans?"

"We'll have our daughter and her current friend, of course, and we've invited the Carmichaels and their houseguest. Do you see much of Willard and Danielle?"

Not if I can help it, Qwilleran thought. Politely he said, "Our paths don't seem to cross very often." It was the Lanspeaks who had introduced him to the new banker and his flashy young wife. Her frank flirtiness, sidelong glances, raucous voice, and breathy stares at his moustache annoyed him.

"I'm afraid," Carol said regretfully, "that Danielle isn't adjusting well to small-town life. She's always comparing Pickax to Detroit and Baltimore, where they have *malls!* Willard says she's homesick. That's why they invited her cousin from Down Below to spend the holidays." She lowered her voice. "Step into my office, Qwill."

He followed her to the cluttered cubicle adjoining the women's department.

"Sit down," she said. "I feel sorry for Danielle. People are saying unkind things, but she's asking for it. She looks so freaky! By Pickax standards, at any rate. Skirts too short, heels too high, everything too tight, pounds of makeup, hair like a rat's nest . . . ! It may be fashionable Down Below, but when in Rome —"

"She needs a mentor," Qwilleran interrupted. "Couldn't Fran Brodie drop a few hints? She's glamorous and yet has class, and she's helping Danielle with her house."

"Fran's been dropping hints, Qwill, but . . ." Carol shrugged. "You'd think her husband would say something. He's an intelligent man, and he's fitting right into the community. Willard has joined the chamber of commerce and the Boosters Club and is helping to organize a gourmet club. Yet, when Larry submitted his name to the country club for membership, nothing happened. They never sent the Carmichaels an invitation! We all know why. Danielle's flamboyant manner of dress and grooming and deportment raises eyebrows and causes snickers. They call her voice cheap. It *is* rather strident."

"Rather," Qwilleran said. It was unusual for Carol to be so critical and so candid.

"Well, let me know if you think of something we can do . . . Shall I gift-wrap Polly's suit and blouse?"

"Please. I'll pick them up later. Go easy on the bows and jingle bells."

He next went to Amanda's Design Studio, hop-

21

ing to find a decorative object for the Rikers and hoping that Fran Brodie would be in-house. The police chief's daughter was out, unfortunately, and her cantankerous boss was in charge. Amanda Goodwinter was a successful business-woman and a perennial member of the Pickax City Council, always re-elected because of her name. The Goodwinters had founded Pickax in the mid-1800s.

Amanda's greeting was characteristically blunt. "If you're looking for a free cup of coffee, you're out of luck. The coffeemaker's on the blink." Her unruly gray hair and drab, shapeless clothing were considered "interestingly individual" by her loyal customers. Her political enemies called her the bag lady of Pickax.

To tease her, Qwilleran said he wanted to buy a knickknack for a gift.

She bristled. "We don't sell knickknacks!"

"Semantics! Semantics! Then how about a bibelot for Arch and Mildred Riker?"

She huffed and scowled and suggested a colorful ceramic coffeepot, its surface a mass of sculptured grapes, apples, and pears.

"Isn't it a trifle gaudy?" Qwilleran complained.

"Gaudy! What are you saying?" Amanda shouted in her council chamber voice. "It's Majolica! It's hand-painted! It's old! It's expensive! The Rikers will be crazy about it!"

"I'll take it," Qwilleran said, knowing that Mildred was a collector with an artist's eye and Arch was a collector with an eye for the bottom line. "And I'd like it gift-wrapped, but don't fuss."

"I never fuss!"

For the other names on his list he relied on the new Sip 'n' Nibble shop. They would make up gift baskets of wine, cheese, and other treats and deliver them anywhere in the county by Christmas Eve.

On a whim he also went into the men's store to buy a waggish tie for Riker, who was known for his conservative neckwear. It was bright blue with a pattern of lifesize baseballs, white stitched in red. He hoped it would get a laugh.

His final stop was the Pickax People's Bank to cash a check, and the sight of the famous moustache created a stir. Customers, tellers, and security personnel smiled, waved, and greeted him:

"Merry Christmas, Mr. Q!"

"All ready for Santa, Mr. Q?"

"Finished your Christmas shopping, Mr. Q?"

He responded with courteous bows and salutes and took his place in line.

The gray-haired woman ahead of him stepped aside. "Are you in a hurry, Mr. Q? You can go first."

"No, no, no," he remonstrated. "Thank you, but stay where you are. I like to stand in line behind an attractive woman."

The commotion brought a man striding from an inner office with hand outstretched. "Qwill! You're the exact person I want to see! Come into my office!" The new banker had the suave manner, expensive suit, and styled hair of a newcomer from Down Below.

Qwilleran followed him into the presidential suite and noted a few changes: a younger secretary, more colorful furnishings, and art on the walls.

"Have a chair," Carmichael said. "I hear you're living in Indian Village now."

"Only for the winter. The barn's not practical in cold weather. How about you? Have you moved into your house?"

"No, we're still camping out in an apartment at the Village. Danielle has ordered a lot of stuff for the house, but it takes forever to get delivery. Expensive as hell, too, but that's all right. My sweetheart likes to spend money, and whatever keeps her happy keeps me happy . . . Say, are you free for dinner tonight? I've been wanting us to get together."

Qwilleran hesitated. "Well . . . it's rather short notice, you know." Willard, he decided, was okay, but the googly-eyed Danielle made him uncomfortable.

Carmichael went on. "I'm baching it tonight. Danielle is taking our houseguest to Otto's Tasty Eats — a vile restaurant, if you ask me — so I told her I had to work. Her cousin is spending the holidays with us."

"Well . . . with a little judicious finagling . . . I could manage to be free. Where would you like to go?"

"Where could we get pasties? I've never had a pasty. I don't even know what it is."

"It's the official specialty of Moose County, dating back to mining days," Qwilleran said. "And it's pronounced to rhyme with *nasty*, by the way."

"I stand corrected," the banker said.

"It's an enormous meat-and-potato turnover — okay for a picnic but not for a civilized dinner. Have you been to Onoosh's café?"

"No, Danielle doesn't like Mediterranean. When I was in Detroit, though, I used to haunt Greektown for shish kebab, taramasalata, and saganaki . . . Oopah! Oopah!"

"That's the spirit!" Qwilleran said. "Suppose we meet at Onoosh's whenever you're free. I have to go home and . . . feed the cats." He was wearing knockabout clothes, but if he had said, "I want to go home and change," Willard would have said, "Don't bother. Come as you are. I'll take off my tie."

Going home to feed the cats was an excuse that was never challenged.

# 2

Qwilleran drove home to Indian Village in his four-wheel-drive vehicle, considered advisable for winter in the country. Having traded in his compact sedan for a medium-size van, he was pleased to find it convenient on many occasions, such as trips to the veterinarian with the cats' travel coop. It was almost new — only thirty thousand miles — and Scott Gippel had given him a good trade-in allowance.

Indian Village on Ittibittiwassee Road was well outside the Pickax city limits. It was debatable whether the drive was more beautiful in summer's verdure or winter's chiaroscuro, when bare trees and dark evergreens were silhouetted against the endless blanket of white. Along the way was the abandoned Buckshot mine and its ghostly shafthouse, fenced with chain-link and posted as dangerous. Just beyond was the bridge over the Ittibittiwassee River, which then veered and paralleled the highway to Indian Village and beyond.

Geographically and politically the Village was in Suffix Township; psychologically it was in a world of its own, being an upscale address for a variety of interesting residents. At the entrance, a gate gave an air of exclusivity, but it was always open, giving an air of hospitality. The buildings were rustic board-and-batten compatible with the wooded site, summer and winter, starting with the gatehouse and the clubhouse. Apartments were clustered in small buildings randomly situated on Woodland Trail. Condominiums in strips of four contiguous units extended along River Lane, close to the water that rushed over rocks or swirled in pools. Even in winter a trickle could be heard underneath the snow and ice.

As Qwilleran neared his own condo in Building Five, he began to think about his housemates. Would they greet him excitedly? — meaning hungrily. Would they be dead asleep on the sofa, curled together in a single heap of fur? Would they have pushed the phone off the hook, or upchucked a hairball, or broken a lamp during a mad chase?

Before unlocking his own door, he delivered the groceries he had picked up for Polly. He had a key to her unit at the other end of the row. Even while unlocking her door he began talking to her watchcat, Bootsie, explaining that he was there on legitimate business and would simply refrigerate the perishables and leave.

His own Siamese were sitting in the window overlooking the riverbank, sitting contentedly on their briskets, listening to the trickle beneath the snow and ice. The wintry sun bounced off the white landscape, making a giant reflector that illuminated their silky fawn-colored coats and accentuated their seal-brown points.

"Hello, you guys," Qwilleran said. "How's

everything? Any excitement around here? What's the rabbit count today?"

Languorously, both cats stood up, humped their backs in a horseshoe curve, and then stretched two forelegs and one hind leg. The male was Kao K'o Kung (Koko, for short) — the "smart cat" in Brodie's book. He was sleek and muscular with a commanding set of whiskers and intense blue eyes that hinted at cosmic secrets. Yum Yum, the female, was delicate and outrageously affectionate. Her large, limpid blue eyes were violet-tinged. Being Siamese, they were both highly vocal, Koko yowling a chesty baritone and Yum Yum uttering a blood-chilling soprano shriek when it was least expected.

Qwilleran brought in the gift-wrapped packages from his van, read the mail picked up at the gatehouse, made some phone calls, fed the cats, and changed into a tweed sports coat over a turtleneck jersey. Polly had told him he looked particularly good in turtlenecks; their simplicity was a foil for his handsome moustache. He was half pleased and half annoyed by everyone's preoccupation with his unique facial adornment. Fran Brodie called it a Second Empire moustache, as if it were a piece of furniture.

What no one knew, of course, was its functional significance to its owner. Whenever Qwilleran suspected that something was false or out-of-order in any way, he felt a tingling sensation on his upper lip. Experience had taught him to pay attention to these signals. Sometimes he would tamp his moustache, pound it with his fist, comb it with his knuckles, or merely stroke it thoughtfully, depending on the nature of the hunch.

Polly, who was in the dark about this phenomenon, would say, "Are you nervous about something, dear?"

"Sorry. Only a silly habit," he would reply. He did, however, heed her suggestion about turtlenecks.

Tonight, Qwilleran took one last look in the full-length mirror, said good-bye to two bemused animals, and drove to Onoosh's Mediterranean Café in downtown Pickax.

Onoosh Dalmathakia and her partner had come from Down Below to open their restaurant, and it had received good coverage from the *Moose County Something* and the *Lockmaster Ledger* in the adjoining county. According to the publicity, the atmosphere was exotic: small oil-burning lamps on brass-topped tables, Mediterranean murals, and hanging lights with beaded fringe. In the kitchen Onoosh herself was training local women to roll stuffed grapeleaves and chop parsley — by hand — for tabbouleh. The reporter who interviewed her for the *Something* said she spoke with a fascinating Middle Eastern accent that seemed just right with her olive complexion, sultry brown eyes, and black hair. Her partner had a Middle American accent, being a sandy-haired native of Kansas.

Qwilleran had not tried the restaurant before suggesting it to the banker. When he arrived, he felt transported halfway around the globe by the aroma of strange spices and the twang of ethnic music. Two waitpersons were hurrying about, wearing European farmer smocks but looking like students from the community college.

Carmichael waved from a corner booth, where he was sipping a Rob Roy. "Hard day!" he said. "I needed a head start. You're my guest tonight. What would you like to drink?"

Qwilleran ordered his usual Squunk water on the rocks with a twist, explaining that it was a local mineral water, said to be the fountain of youth.

"It must be true," Carmichael said, "because you certainly look fit. How does it taste?"

"To tell the truth, Willard, it could be improved by a shot of something, but I've sworn off shots of everything."

"Call me Will," the banker said. "I should give up the hard stuff myself. I gave up smoking two years ago, but do you want to hear something stupid? I never travel in a plane without two packs of cigarettes in my luggage — for luck."

"If it works, don't apologize."

"Well, I haven't been in a plane crash, and they never lost my luggage!"

"How's your lovely wife?" Qwilleran asked. It was the polite thing to say and in no way reflected his personal opinion.

"Oh, she's all involved in decorating the new house, and Fran Brodie is really taking her for a ride. That's okay with me. Anything to keep peace in the family!"

"A wise attitude!" Qwilleran gave the sober nod of one who has been there.

"Were you ever married, Qwill?"

"Once. Period . . . You bought the Fitches' contemporary house, as I recall."

"I'm afraid I did — the one that looks like the shafthouse of an abandoned mine. No wonder it was on the market for three years! It's ugly as sin, but Danielle likes anything that's modern and *different,* so I acquiesced."

Qwilleran thought, She's spoiled; she has a mouth made for pouting, and a voice made for complaining. He asked, "How long have you two been married?"

"Not quite a year. My first wife died three years ago, and I was living alone in a big house. Then I went to Baltimore on business and met Danielle in a club where she was singing. It was love at first sight, let me tell you. She doesn't have a great voice, but she's one gorgeous woman! So I brought her back to Michigan."

"What made you move up here?"

"That's a story! I'd been wanting to get away from the fast track and the pollution and the street crime. I'd been mugged twice and had my car hijacked once, which was par for the course. But then I was robbed by a fast-food restaurant, and that was the clincher. I was ready for River City, Iowa."

"Robbed *by* the restaurant or *in* the restaurant?" Qwilleran was a stickler for the right word.

31

"*By* the restaurant, I'm telling you. It was Sunday, and Danielle had gone to Baltimore for a visit. In the evening I went out to get a burger and fries but forgot my bill clip, so I stopped at an ATM across from the restaurant. When I ordered my burger, I paid with a twenty but got change for a five. I pointed out the error. The counter girl called the manager. He took the cash drawer away to count it and brought it back faster than you can count your fingers. He said the cash box showed I'd paid with a five. All I had on my person that night was a twenty from the ATM, but how could I prove it?" Willard stopped to finish his drink.

Qwilleran said, "Don't stop now. What did you do?"

"Nothing I'm particularly proud of. I called him a crook and threw the whole tray at him. I hope the coffee was scalding hot! . . . That's the story! The next day I contacted an executive placement agency, and here I am!"

"You're safe here. We don't have fast fooderies."

"That puzzles me," the banker said. "There's money to be made in this county if you wanted to build a mall and bring in fast foods. . . . But look here! I'm gassing too much. Let's order some appetizers and another drink." He ordered hummus and asked to have the pita served warm.

Qwilleran ordered baba ghanouj and said to the server, "Would you ask Onoosh if she can make meatballs in little green kimonos?"

In less than a minute she came rushing from the kitchen in her white apron and chef's toque. "Mr. Qwill!" she squealed. "It's you! I knowed it was you!"

He had risen, and she flung her arms around him. A radiant smile transformed her plain face, and her tall hat fell off. It was an emotional scene, and — in Pickax style — the other diners applauded.

"Just an old friend," Qwilleran explained after she had returned to the kitchen.

The banker asked, "Do you think a Mediterranean restaurant will go over in a town like this?"

"I hope so. It's backed by the Klingenschoen Foundation as part of the downtown improvement program. Also, Polly Duncan tells me that Middle Eastern cuisine is on-target healthwise."

"I've met your Polly Duncan, and she's a charming woman," Willard said with a note of envy. "You're a lucky man. She's attractive, intelligent, and has a beautiful speaking voice."

"It was her voice that first appealed to me," Qwilleran said. " 'Soft, gentle, and low,' to quote Shakespeare. And it's the first time in my life that I've had a friend who shared my literary interests — a great feeling! Also, I'm constantly learning. Jazz used to be the extent of my music appreciation, but Polly's introduced me to chamber music and opera." He stopped to chuckle. "She hasn't converted me to bird-watching, though, and I haven't sold her on baseball — or Louis Armstrong."

"I understand you've bought separate condos in the Village. Have you ever thought of —"

"No," Qwilleran interrupted. "We like our singlehood. Besides, our cats are incompatible."

"While I'm asking nosey questions, mind if I ask another? . . . The Klingenschoen Foundation seems to have poured millions into Moose County — schools, health care, environment, and so on. What's the source of their wealth?"

Qwilleran explained simply: "The K family made their fortune here during the boom years of Moose County — in the hospitality business, you might say. A later generation invested wisely. The family has died out now, and all the money has gone into the K Foundation."

"I see," said the banker, eyeing Qwilleran dubiously. "My next nosey question: Is it true that *you* are the K Foundation?"

"No, I'm just an innocent bystander." How could a journalist explain to a banker that money is less interesting than the challenge of deadlines, exclusives, and accurate reporting?

Their dinner orders were taken, and both men chose the lentil soup with tabbouleh as the salad course, followed by shish kebab for Will and stuffed grapeleaves for Qwill.

The conversation switched to the gourmet society that was being organized. "Cooking is my chief pleasure," the banker said. "It's relaxing to come home from the play-it-cool bank environment and start banging pots and pans around. Danielle hates the kitchen, bless her heart . . .

She's bugging me to grow a moustache like yours, Qwill. She says it's sexy, but that isn't exactly the bank image . . . Have you ever been to Mardi Gras? She talked me into making reservations, although I'd rather take a cruise."

Qwilleran, as a journalist, was a professional listener, and he found himself practicing his profession. Willard seemed to need an understanding and sympathetic ear. He said, "When we move into our house, we want to get a couple of Siamese like yours — that is, if I can talk Danielle into it. The Village doesn't allow cats in apartments."

"I know. That's why I bought a condo."

"I'll bet your cats miss the barn."

"They're adaptable."

"Are they a couple?"

"No, just friends."

Willard said, "I have two grown sons in California, but I'd like to start a second family. At my age I think I could father some smart offspring, but Danielle isn't keen about the idea." He shrugged in resignation.

The conversation slowed to a desultory pace after the entrées were served. Once in a while Willard would ask a question. "Were you ever an actor? You've got a trained voice."

"In college I did a few plays."

"Fran Brodie wants Danielle to join the theatre club. Fran's a good-looking woman. Why isn't she married?"

"Who knows?"

"Amanda Goodwinter's an oddball."

"More bark than bite. The voters love her."

"And how about George Breze? What do you know about him?"

"He always wears a red feed cap, and no one knows what's underneath it, if anything," Qwilleran said. "A few years ago he had the gall to run for mayor. The locals call him Old Gallbladder. He polled only two votes."

"He seems to make money," the banker said, "but he strikes me as a shady character. And he's just taken an apartment in the Village!"

"There goes the neighborhood!"

"The apartments aren't very well built. How are the condos?"

"Ditto. I tell the cats not to go around stamping their feet."

After a while, Willard said, "I'd like to get your opinion, Qwill, on an idea that Danielle's cousin and I have been kicking around. We think those old houses on Pleasant Street could and should be restored for economic purposes and the beautification of the city."

"Does she have an interest in preservation?" Qwilleran asked in some surprise.

"My dear wife couldn't care less!"

"I mean her cousin."

"Danielle's cousin is a guy. He's a restoration consultant Down Below, and he's amazed at the possibilities here. Do you know the Duncan property on Pleasant Street?"

"Very well! Lynette Duncan is Polly's sister-in-

36

law. She recently inherited the house, an unspoiled relic of the nineteenth century."

"Right! We met Lynette at a card party in the Village, and she invited us to Sunday brunch. She has a fabulous Victorian house! In fact, the entire street is a throwback to the late 1880s. 'Carpenter Gothic' is what Danielle's cousin calls it."

" 'Gingerbread Alley' is what the local wags have named Pleasant Street," Qwilleran said.

Will Carmichael put down his knife and fork and warmed to his subject. "What's good is that the property owners haven't modernized with vinyl siding and sliding glass doors. The way we see it, Pleasant Street could become a mecca for preservation buffs, with houses operating as living museums or bed-and-breakfasts. There's money to be made in that field today. My bank would offer good deals on restoration loans . . . How does it strike you?"

"It strikes me as a huge undertaking," Qwilleran said. "Exactly what does a restoration consultant do, and what is his name?"

"Carter Lee James. Perhaps you've heard of him or seen his work in magazines. He appraises the possibilities, supervises the restoration, and helps get the houses registered as historic landmarks. He knows the techniques, sources, and — most important — *what not to do!* Can you imagine Pleasant Street with a bronze plaque in front of every house? It would be a unique attraction — not for hordes of noisy tourists but for serious admirers of nineteenth-century Americana."

They ordered spicy walnut cake and dark-roast coffee, and the banker continued. "Lynette has a fortune in antiques in her house — all inherited, she says."

Qwilleran, whose personal preference was for contemporary, remembered the ponderous furniture, dark wall coverings, velvet draperies, ornate picture frames, and skirted tables at Lynette's house. Polly had recuperated there after her surgery. He tried to find something upbeat to say. "Lynette is the last of the Duncans-by-blood. It's a highly respected name around here. The Duncans were successful merchants in the boom years, and they prospered without exploiting the mineworkers."

"That's to their credit." Willard was gazing thoughtfully into his coffee. "I imagine she doesn't have to work . . . yet she tells me she holds down a nine-to-five job."

"Lynette likes to keep busy. She's also active in volunteer work. Volunteerism is big in Pickax. You should get Danielle involved."

With a humorous grimace her husband said, "If it means visiting the sick, I don't think my dear wife would qualify." For a few minutes he occupied himself with the check and a credit card, then said, "We'll have to get together during the holidays. You should meet Carter Lee. You'll be impressed. Personable guy. Fine arts degree. Graduate study in architecture . . . Do you play bridge?"

"No, but Lynette has told me about the Village

bridge club and the big glass jar."

It was an antique apothecary jar about a foot high, with a wide mouth and a domelike stopper. At Village card parties each player dropped a ten-dollar bill into the jar and rubbed the stopper for luck. Bridge players, Qwilleran had reason to believe, ranked with athletes, sports fans, actors, sailors, and crapshooters as creatures of superstition. To the credit of the bridgehounds at Indian Village, they also contributed their winnings to the jar, and when it was full, the total sum was donated to the Moose County Youth Center. He remarked to Willard, "I hope you've contributed generously to the jar."

"I've had a little luck," he admitted. "Lynette is a consistent winner, though. And Carter Lee's pretty good . . . Danielle should stay home and watch TV."

It was time to say goodnight. Qwilleran had genuinely enjoyed the conversation and the food. He thanked his host and added, "It's my turn to treat — the next time you're baching it." The qualifying clause was tacked on casually, but he hoped it registered.

The two men drove home in their respective vehicles, both of them vans. On the way, Qwilleran recalled the banker's remarks about his "dear wife" and feared the marriage was doomed. It had been too hasty. Too bad . . . Willard was interesting company, although nosey. He was certainly enthusiastic about Pleasant Street . . . The country club situation was unfortunate. No doubt he was a golfer. It was good news about the gourmet society, however.

Qwilleran glanced at the clock on the dashboard and tuned in the hourly newsbreak on WPKX. First he heard the high-school basketball scores. Then came Wetherby Goode with his forecast and usual silliness:

"Boots — boots — boots — boots — sloggin' through the snow again." He always had a parody of a song or nursery rhyme or literary work to fit the occasion. Some of his listeners, like Lynette Duncan, thought he was terribly clever; others wished for better forecasts and fewer cultural allusions.

After Wetherby's prediction of more snow, the newscaster came in with a bulletin:

"A disturbing incident has just been reported in Indian Village. A sum of money estimated at two thousand dollars has been stolen from an unlocked cabinet in the clubhouse. It was being collected in a large glass jar by members of the bridge club, for donation to the Moose County Youth Center. Police are investigating."

Qwilleran huffed into his moustache and snapped off the radio, thinking, Brodie was right; it's escalating . . . The editorial was right; it's time to lock up!

## 3

On December 24, Qwilleran went downtown at noon to celebrate with the staff of the *Moose County Something*. They were having the afternoon off, but first there was the office party. It featured ham sandwiches from Lois's Luncheonette, a sheet cake from the Scottish bakery, coffee, and year-end bonuses. Arch Riker was beaming as he handed out the envelopes with a ho-ho-ho.

Qwilleran said to him, "This is a far cry from the wild office parties we had Down Below. They were all booze, no bonuses."

"Don't remind me!" Riker protested. "I've been twenty-five years trying to forget my first one at the *Daily Fluxion*. Rosie and I were just married, and the whole Riker family was celebrating Christmas Eve at our house — with a potluck supper and me in a Santa suit handing out presents. That was the plan, anyway. I had to work all day, but it got whispered around that every department was holding open house. Bring your own glass! At five o'clock we all started making the rounds to Editorial, Sports, Women's, Photo Lab (that was the worst), Advertising, Circulation — the whole shebang! Everyone was wallowing in holiday cheer, and I completely forgot my wife and family! By the time some guys took me home in a cab, I flaked out and woke up the next morning. Oh, God! I was in the doghouse for a year!"

Qwilleran said, "You weren't the only heel. That's why firms outlawed office parties. There's nothing like a lawsuit to grab the corporate attention."

Then Hixie Rice, the promotion director and a resident of Indian Village, pulled him aside. "Did you hear about the theft?" she whispered.

"The Pickax Picaroon strikes again! When was the money last seen?"

"The night before. We'd had our Christmas bridge party, and everyone was extra generous. Then we put the jar away in the manager's office as usual, camouflaged with a shopping bag."

"But all the players know where it's kept — right? Someone was waiting for it to fill up. Who are these players?"

"Mostly residents of the Village, but a few guest-players as well, who drive out from Pickax or wherever. Ironically, the shopping bag was gone, too. They must have used it to carry the money. According to the denomination of the bills, it could be as much as two thousand . . . Do you have a noodle, Qwill?"

"Yes. Let's get some ham sandwiches before the vultures from the city room eat them all."

After the camaraderie of the office party, Qwilleran was reluctant to leave the festive downtown scene, where shoppers were hurrying faster and carolers were singing louder. He picked up a few extra gifts: perfume for Polly, a scarf for Mildred, and a few small cans of smoked turkey pâté and gourmet sardines for the cats he knew.

The first can went to the longhair at the used book store. The bookseller was overwhelmed, saying it was the first Christmas present Winston had ever received. Eddington Smith was a gentle little old man who loved books, but not for their content. He loved them for their titles, covers, illustrations, paper quality, and provenance. He slept and cooked meals and repaired books in a room at the back of the store.

Slyly he said to Qwilleran, "I know what Santa's bringing you!"

"Don't tell me. I want to be surprised."

"It's an author you like a lot."

"That's good."

"I could tell you his initials."

"Please, Eddington, no clues! Just show me what's come in lately." He never left the store without buying something.

The bookseller puttered among opened and unopened cartons until he found a box from the estate of a professor of Celtic literature, who had spent his last years in Lockmaster; the area reminded him of Scotland. "Beautiful bindings," he said. "Most printed on India paper. Some very old but the leather is well cared for . . . Here's one published in 1899."

Qwilleran looked at it. The title was *Ossian and the Ossianic Literature*, and it was written by A. Nutt. "I'll take it," he said, thinking he might give it to Arch Riker for a gag. As he left the store, he called out, "Merry Christmas, Edd! When I die, I'm leaving you all my old books."

"I'll be the first to go," the old man said earnestly, "and I'm leaving you my whole store. It's written in my will."

He mentioned his purchase to Polly Duncan that evening. They met at her place for their traditional Christmas Eve together. "I bought a book on Ossian today at Eddington's. The author was someone by the name of Nutt. Wasn't there a scandal concerning Ossian in Samuel Johnson's time?"

"Yes, and quite a controversy," she said. "An eighteenth-century poet claimed to have found the third-century poems of Ossian. Dr. Johnson said it was a hoax."

After serving a low-fat supper, she offered Qwilleran a choice of pumpkin pie or fruitcake with a scoop of frozen yogurt.

"Is there any law against having both?" he asked.

"Qwill, dear, I knew you'd say that! . . . By the way, Lynette has been chiding me for calling you 'dear.' She says it's old-fashioned."

"You're the only one in my whole life who's ever called me that, and I like it! You can quote me to your sister-in-law. For someone who hasn't had a love affair for twenty years, she hardly qualifies as an authority on affectionate appellations."

They listened to carols by Swiss bell-ringers and French choirs. He read Dickens's account of the Cratchits' Christmas dinner. She read Whittier's *Snow-Bound*. In every way it was an enjoyable evening, unmarred by any hostility from Bootsie. (The husky male Siamese, who considered Qwilleran a rival for Polly's affection, had been sequestered in the basement.) Perhaps the occasion was made more poignant by Polly's recent crisis, when they feared they might never have another Christmas Eve together. The blissful evening ended only when the banging on the basement door became insufferable.

On Christmas morning Qwilleran's telephone rang frequently as friends called to thank him for their gift baskets. One of them was a fun-loving, gray-haired grandmother: Celia Robinson. She was his neighbor when he lived in the barn and she supplied meatloaf, macaroni and cheese, and other home-cooked fare that he could keep in the freezer.

"Merry Christmas, Chief! Thank you for the goodies! And Wrigley thanks you for the gourmet sardines. He sends greetings to Koko and Yum Yum. Are they having a good Christmas?"

"They had some of your meatloaf, and that made their day." This mild quip occasioned a burst of merry laughter.

"Guess what, Chief!" She called him "Chief" for reasons that only he and she understood. "My grandson is here for the holidays."

"Clayton?" He knew about the fourteen-year-old science and math whiz who lived on a farm in Illinois.

"I picked him up at the airport yesterday afternoon. Mr. O'Dell came to supper, and we all opened presents and had a good time. Then we floodlighted the yard and built a big snowman. Today Clayton went to your barn on snowshoes and checked it out. Everything's okay. No damage. Today we're having dinner with Virginia Alstock's family. Her kids are about Clayton's age."

While she was talking, Qwilleran was thinking. He had never met the fourteen-year-old science and math whiz who had helped solve the Euphonia Gage case in Florida, and he felt obliged to extend some form of hospitality, although he was not fond of the underage bracket. He said, "Would your grandson like to go along with me on an assignment for the paper?"

"Oh, Chief! He'd love it! He's outside now, using the snowblower, but I'll tell him when he comes in. He'll be thrilled! It might change his life! He might decide to be a newspaperman!"

"Tell him to stick with cybernetics. It pays better. Does he have a camera?"

"Yes. A new one his dad gave him for Christmas. And he has the little tape recorder he used in Florida."

"Good! He can pose as my photographer. Tell him to pick up a roll of film, and I'll pay for it. Meanwhile, I'll set up an interview and call you back."

"Shall I cut his hair?" Celia asked.

"Not necessary," Qwilleran said. "Photographers aren't expected to look too civilized."

Her laughter was still resounding as they hung up.

Then Polly called to discuss how they should dress for dinner.

"Arch will be wearing his twenty-year-old red wool shirt," Qwilleran said, "so I suggest we go in sweaters."

Polly's staff had given her a white sweater embroidered with red cardinals and green holly — livelier than her usual garb, but Polly herself was livelier since her surgery. Qwilleran had a new sweater, ordered from Chicago, that looked like an Oriental rug — high style for a man whose peers Down Below used to call a lovable slob.

"I'll pick you up at one o'clock," he said. "Bundle up, and we'll walk. It isn't windy."

"Do you know who's just moved into the unit next to you, Qwill?"

"A husky man. Drives a large van."

"That's Wetherby Goode!"

"No! What did I do to deserve that clown for a neighbor?"

"Do I detect inter-media jealousy?" she said, teasing gently. "Most radio-listeners think he's entertaining. It's not all about dew point and barometric pressure. One windy day he sang 'Rockabye Baby.' After an ice storm he quoted from *The Rime of the Ancient Mariner*. One of his listeners had sent it in: *The ice was here, the ice was there, the ice was all around.* People are afraid he'll run out of quotes."

"Well, if you have to have a gimmick with your weather, I guess that's as good as any," Qwilleran acknowledged. "Who lives next to you?"

"The Cavendish sisters, retired teachers, very quiet."

At one o'clock they started out for the Riker condo in Building Two, muffled in down jackets, scarfs, woolly hats, mittens, and boots. They walked hand-in-hand as they had done during her first post-surgery outings. Now it had become a pleasant custom to both of them; to observers it was romantic grist for the gossip mill.

Polly had a red wool scarf, six feet long, wrapped around her chin and ears and trailing front and back. "A present from Lynette," she said.

"What did you give her?"

"A set of violet-scented soap, bath oil, and cologne. Violet is all she ever wears."

"I always wondered what that aroma was on Pleasant Street. I thought it was furniture polish."

"Oh, Qwill, you're wicked! Violet is a lovely scent. To simplify my Christmas shopping I mailed the same thing to my sister in Cincinnati, and she phoned this morning to say how much she liked it."

"Do people on your gift list ever call to say they hate what you gave them?"

"Now you're being the cynical journalist!"

Arriving at their destination, they were greeted at the door by a committee of three: the beaming host in a red wool shirt, the plump and pretty hostess in a chef's apron, and their cat in his usual tuxedo with white shirtfront and spats. Toulouse looked slyly satisfied with his lot, like an alley-smart stray who has found a home with the food writer of a newspaper. The two women hugged, and each told the other she looked wonderful. The men, friends since childhood, had only to make eye contact to express all that needed to be said.

There was a Scotch pine tree in the living room, trimmed like the one at their wedding the previous Christmas: white pearlescent ornaments, white doves, white streamers. The festively wrapped packages under the tree included those sent over by Polly and Qwilleran. The aromas were those of pine boughs, roasting turkey, and hot mulled cider.

Mildred removed her apron and joined the others around a low party table loaded with hot and cold hors d'oeuvres.

Polly said, "I always feel so secure when I come to dinner here. Mildred doesn't fuss in the kitchen; she doesn't expect anyone to help; and everything turns out perfectly: the hot foods hot and the cold foods cold."

"Hear! Hear!" Qwilleran said.

As the four busied themselves with the hors d'oeuvres, conversation came in short bites:

About the theft: "An inside job! An outsider could have stolen it only if an insider talked on the outside."

About Lynette: "Suddenly she's looking ten years younger! Is she in love? . . . She was jilted twenty years ago and hasn't dated since . . . Maybe it's Wetherby Goode. She thinks he's cute."

About George Breze: "What's he doing in Indian Village? . . . His house on Sandpit Road is up for sale . . . His wife left him. Why did she stay as long as she did?"

About the Carmichaels: "Big difference in their ages . . . He's an asset to the community, but she's a misfit . . . Someone should talk to her about her wardrobe."

Polly said, "She has such a pouty mouth! Is it natural?"

"It's what they call a fish-mouth," Mildred said. "You can have it done."

"My wife is so worldly," said Arch.

Toulouse walked into the room with a solemn tread and rubbed against the cook's ankles as a reminder that the turkey was ready. Mildred served it with a brown-rice-and-walnut stuffing, twice-baked sweet potatoes with orange glaze, sesame-sauced broccoli, and two kinds of cranberry relish.

"I feel compelled to serve two kinds," she said, "or the turkey will be dry and the stuffing will be soggy. It's just a superstition."

"It's absurd," said her husband, "but I don't fight it."

Qwilleran claimed he had never been superstitious. "As a kid, I deliberately walked under ladders and stepped on cracks in the sidewalk."

"And look how he turned out!" Riker said. "Luckiest guy in the northeast central United States."

In pioneer days, Mildred related, it was unlucky to whistle in the mines, kill a woodpecker in a lumber camp, or drop a knife on the deck of a fishing boat.

"Today," Polly said, "we observe superstitions half in fun and half hopefully. Lynette always wears her grandmother's ring to play bridge, and she almost always wins."

"Anything will work if you think it will," Qwilleran said. "With the ring on her finger, she expects to win — a positive attitude that enables her to think clearly and make the right moves."

"The *right bids*," Arch corrected him. "You're thinking of chess."

With a wink at the others, Mildred said, "Arch always puts on his right shoe before the left."

"It has nothing to do with superstition. It has everything to do with efficiency," he explained. "It's the result of a lifelong time-and-motion study."

"You never told me that," she said innocently.

"But if you accidentally put on the left shoe first, you take it off and start over."

"Who needs Big Brother? I've got Big Wife monitoring my behavior."

"Ooh! I'm going on a diet after the holidays," Mildred said.

"Isn't it strange," Polly remarked, "how many superstitions have to do with the feet, like putting a penny in your shoe for luck or wearing mismatched socks to take an exam? Bootsie gives his paw three licks — no more, no less — before starting to eat."

"Will someone explain to me," Qwilleran asked, "why Koko always eats with his rear end pointed north? No matter where he's being fed, he knows which way is north. And Yum Yum always approaches her food from the left. If something's in the way and she has to do otherwise, she throws up."

Arch groaned. "This conversation is getting too deep for me. Let's have dessert."

After the plum pudding had been served and after the coffee had been poured, the presents were opened — not in a mad scramble but one at a time, with everyone sharing the suspense.

The first — to Qwilleran from the Rikers — was an odd-shaped package about four feet long. "A short stepladder," he guessed. "A croquet set." It proved to be a pair of snowshoes. "Great!" he said. "There are snow trails all around here! It's just what I need to get some exercise this winter!" And he meant it.

Polly was thrilled with her suede suit and silk blouse, and the Rikers whooped in unison over the Majolica coffee pot. Then Arch unwrapped his baseball tie and exploded with laughter, while Mildred screamed in glee.

Qwilleran said, "It was supposed to be a joke, but I didn't know it was that funny!" He understood their reaction when, a few minutes later, he opened a long, narrow giftbox from Arch. It was a baseball tie.

The largest box under the tree — to Qwilleran from Polly — was a set of leather-bound books by Herman Melville, a 1924 printing in mint condition. Included were novels that Qwilleran, a Melville buff, had never been able to find. He dug into the box excitedly, announcing title after title, and reading aloud some of the opening lines.

"Okay," Arch said, "you've got all winter to read those books. Let's open some more presents."

Also for Qwilleran was an opera recording from Polly: *Adriana Lecouvreur* with Renata Tebaldi . . . Toulouse gave Koko and Yum Yum a gift certificate good at Toodle's fish counter . . . Arch gave Mildred a three-strand necklace of onyx beads accented with a cartouche of gold-veined lapis lazuli.

The last gift under the tree was tagged to Qwilleran from Bootsie. "It's a package bomb," he guessed. After unwrapping it with exaggerated care, he exclaimed, "I can only quote the bard: *I am amazed and know not what to say!* It's a spor-ran!"

"You could have fooled me," said Arch. "I thought it was something for cleaning the wind-shield."

"A sporran, for your information, Arch, is a fur pouch worn with a kilt by men in the Scottish Highlands. It's used to carry money, car keys, driver's license, cigarettes, lighter, credit cards, sunglasses, and possibly a sandwich." He turned to Polly. "How did Bootsie find out I'd bought a kilt?"

"Everyone in town knows it, dear. There are no secrets in Pickax."

"Well, we're now a two-sporran family. Yum Yum has a cat-size sporran attached to her un-derside. It flaps from side to side when she trots, but hers is real fur. I think this one can be ma-chine-washed and tumble-dried."

When dusk fell and the gaslights on River Lane began to glow, it was snowing, so Arch drove Polly and Qwilleran home with their loot and foil-wrapped packs of turkey for their cats. Qwilleran minced some before going to Polly's for mint tea and a recap of the afternoon:

"Carol gets the credit for selecting your suit, Polly."

"Mildred made your sporran, Qwill."

"The snowshoes are good-looking enough to hang on the wall when I'm not using them."

"Did you know Adriana was the last role Tebaldi sang before she retired?"

"Eddington Smith searched a whole year for a Melville collection. This one turned up in Boston."

It had stopped snowing when Qwilleran finally went home, and he was surprised to find footprints in the fresh snow on his front walk, leading to and from his doorstep. They were a woman's footprints. There were no tire tracks. She lived in the Village and had walked. Who in the Village would pay a call without phoning first or being invited? Not Hixie or Fran. Certainly not Amanda Goodwinter. Opening the storm door, he found a gift on the threshold, wrapped in conservative holly paper and about the size and weight of a two-pound box of chocolates. He felt obliged to quote Lewis Carroll: *Curiouser and curiouser!* He carried it indoors, hoping it was not chocolates.

The Siamese, dozing on the sofa, raised their heads expectantly.

"Three guesses!" he said to them as he tore open the paper. It was a book with an unusual binding: leather spine and cloth-covered boards in a red and green Jacobean design, leafy and flowery. The gold tooling on the spine spelled out *The Old Wives' Tale.*

"Hey," he yelped, alarming the cats. Arnold Bennett was one of his favorite authors, and this was considered his best novel. It was obviously a special edition of the 1907 book, with heavy quality paper, deckled edges, and woodcut illustrations. There was a note enclosed:

Qwill — You mentioned Bennett in your column last week, and I thought you'd like to have this precious book from my father's collection.
— Your Number-One Fan — Sarah

Qwilleran was flabbergasted. Sarah Plensdorf was the office manager at the *Something* — an older woman, rather shy. She lived alone in the Village, surrounded by family treasures.

Clutching the book, he dropped into his favorite easy chair and propped his feet on the ottoman. Koko and Yum Yum came running. Reading aloud was one of the things they did together as a family.

Bennett had been a journalist, and his novels were written in an unromantic style with detailed descriptions. As Qwilleran read, he dramatized with sound effects: the resounding call of the cuckoo in the English countryside, the clanging bell of the horse-car in town, the snores of Mr. Povey, asleep on the sofa with his mouth wide open. (He had taken a painkiller for his aching tooth.) When the prankish Sophie reached into the gaping mouth with pliers and extracted the wobbly tooth, Mr. Povey yelped, Qwilleran yelped, Yum Yum shrieked. But where was Koko?

Some muttering could be heard in the foyer, where Qwilleran had piled all the Christmas gifts;

Koko was doing his best to open the carton containing the set of Melville's works.

Was he attracted to the leather bindings? Did he detect codfish on a set of old books from Boston? Could he sense that the box contained a novel about a whale? He was a smart cat, but was he that smart?

Koko did indeed have a baffling gift of extrasensory perception. He could tell time, read Qwilleran's mind, and put thoughts in Qwilleran's head. All cats do this, more or less, at feeding time. But Koko applied his powers to matters of good and evil. He sensed misdeeds, and he could identify misdoers in an oblique sort of way. Melville's novels were concerned with good and evil to a large degree; was Kao K'o Kung getting the message?

Was it coincidence that he pushed *The Thief* off the bookshelf when Pickax was plagued with petit larceny — and some not so petit?

Trying to find answers to such questions could drive a person mad, Qwilleran had decided. The sane approach was to be receptive, open-minded. There was one clue, however, that he had divined: Normal cats have twenty-four whiskers on each side, eyebrows included. Koko had thirty!

# 4

Between Christmas and New Year's, Qwilleran took Celia Robinson's grandson out on an assignment. He had been scheduled to interview an innkeeper in Trawnto Beach, but a dowser in Pickax seemed more likely to interest a future scientist. Furthermore, the dowser lived nearby, and Qwilleran could avoid sixty miles of driving in the company of a precocious fourteen-year-old. Admittedly, summer would be more appropriate for a dowsing story, but the interview could be conducted during Clayton's visit and put on hold. Then, after spring thaw, Qwilleran could return for a demonstration of the mysterious art.

When he drove into Celia's parking lot, he saw Clayton on the snowblower, spraying his grandmother with plumes of white flakes, while she pelted him with snowballs in gleeful retaliation. Brushing snow from their outerwear, they approached Qwilleran's car, and Celia made the introductions: "Mr. Qwilleran, this is my famous grandson . . . Clayton, this is the famous Mr. Q. I call him 'Chief.' "

"Hi, Chief," the young man said, thrusting his hand forward. His grip had the confidence of a young teen who is expecting a scholarship from M.I.T.

"Hi, Doc," Qwilleran replied, referring to his role in the Florida investigation. He sized him up as a healthy farm-bred youth with an intelligent face, freshly cut hair, and a voice deeper than the one on last year's tape recording. "Got your camera? Let's go!"

"Where are we off to, Chief?" Clayton asked as they turned into Park Circle.

"We're going to Pleasant Street to interview Gil MacMurchie. His ancestors came here from Scotland about the time of Rob Roy. Do you know about Rob Roy? Sir Walter Scott wrote a novel with that title."

"I saw the movie," Clayton said. "He wore skirts."

"He wore a kilt, customarily worn by Scottish Highlanders for tramping across the moors in wet heather, and also as a badge of clansmanship. During the Jacobite rebellion, clans were stripped of their names and kicked off their land. Rob Roy had been chief of the MacGregor clan but changed his name to Campbell. 'Roy' refers to his red hair."

"How do you know all that?"

"I read. Do you read, Doc?"

"Yeah, I read a lot. I'm reading Einstein's *Philosophy of Civilization.*"

"I'm glad you're not waiting for the movie . . . Mr. MacMurchie is retired from the plumbing and hardware business, but he's still active as a dowser. Know anything about dowsing? Scientists call it divining. It's also known

59

as water-witching."

"Sure, I know about that! When our well ran dry, my dad hired a water-witch. He walked around our farm with a branch of a tree and found underground water. I don't know how it works."

"No one knows exactly, but there are plenty of guesses. Geologists call it an old wives' tale."

"What does that mean?"

"Folklore . . . superstition. Yet proponents of dowsing say it works, in spite of the controversy."

Pleasant Street was an old neighborhood of Victorian frame houses ornamented with quantities of jigsaw trim around windows, porches, rooflines, and gables. The large residences had been built by successful families like the MacMurchies and Duncans in the heyday of Moose County.

"This street looks like Disneyland," said Clayton. "It doesn't look real."

"There may be no other street in the United States with so much gingerbread trim still intact. Right now there's a proposal to restore all the houses and have it recognized as a historic neighborhood."

Qwilleran parked in front of a neat two-tone gray house that still had a stone carriage step at the curb. The sidewalk and the steps of the house had been recently broomed, showing the streak-marks of the broom straw in the snow.

As they walked up the front steps, Clayton asked, "What kind of pictures shall I take?"

"Close-ups of Mr. MacMurchie and his dowsing stick, plus anything else that looks interesting. If you get some good shots, the paper might do a picture spread and give you a credit line."

Clayton had never seen a doorbell in the middle of the door, and he snapped a picture of it. He had never heard the raucous clang it made, either.

"Remember, Doc," Qwilleran said. "I ask the questions; you click the camera, but do it unobtrusively."

"Do you tape the interview?"

"If he gives permission; that's our paper's policy. But I take notes, whether we tape or not. When I was younger, I could commit a whole interview to memory, and it would be printed verbatim without error. But that was just showing off."

The man who responded to the bell was a leathery-faced Scot whose red hair was turning sandy with age. "Come in! Come in, Qwill" was his hearty welcome.

"Gil, this is my photographer, Clayton Robinson."

"Hiya, there! Let's go right back to the kitchen. There's some folks from the bank working in the front rooms. All my dowsing gear is laid out on the kitchen table."

A long hall extended through to the rear, similar to that in the Duncan house. Lynette's furnishings were stubbornly Victorian, however; this collection represented the taste of passing generations and the fads of recent decades: a little William Morris, a little Art Deco, a little Swedish modern, a little French provincial, a little Mediterranean.

As the trio walked down the hall, Qwilleran glimpsed antique weapons in a glass-topped curio table . . . a small black dog asleep on the carpeted stairs . . . a man and a woman examining one of the parlors and making notes.

"Excuse the mess," the dowser apologized when they reached the kitchen. "My wife passed away last year, and I'm no good at housekeeping. I'm getting ready to move into a retirement complex, and I'm selling the house and most of my goods. Willard Carmichael at the bank said I can get more for the house if I fix it up so that it's historic. You know Willard, don't you? He sent this out-of-town expert over here today to figure out what needs to be done and what it'll cost. Sounds pretty good to me! . . . Pull up a couple of chairs. Do you want me to explain this gear? Or do you want to ask questions?"

Laid out on the table was an array of forked twigs, L-shaped rods, barbed wire, string, even a wire coat hanger.

"Let's talk first," Qwilleran suggested, setting up his tape recorder. "How long have you been dowsing, Gil? . . . I'll tape this, if you don't mind."

"Ever since I was a kid and my granddad showed me how to hold the forked stick. He found good water for folks, and also veins of iron ore and copper. The mines closed a long time ago, but folks always need good drinking water. When there's a drought, some wells run dry.

62

When a new building's going up, they have to know if there's water down there and how many gallons a minute they can get."

Qwilleran asked, "Considering new technology, is water-witching a dying art?"

"No way! No way! My grandson's been finding water since he was twelve. It's a gift, you know, and you pass it on, but it skips a generation. My father couldn't find water to save his life! My son can't either. But my grandson can. See what I mean?"

Occasionally there was the soft click of a camera and a flash of light.

"How often are you called upon to use this skill?"

"All depends. I'm a licensed plumber, and my wife and me ran the hardware store for years, but I'd always go out and dowse if somebody wanted me to. Still do."

"Are you always successful?"

"If the water's down there, by golly I'll find it! Sometimes it just ain't there! Either way, I never charge for my services, and I've made a lot of friends. Of course, I've made enemies, too. There's a well-driller in Mooseville who hates my guts. He'll drill a couple of dry holes, and then I'm called in and I find water with my little forked stick. Drives the guy nuts!" MacMurchie stopped to enjoy a chuckle. "Then there's an old biddy in Kennebeck who says it's the work of the devil. But just wait till her well runs dry and see who she calls!" The dowser slapped his knee and had another laugh. "If she calls me, I'm gonna go out there with one of them Halloween masks with red horns."

"How about the scientists? The geologists?"

"Oh, them! Just because they can't explain it, they think it's all superstition. How about you, Qwill? What's your honest opinion?"

"I'll reserve my opinion until next spring when you give a demonstration. Meanwhile, what are these gadgets?" He waved his hand at the odd assortment on the kitchen table.

"Okay. Here's the famous forked twig — goes back hundreds of years. Can be birch, maple, willow, apple, whatever. Should be fresh, with the sap in it . . . So you hold it in front of you, stem pointing up. The two forks are in your hands, palms up — like this." The camera clicked. "You walk across the ground, concentrating. You pace back and forth. Suddenly the stick quivers, and the stem swings down and points to the ground. There's a vein of water under your feet!"

"Uncanny!" Qwilleran said. "How far down?"

"Could be twenty, forty, sixty feet. If I say it's down there, all you gotta do is drill — or dig. My granddad dug wells by hand, as deep as eighty feet! Sent the mud up in buckets."

Qwilleran heard voices in the next room: the rumble of a man's voice and a woman's shrill laughter. Catching Clayton's eye, he jerked his head in that direction, and the young photographer quietly left the room.

"Are there any women dowsers, Gil?"

"In some places. Not here."

"Explain these other gadgets."

"They'll all find water, but mostly it depends on the dowser. Nothing works if you're just fooling around, or if you don't feel too good, or if you think it's really a lot of baloney." MacMurchie looked up suddenly, over Qwilleran's shoulder, and said, "Yes, Mr. James. Want to see me?"

A deep, pleasant voice said, "We're leaving now. We'll be back tomorrow to appraise the upstairs. I think you have a gold mine here. Don't let me disturb you. We can find our way out."

Qwilleran had his back to the voice and saw no reason to turn around.

"Nice fella," the dowser said as footsteps retreated and a woman's laughter drifted back to them.

Qwilleran stood up and pocketed his recorder. "This has been very enlightening. I'll look forward to the demonstration in the spring . . . Where's my photographer? Let's go, Clayton."

"Here I am — in the dining room. I've found a friend." He was sitting cross-legged on the floor, and a black schnauzer was curled on his chest, looking up at him with a shameless expression of devotion.

"That's Cody," said MacMurchie. "You can have her if you want. I can't have a pet where I'm going. She's a sweet little girl. She was my wife's."

Clayton said, "I live on a farm. She'd like it there. Can I take her on the plane, Chief?"

65

"Better discuss it with your grandmother."

While Clayton took a few pictures of Cody, the two men walked toward the front door, and Qwilleran asked about the weapons in the curio table.

"They're Scottish dirks — longer than daggers, shorter than swords." He lifted the glass top and removed a dirk from its scabbard. "See these grooves in the blade? They're for blood. Those Highlanders thought of everything." There were also two silver pins three inches in diameter, set with stones as big as egg yolks — a kind of smoky quartz. "Those are brooches to anchor a man's plaid on his shoulder. The stones are cairngorms, found only on Cairngorm mountain in Scotland. We call the brooches poached eggs. Sorry to say, I've got to unload all this stuff. No room in my new place. I'll only keep the dirk with the silver lion. It was a gift from my wife."

"How much do you want for all the others?" Qwilleran asked.

MacMurchie rolled his eyes toward the ceiling. "Well . . . let's see . . . four dirks with brass hilts and leather scabbards . . . and two silver brooches . . . You could have 'em for a thousand, and I'd throw in the table."

"I wouldn't need the table, but I'll think about the others and let you know."

"Are you going to Scottish Night at the lodge?"

"They've invited me, and I've bought a kilt, but so far I haven't had the nerve to wear it."

"Wear it to Scottish Night, Qwill. There'll be

twenty or thirty fellas in kilts there, and you'll feel right at home. I'll lend you a knife to wear in your sock. You have to have a knife in your sock to be proper."

"Isn't it considered a concealed weapon?"

"Well, Andy Brodie wears one to Scottish Night, and he never got arrested. When you go in, you show it to the doorman, that's all. Wait a second." MacMurchie disappeared and returned with a stag-horn-handled knife in a scabbard. "You borrow this, Qwill. It's lucky to wear something borrowed."

Qwilleran accepted, saying it was a good-looking knife.

"It's called a dubh, but it's pronounced 'thoob.' "

They said good-bye. Qwilleran told Cody she was a good dog. He and his photographer drove away from Pleasant Street.

"That was cool," Clayton said.

"How'd you like to stop at the Olde Tyme Soda Fountain for a sundae?"

It was a new addition to downtown Pickax, part of the revitalization sponsored by the K Fund. A light, bright shop with walls and floor of vanilla white, it had small round tables and a long fountain bar in chocolate-colored marble. Customers sat on "ice cream" chairs or high stools of twisted wire, with strawberry red seats. Sundaes were called college ices; sodas were called phosphates; banana splits remained banana splits. That was Clayton's choice. Qwilleran had a double scoop of coffee ice cream. Everything was served in old-style ice cream dishes of thick molded glass.

"Did you shoot the whole roll?" Qwilleran asked.

"No, I've got a few exposures left. I'm leaving tomorrow, so I'll send you the prints. I hate to go. Grandma's a lotta fun."

"Did you get a look at the people from the bank?"

"Yeah, he was okay, but she was weird."

"In what way?"

"I don't know. Just weird. Her voice — it sounded kind of electronic."

An apt description of Danielle Carmichael, Qwilleran thought. "What were they doing?"

"He was walking around and measuring things and talking, and she was writing down what he said. I turned on my recorder. Want me to send a transcript when I get home?"

"Good idea! Did you enjoy your holiday?"

"Yeah, lotsa fun, lotsa food. Grandma remembered all my favorites. Do you think she'll marry Mr. O'Dell?"

"I don't know. Both have a very positive attitude. They both like to help people. They might make a good match."

Clayton was lost for a while in deep thought as he tackled the complexities of a banana split.

Then Qwilleran questioned him about life on the farm. It was a poultry factory. There were no farm animals, just watchdogs and barn cats, but no indoor pets. Clayton had a stepmother who wouldn't allow animals in the house.

"I'd like to come up here and live with Grandma and go to Pickax High School. It's cool!" he said. "My stepmother wouldn't mind, but my dad doesn't want me to."

As they pulled into Celia's parking lot, Clayton said, "Thanks a lot, Chief. It was cool."

When Qwilleran returned home, he noticed heavy vehicle tracks and large footprints in the recently fallen snow around his condo, but he was not alarmed. It meant that some long-awaited furniture had been delivered. Fran Brodie, who knew his likes and dislikes, had been able to supply the basics for his condo, but additional items were straggling in. She had bought certain items of old pine farm furniture, almost contemporary in its simplicity, and had stripped the finish to a honey color. A light interior was a good choice for a building nestled in the woods. The walls were off-white, and honey was the color of the pine woodwork.

Qwilleran's unit had a lofty living room with large windows overlooking the river. On the opposite wall was a balcony with two bedrooms, and below it were the kitchen and dining alcove. He would use the alcove as an office, and he needed a table or desk surface large enough for typewriter, lamp, papers, books, files, and two supervisory cats.

On this day, as soon as he unlocked the door, Koko notified him that something had been

69

added, yowling and running back and forth to the office alcove. The writing table was indeed large, and it had character. One could imagine that families had been fed on its ample surface, bread had been kneaded, tomatoes had been canned, babies had been bathed, sheets had been ironed, and letters had been written to loved ones during the Spanish American War. There was also a huge stripped-pine cupboard with open shelves above and cabinet below.

Qwilleran lost no time in loading the shelves with books recently purchased or brought from the barn. One shelf he reserved for the Melville set, volumes one to twelve, numbered in chronological order: *Typee*; *Omoo*; *Mardi*; *Redburn*; *White-Jacket*; *Moby-Dick*; *Pierre*; *The Piazza Tales*; *Israel Potter*; *The Confidence-Man*; *Billy Budd*; and *Weeds and Wildings*, the last being a book of poems. He could hardly believe his good fortune.

Koko was impressed, too. During the evening, when it was time for another reading from *The Old Wives' Tale*, only one cat reported. Koko was curled up on the shelf with the leather-bound volumes. Had he become a literary critic? Was he saying that Melville was a better writer than Bennett?

 5

On the last day of the year it snowed as usual, and high winds were predicted. Wetherby Goode advised New Year's Eve celebrants to stay off the highways if possible. *Then blow ye winds, heigh ho!* was his quotation for the day.

In Indian Village it was customary for neighbors to celebrate with neighbors, and there were numerous at-home parties. For those who liked elbow-to-elbow conviviality, there was a late-night get-together at the clubhouse: light supper, champagne at midnight, no paper hats, no noise-makers. Earlier, Qwilleran and Polly and two other couples would dine with the Exbridges.

Don Exbridge, the X in XYZ Enterprises, was the developer responsible for Indian Village, and he and his new wife lived in Building One. They had a double unit, said to be quite posh, with gold faucets and all that. Qwilleran wondered if the Exbridges' windows rattled when the wind blew, *heigh ho,* as they did in Building Five. He wondered if the floors bounced like trampolines, and if the Exbridges could hear the plumbing next door. He enjoyed a recurring fantasy: The K Fund would buy Indian Village — the only planned, upscale community in the county — then tear it down and build it right.

The Exbridges proved to be charming hosts, and the dinner was excellent. They had a cook and houseman in addition to gold faucets. Qwilleran kept his ear tuned to the fenestration, but there was no rattle even when the wind swayed the trees frighteningly. As for the floors, they were hardwood with Oriental rugs — not plywood with wall-to-wall carpet. The plumbing was discreetly quiet.

There was much conversation about the theft of the bridge club's money. The new clubhouse manager, Lenny Inchpot, had been questioned by the police; the money jar was kept in a cabinet in his office. Also questioned were officers of the clubhouse association and the maintenance crew of the building. All agreed there was too much casual traffic in and out. The premises were available for rental, and there were catered parties, lectures, classes, art exhibits, and the like. There was a TV lounge, and there was a room with exercise equipment. Anyone could walk in and watch a soap opera or pump a little iron. There was even a cash bar during certain hours. Locking the doors and issuing keys to members would be the first move.

When the time came to ring in the New Year, scores of residents converged on the clubhouse. The main hall had the air of a ski lodge, with a lofty wood-paneled ceiling, exposed beams, and a big stone fireplace. Windows overlooked the floodlighted woods, enchanting in winter white.

Indoor trees and baskets of ferns, with all the green perfection of plastic, were banked in corners. Silver letters were strung across the chimney breast spelling H-A-P-P-Y N-E-W Y-E-A-R.

Since dress was optional, it ranged from jeans to black tie. Polly was wearing her terra-cotta suit, admired by everyone, and Qwilleran was in suit and tie. He and Arch had considered wearing their baseball ties, but their women vetoed it; the Exbridges would not be amused. Amanda Goodwinter was there in her thirty-year-old dinner dress; she considered large parties an abomination but attended for commercial and political reasons. A husky man who looked dapper in a double-breasted suit wore a large lapel button inscribed: HIT ME! I'M THE WEATHER GUY!

Willard Carmichael and his houseguest wore dinner jackets. Danielle was spectacular in a low-cut, high-cut cocktail sheath, leading Arch Riker to mumble, "You'd think a banker could afford to buy his wife something longer."

"At least she has good legs," Qwilleran mumbled in reply, "but she makes Lynette look like a prison matron."

In a navy blue taffeta shirtdress with her grandmother's jewelry, Lynette had dined with the Carmichaels. She reported that Willard had prepared a delicious beef Wellington; Danielle's cousin was adorable; his deep voice gave her goosebumps; even his name was romantic: Carter Lee James. All the women were talking about him, she said.

For several years Qwilleran had been the pick

of Pickax, as far as eligible bachelors were rated. One woman had donated fifteen hundred dollars to charity for the privilege of having dinner with him. Although he appreciated compliments on his writing, the adulation centering around his moustache was cloying. He would be glad to share his lionization with the new fair-haired boy in town.

When Lynette pointed him out, Qwilleran recognized him as the man who had been measuring the MacMurchie house; his voice was indeed ingratiatingly pleasant. He had blond hair, medium good looks, and a relaxed way with strangers, young and old, men and women. Compared to his blockbuster cousin, he seemed quite acceptable by Pickax standards.

"His hair's bleached," Amanda muttered to Qwilleran.

Polly said, "He has a frank, boyish way of looking at one that's quite disarming."

Lynette said, "All his shirts and sweaters are monogrammed."

"How do you know?" Qwilleran asked.

"He's been playing bridge with us, and I had the three of them to Sunday brunch once. Carter Lee is crazy about my house!"

Danielle was in a giddy mood. Her electronic laugh frequently pierced the even level of background conversation.

Her husband, too, was in high spirits, saying, "That suit looks fabulous on you, Polly! . . . Hixie baby, we've gotta do lunch . . . Qwill, my wife wants me to grow a moustache like yours. Don't you think I'm more the Charlie Chaplin type?"

Hixie Rice grabbed Qwilleran's arm. "An anonymous donor has sent a check for fifteen hundred to cover the theft from the money jar! It's drawn on a Chicago bank. Does that mean it's from the Klingenschoen Foundation?"

"Don't ask me," he said. "They never tell me anything."

She was circulating with a tape recorder, collecting New Year's resolutions for the monthly newsletter, *The Other Village Voice.* Qwilleran told her he was going to write a book. Mildred declared she would lose thirty pounds. Polly resolved to find a playmate for Bootsie. Lynette, the confirmed single, amused bystanders by saying, "This is the year I get married." Danielle was determined to buy a kinkajou. Her husband said he was determined to get his wife pregnant.

Then Wetherby Goode surprised the crowd by sitting down at the piano and playing cocktail music, while Danielle surprised them further by singing ballads.

Lynette said, "I didn't know Wetherby could play."

Polly said, "I didn't know Danielle could sing."

"She can't," Qwilleran muttered as he returned to the buffet for seconds. Standing in line behind Amanda, he said, "I didn't hear your New Year's resolution."

"They wouldn't print mine," she said grouchily. "I'm campaigning to eliminate those family

75

newsletters that people do on home computers and send out instead of Christmas cards! Whatever happened to those beautiful reproductions of Raphael and Murillo? All we get is a long, sickening report on family reunions, weddings, scholarships, vacations, holes-in-one, and new babies! Who cares if Uncle Charlie was elected president of the bowling club? I never even heard of Uncle Charlie!"

"You're absolutely right!" Qwilleran liked to encourage her tirades. "They never tell you that Junior was kicked out of college for cheating, and Daddy lost his job, and Cousin Fred was arrested for driving while impaired."

"Next year," she said, with a conspiratorial punch in his ribs, "you and I will make up a phoney newsletter that's nothing but bad news, and we'll send it to every name in the Pickax phone book!"

"We'll sign it: Ronald Frobnitz and family," he said.

Later, Riker asked him, "What were you two talking about? No one's seen her laugh since George Breze ran for mayor and got two votes!"

"Just nonsense," Qwilleran said. "You know Amanda."

Then Willard Carmichael approached him. "Qwill, have you met Danielle's cousin yet?"

"I've been watching for an opportunity, but he's always surrounded."

"Come with me. We'll bust in."

The visiting celebrity stood with his back to the

fireplace, answering questions calmly and modestly.

"Excuse me," Willard said loudly. "Carter Lee's visit won't be complete until he shakes hands with the hand that writes the 'Qwill Pen' column."

The group moved aside, and the two men gripped hands heartily.

"Welcome to Moose County," Qwilleran said. "I hope you brought your snowshoes."

"Snow or no snow, I'm glad to be here," the visitor said with sincerity. "I've been reading your column. Let me compliment you."

"Thank you. Perhaps we could arrange an interview in the coming week. I understand you have some interesting proposals to make."

"Well, I have to be in Detroit for a few days to finish up some business, but then I'll return, and we'll see what happens."

Willard said, "I'll be down there at the same time, and I'll make sure he comes back. We need him."

Mildred, overhearing them, said, "Willard, how can you miss the first dinner of the gourmet society? It was all your idea!"

"I feel worse than you do," he said, "but I have to attend a seminar. Technology is advancing at such a breakneck speed that bankers have to go back to school every year."

Danielle said, "He wanted me to go with him, but it would be so boring!"

The conversation was interrupted by an announcement by Wetherby Goode in his radio voice: "Who wants to bring in the New Year? To guarantee good luck in the next twelve months, the first one to enter the building after the stroke of twelve has to be a male — cat, dog, or human."

"Bosh!" a woman's voice shouted.

"It's an old custom, Amanda. You know that."

"Well, you brought in the New Year last January, and we had a hurricane, an explosion on Main Street, and a financial disaster!"

"Take a vote!" Hixie yelled above the hubbub of dissension.

"Okay," Wetherby said, "all in favor of a female bringing in the New Year . . . ?"

"Yea!" chorused all the women present.

"Opposed?"

The men thundered an overwhelming negative.

"Why not alternate?" Qwilleran shouted.

"Now there's a man with some sense!" said Amanda, starting for the exit. "As a member of the city council, I consider it my duty to bring in the New Year."

There were protests.

"Let her go!" said a man who had opposed her in the last election — and lost. "Maybe she'll catch pneumonia."

The women booed.

"Amanda, take your coat," Wetherby cautioned. "The wind chill is thirty below!"

The commotion subsided as everyone waited for the magic hour. Champagne corks were popping. The big clock over the bar was ticking. Wetherby was counting down the seconds. The hands reached twelve, and the crowd shouted "Happy New Year!"

Wetherby Goode played "Auld Lang Syne" as the new year was ushered in by Amanda Goodwinter. And Qwilleran, with the instincts of a veteran reporter, went around asking for prognostications for the coming twelve months.

"We'll see a sudden end to thievery at the local level," Riker predicted.

"Our First Annual Ice Festival will be a whopping success!" Hixie declared.

"Carter Lee's plans for Pleasant Street will be a national sensation," Willard said.

As the guests started bundling into their stormwear and trooping out into the snow, firecrackers and gunshots could be heard in the distance. Everyone was happy, except Carter Lee James. He discovered his lambskin car coat had been taken from the coatroom.

The New Year's Eve incident was reported to the police, and the residents of Indian Village were in a furor. They were embarrassed that it had happened to a visitor from Down Below — and worried that he might decide not to return — and indignant that two such incidents had occurred in their squeaky-clean neighborhood. Qwilleran tried to discuss the matter with Brodie but was brushed off — a sure indication that the police were on the trail of a suspect.

Qwilleran had his own suspicions. George Breze had recently moved into the Village. With

79

his red cap, overalls, and noisy pickup truck, he was an incongruous figure in the white-collar community. On Sandpit Road outside Pickax he had an empire of marginal commercial ventures behind a chain-link fence. It was under seven feet of snow in winter, and only the "office" was accessible — a shack with a pot-bellied stove. Yet in both winter and summer it was a hangout for kids. When the police dropped in from time to time, the kids were always reading comic books and playing checkers, and Red Cap was busy at his desk. On the same property was a large Federal-style house where Breze had lived with his wife until recently, when she went off with a hoe-down fiddle-player from Squunk Corners. That was when he moved to Indian Village.

Qwilleran had a strong desire to investigate this lead, considering Red Cap a latter-day Fagin, but he had to postpone extracurricular activity and work on the "Qwill Pen." Finding subject matter in winter was a greater problem than in summer, and this year he had encountered a few dead ends. The dowsing story was on hold until spring thaw; a piece on mushroom-growing had hit a credibility snag; it was too soon to write about the Ice Festival; Carter Lee was not ready.

In a quandary, Qwilleran paced back and forth across a floor that bounced more than usual. Suddenly there was a crash near the front door, and two cats fled from the foyer, either frightened or guilty. He had hung his snowshoes on the foyer wall, with their tails crossed, and the Siamese had ventured to investigate something new.

First, he phoned Polly at the library, asking if there might be a book on the fine points of snowshoeing and, if so, would she bring it home? Meanwhile he gave the sport a try. He was clumsy. He tripped. His right shoe stepped on his left shoe. After he got the hang of it, he enjoyed tramping through the silent woods, although certain thigh muscles protested. When he wrote his column on the joys of snowshoeing, it began: "Did you ever try walking through snow with your feet strapped to a couple of tennis rackets?"

Qwilleran was one of those invited to join the Nouvelle Dining Club. The prospectus — signed by Mildred Riker, Hixie Rice, and Willard Carmichael — stated: "We are committed to quality rather than quantity, pleasing the palate with the natural flavors of fresh ingredients seasoned with herbs, spices, and the essence of fruits and vegetables."

For each monthly dinner, a committee would plan the menu, assign cooking responsibilities, and provide the recipes. One member would host the event and serve the entrée. Others would bring the appetizers, soup, salad, and dessert courses. Expenses would be prorated.

Qwilleran signed up, volunteering for the wine detail, and he and Polly attended the first dinner one evening in January. It was held at the Lanspeaks' picturesque farmhouse in West Middle Hummock. Twelve members assembled in the country-style living room and talked about food as they sipped apéritifs.

Mildred entertained listeners with an account of her first cooking experience at the age of eleven. "I was visiting my aunt and was watching her make BLT sandwiches for lunch. Just as she started the bacon, the phone rang and she left the room, saying, 'Watch the bacon, Millie.' I did what she told me; I watched the strips turn brown and shrink and curl up. She kept yakking on the phone, and I kept watching the frying pan, and the bacon kept getting smaller and blacker. Just as I was opening a window to let out the smoke, my aunt came running. 'I told you to watch the bacon!' she screamed."

Everyone laughed, except Danielle Carmichael, who looked puzzled. Foodwise she was at age eleven, according to her husband. Since he and Carter Lee had left for Detroit, she had driven to the dinner with Fran Brodie. Hixie Rice and Dwight Somers had carpooled with the Rikers. The Wilmots lived nearby.

For the sit-down courses, three tables-for-four were set up in the family room. There were place cards, and Qwilleran found himself seated with Mildred, Hixie, and Pender Wilmot. He noted that Riker and Dwight were the lucky ones, seated with Danielle. At each place there was a printed menu:

Smoked whitefish on triangles of
spoon bread with mustard broccoli coulis

Black bean soup with conchiglie (pasta shells)
Roast tenderloin of lamb in a crust of pine
nuts, mushrooms, and cardamom
Purée of Hubbard squash and leeks
Pear chutney
Crusty rolls
Spinach and redleaf lettuce tossed
with ginger vinaigrette and garnished
with goat cheese
Baked apples with peppercorn sauce

Mildred said, "The menu is built around local products: lamb, whitefish, beans, squash, goat cheese, pears, and apples. It's such a pity that Willard couldn't be here. I wonder what he's having for dinner tonight."

"If he's in Detroit," Qwilleran said, "he'll be headed for Greektown."

Hixie asked, "Do you think Carter Lee will ever come back?"

"I hope so," Mildred said. "He's such a gentleman, and that's unusual in one of his generation."

"He has personality-plus, and he's not married."

"If you're staking out a claim, Hixie, I think you'll have to stand in line."

"Seriously," said Pender, "I see him as a visionary. I hope his plans for Pleasant Street come to fruition. It would be a stimulating triumph for the whole city."

Qwilleran said, "He's like some actors I've

known: laid back but fired with an inner energy that produces a great performance. I'm looking forward to interviewing him when he returns."

Pender asked about the status of the late Iris Cobb's cookbook. The long-lost recipe book was being edited for publication by Mildred. She said, "I'm running into a problem. Only about two dozen recipes are original with her; the rest are photocopied from cookbooks by Julia Child, James Beard, and others."

Pender said, "You'll have to get permission to reprint, or risk being sued for plagiarism."

Hixie had an idea. Hixie always had an idea. "Make it a coffee table book with large color photos on slick paper — large format, large print, and only her own creations. If it's going to be a memorial to Iris, make it spectacular."

Mildred said she would be happy to prepare the dishes. "Do you think John Bushland could shoot them?"

"It would be better to hire a specialist. I used to work with food accounts Down Below, and we'd fly in a photographer and food stylist from Boston or San Francisco. They'd use real food, but they'd glue it, oil it, paint it, sculpture it, spray it, pin it, sew it . . ."

"Stop!" Qwilleran said. "You're ruining my appetite!" He uncorked the wine and poured with an expert twist of the wrist when the lamb was served.

Pender complimented him. "Done like a professional sommelier!"

"I worked as a bartender when I was in college," Qwilleran explained. "I'm still available for private parties."

Before the forks could be raised, Larry stood and proposed a toast to Willard Carmichael. "To our absent friend and mentor! May he live all the days of his life!"

The entrée was a taste sensation, especially the vegetable accompaniment. "I'll never eat mixed peas and carrots again!" said Qwilleran. At his table they began to talk about the best food they had ever eaten — and the worst.

Hixie said, "My worst was at a place between Trawnto Beach and Purple Point. I was driving around the county on ad business and hadn't eaten, so I stopped at a real *shack* that advertised pasties and clam chowder. It was mid-afternoon. The place was empty. A heavy woman came from the kitchen, and I ordered the chowder. She waddled back through the swinging doors, and I waited. Pretty soon a school bus stopped, and a young boy rushed through the door and threw his books on a table. Right away a voice yelled, 'Baxter! Come in here!' He rushed into the kitchen and rushed out again, and I saw him running down the highway. Still no chowder.

"Baxter returned with a bag of something which he tossed through the swinging doors before sitting down to do his homework. I began to hear cooking noises, so that was reassuring. In a while, the woman screamed for Baxter again, and he rushed into the kitchen and came out carrying a bowl with a spoon in it. He carried it very carefully with two hands and set it down in front of me. I looked at it and couldn't believe what I saw. It was watery, dirty gray, and appeared to be curdled, and there were lumps in it that looked like erasers from old lead pencils . . . I rushed from the premises."

Qwilleran said, "Too bad you didn't get the recipe."

"I think it was a quart of water, a package of instant mashed potatoes, and a can of minced clams," she said. "Serves four."

Just as the dessert course was being served, the telephone rang, and Carol went to the kitchen to answer it. She returned immediately with a look of anxiety and whispered to Fran Brodie, who jumped up and left the room.

Qwilleran stroked his moustache. There was something about this pantomime that worried him. Glancing toward the kitchen door, he saw Fran beckoning him. Now it was his turn to excuse himself and leave the table. She said a few words to him before he went to the phone.

In the family room the baked apples with peppercorn sauce were untouched. There was a murmur of concern.

Qwilleran returned and touched Larry's shoulder, and the two of them went to the foyer. Carol joined them for a moment of conference. Then the Lanspeaks together went to Danielle and led her across the foyer to the library.

"What's the trouble, Qwill?" Mildred asked

when he sat down again.

"Andy Brodie called. He knew Fran was here with Danielle. It's bad news. Very bad! The Detroit police got in touch with him. You know Willard left yesterday to attend a conference —"

"An air crash?" Mildred asked, clutching her throat.

"No, he arrived safely and was registered at a hotel. Apparently he was walking to a restaurant when he was mugged. And shot . . ."

"Fatally?" Pender asked under his breath.

"Fatally."

"Oh, my God!" Mildred said in a horrified whisper.

"They're trying to break the news to her gently."

At that moment there was a shriek from the library.

Larry returned to the room and faced the diners. "Friends," he said, "you won't feel like eating your dessert."

# 6

The WPKX bulletin about the homicide sent the entire county into shock and rage, and individuals wanted to share their feelings with others. When thwarted by busy signals on the phone, they went out in the snow and cold to gather in public places and bemoan the loss of Willard Carmichael, who had died in such an unthinkable way. Qwilleran, with his usual compulsion to take the public pulse, joined them and listened to their comments:

"Those cities Down Below are jungles! He shouldn'ta went there!"

"We've lost a good man. He would have been an asset to the community. He attended our church."

"What'll happen now? He was married to that young girl. They'd bought the Fitch house."

"I feel sorry for his wife. We shoulda been nicer to her, even though she didn't fit in."

"If she moves back Down Below, she's nuts!"

"The church'll send their Home Visitors to call on her and try to give her some comforting thoughts."

With grim amusement Qwilleran visualized Danielle receiving these well-intentioned visitors with their "comforting thoughts." That alone would drive her back Down Below, where her citified wardrobe would be appreciated, and where she could buy a kinkajou. No doubt Willard had provided for her generously.

While downtown he stopped at the design studio, expecting Fran Brodie to be up-to-date on developments. The husky delivery man was there alone. "She flew Down Below with that woman," he said. "I'm mindin' the store till the boss gets back from a call, if that's what she's doin'. I think she's goofin' off."

Qwilleran went to the department store for more details and found the compassionate Carol Lanspeak still distraught. "Fran took Danielle home last night and stayed with her, and my daughter went over and gave her a sedative. Danielle's a good customer of Fran's and feels comfortable with her, so we thought Fran should be the one to take her to Detroit. We got in touch with Carter Lee James, and he's meeting them at the airport and taking care of everything. Fran will stay in the airport hotel tonight and come right home tomorrow. We don't want her wandering around in that city!"

"I predict Danielle won't return," said Qwilleran, influenced by wishful thinking.

"Well, maybe not, but if she does, we want to have a quiet little dinner for her, and we want you and Polly to be there. Danielle likes you, Qwill."

He hoped the day would never come. He had always disliked women who were sexually aggressive. Melinda Goodwinter, broke and in need of a rich husband, had been a problem. Now he feared he would have a merry widow on his trail, winking and pouting and remarking about his moustache. Danielle was not one to wear black for very long, if at all.

His next stop was the newspaper office. It was late morning, and the staff was on deadline. Junior Goodwinter, the young managing editor, was writing an editorial in the nature of a tribute to Willard. Roger MacGillivray was punching out a piece on the banking improvements instituted by the victim. Jill Handley was on the phone collecting laudatory quotes to be used in a human interest feature.

Qwilleran found the publisher at his massive executive desk, juggling two phones. "What's the latest?" he asked when Riker had a breathing space.

"I talked to Brodie. He's in touch with the Detroit police, but I'm afraid Willard is just another statistic. Thousands of homicides go unsolved Down Below."

Qwilleran said, "He had wanted Danielle to go with him. If she had been along, no doubt they would have taxied to the restaurant, and this wouldn't have happened — or, at least, the odds would have been better. If she's sensitive enough or smart enough to figure that out, she could feel guilty."

"Well, we'll never know. She won't come back," Riker predicted, shaking his head soberly.

On his way out of the executive suite, Qwilleran was hailed by Hixie Rice. He went into the promotion office and sat down.

"What do you know?" she asked.

"No more than you do."

"It was a shocker. Willard was a nice guy — cocky but kind of sweet. He worked with Mildred and me on the organization of the club and the dinner menu. What did you think of it?"

"Everything was excellent. I don't know about the dessert. No one felt like eating dessert."

"And wouldn't you know. The dessert was my contribution!" Hixie had a long history of major and minor disappointments, yet she always bounced back. "How about lunch, Qwill? I'll buy and put it on my expense account."

"Those are the words I love to hear."

She started pulling on her boots. "We'll drive to Mooseville and eat at the Northern Lights. That's headquarters for the Ice Festival, and I want to fill you in on the plans. You might get a slant for your column. We'll take my van. How do you like your four-over-four?"

"It uses more gas, and the cats find it a little bumpier."

"Willard drove a Land Rover, and you could probably get a good deal on it. I'm sure Danielle won't keep it. He bought her a Ferrari."

"She flew to Detroit this morning, and I doubt whether she'll come back. She didn't want to move here in the first place," he said.

"But didn't they buy the Fitch house?"

"That was to humor her. I doubt whether Carter Lee will return, either. The Pleasant Street project was half Willard's idea, and the bank was going to finance it. Without him, I don't know . . ."

"Too bad. Carter Lee was a really neat guy. He always wore monogrammed shirts." Then after a few moments' silence, Hixie said, "After some serious reflection I can see why a man of Willard's age would marry a gorgeous young woman like Danielle, but why would she marry him, except for his money?"

"Don't forget," Qwilleran reminded her, "Willard could cook."

They turned onto the lakeshore drive, where beach houses were boarded-up, snowed-in, bleak and forbidding. Mooseville, a teeming fishing village in summer, was chillingly quiet in January, and relentlessly white. Piers protruded blackly from the white frozen lake. On Main Street, where most commercial enterprises were closed, the dark log cabins and pseudo-log cabins had snow in their chinks and on their rooftops. Dark evergreens drooped with their white burden. The fishing fleet and pleasure craft were somewhere else, in dry dock.

They parked at the Northern Lights Hotel, overlooking the expanse of ice that extended to the horizon. Far, far out it was dotted with a row of black fishing shanties, like dominoes. In the dining room there was one waiter and a limited menu: fried fish sandwich with lumber-camp fries and cole slaw.

Hixie said, "The Ice Festival will be a shot in the arm for the shoreline. By the end of January, the ice on the lake will be twenty inches thick at least. All of the activities will take place on the ice: races, tournaments, hospitality, and entertainment."

"What kind of races?"

"Dogsled, snowmobile, motorcycle, cross-country ski, snowshoe, and ice skate. Plows will clear the race tracks and rinks, building up snow barriers as viewing ridges for spectators. Other areas will be cleared for hospitality tents . . . And see those fishing shanties out there? We'll have twice that many for the tournament. They've signed up already. Colleges all over are sending artists to the snow sculpture competition. And there'll be a torchlight parade on Friday night to kick off the whole exciting weekend!"

Qwilleran listened dumbly to her exuberant recital, finally asking, "How many people do you expect?"

"As many as ten thousand."

"What! Where'll they park, for Pete's sake!"

"No problem. Parking will be inland at Gooseneck Creek, where there's lots of open area, frozen solid," she explained glibly. "Shuttle buses will transport people to the ice, where they'll buy admission tickets and get their Festival buttons. The design is a three-inch plastic button with a polar bear on a blue background, a souvenir worth saving. We've ordered fifteen thousand, because people will want to buy extras to take home."

"Where'll they sleep?"

"Most will be day-trippers from the tri-county, but we have lodgings lined up all over Moose County, even in private homes."

"And what are the hospitality tents?"

"They'll sell food and drink, admissions, and tickets for prize drawings. There'll also be a first-aid tent and two EMS ambulances."

Qwilleran said, "I'm impressed, Hixie. Some brilliant brain has thought of all this, and I suspect it's yours."

She pointed to the frozen lake outside the hotel window. "Look out there, Qwill, and imagine flags flying, striped tents, portable johns painted in bright colors, and thousands of people having a wonderful time! Doesn't it make your blood race?"

"It makes me want to move to Mexico," he said.

She pounded his arm with a friendly fist. "I know you, Qwill. You'll wind up loving it! You'll want to hang out here for two days!"

"And how does the newspaper fit into the picture?"

"We're sponsoring it as a public service. That means advancing the money, but costs will be more than covered by admissions, contestants' fees, and raffle tickets. All prizes are donated." Hixie paused for a sobering thought. "Willard was all for it! The bank was donating a microwave."

The fish sandwiches were not bad, and Qwilleran was contemplating a piece of apple pie when Hixie said, "Could I ask you a favor, Qwill?"

"I thought so," he said. "There's no such thing as a free lunch. What do you want me to do?"

"Well, there'll be a couple of thousand people here Friday night, and you're the most famous personality in three counties. Would you be noble enough to act as grand marshal of the torchlight parade?"

"What does that entail?" He remembered his traumatic experience in a Santa Claus suit the previous year. "If it means wearing a polar-bear costume —"

"Nothing like that! You simply ride in a horse-drawn sleigh with the cheering multitude lining the route. They love you, Qwill."

"Yes, but do I love them? All it takes is one ugly kid throwing the first snowball, and then it's avalanche time, with everyone playing hit-the-moustache. No thanks!"

Hixie was only momentarily rebuffed. "Is there any kind of conveyance you could suggest?"

"An army tank," he said. "Or how about a county snowblower with enclosed cab? I could ride in the cab and spray the cheering multitude with snow. I might enjoy that."

"You're not taking this seriously," she chided him.

"Do you know that the temperature drops at night, and the wind comes off the lake, and the

95

wind chill is sixty below? And you're having a parade!"

"Okay, so we have a few details to rethink, but will you be grand marshal?"

"I can't say no, can I? You'd make me walk home. Let's say I'll take it under advisement."

They drove home via Sandpit Road, past George Breze's snow-covered empire, with only a curl of smoke coming from the "office."

"Does Red Cap pay club dues?" Qwilleran asked. "He was conspicuously absent on New Year's Eve."

"He must have clubhouse privileges. He's always in the TV lounge, but no one speaks to him."

"How's Lenny Inchpot working out as club manager? Lois is bursting with pride these days."

"She should be proud! He's very reliable and helpful and even studies at his desk in his spare time. Don Exbridge likes him because he's clean-cut and good with people — the result of having been a hotel desk clerk, I suppose."

"How did Lenny react to the two thefts?" Qwilleran asked.

"He was upset, but Don told him there was nothing he could have done to prevent either of them."

"Do you suspect anyone, Hixie?"

"Yes. It's either Amanda Goodwinter or you."

The day Fran Brodie was due back from Detroit, Qwilleran left a message on her answering machine: "Fran, you must be bushed. Would you like dinner at the Old Stone Mill?"

Around seven in the evening she called back. "You're right, Qwill. I'm even too exhausted to go out to dinner. I just want to take my shoes off and have a cup of cocoa and a graham cracker, but if you want to come over in half an hour, I'll give you a report."

"I'll be there."

Meanwhile he fed the cats and thawed his own dinner: a freezer carton marked M-and-C. This, plus Fran's reference to C-and-GC, gave him an idea for the "Qwill Pen." Comfort food! What did prominent townfolk crave in times of exhaustion, sadness, or frustration? Polly always prepared poached eggs on toast with the crusts cut off. He could imagine the mayor gulping red Jell-O, George Breze wallowing in mashed potatoes and gravy, Amanda Goodwinter gorging on Oreos, Chief Brodie eating chocolate pudding.

As he swallowed his macaroni and cheese, the Siamese sat in quiet bundles on the carpet, not looking at each other, not looking at anything. Abruptly Koko rose, stretched, walked over to Yum Yum and, without apparent malice, bopped her on the head. She winced.

"Stop that!" Qwilleran shouted. "Act like a gentleman!"

Koko strolled nonchalantly from the room.

Picking up the little female and fondling her silky ears, Qwilleran murmured, "Why do you let

him get away with that? Sock him on the nose!"
She purred throatily.

Then it was time to visit Fran. Bundled in
layers of warm clothing, he walked the length of
the Village to her apartment. The young woman
who opened the door wore sweats and no
makeup. She looked pale and frazzled.

"Help yourself in the fridge, if you want anything," she said, flopping on the sofa. The living
room was furnished with items he had seen in the
design studio in times gone by — items that apparently had failed to sell: a houndstooth check
sofa, an elephant cocktail table, a lamp with a
grapeleaf shade.

"Rough day?" he asked sympathetically.

"We really started the Nouvelle Dining Club
with a bang, didn't we? — if you'll pardon the
pun," she said.

"The timing seemed more like fiction than fact."

"Danielle was lucky to be with friends. If she'd
been home alone, Dad would have gone to her
apartment to break the news, cop-style. Even so,
she was hysterical. When we got home, Dr. Diane
was waiting with a hypo, so that helped. In fact,
she slept just fine, but I didn't sleep a wink. Larry
lined up our tickets, and in the morning we took
off. She was groggy until we boarded the jet in
Minneapolis. Then she had a drink and started
to talk. She'd had a hunch something would happen, because he forgot to take the cigarettes he
always packed — for luck."

"Did she feel any guilt?"

"No," said Fran. "After another drink she started putting him down. He called her Danny-girl, which she hates. She'd begged him not to go to the seminar, but his work always came first. He was critical of the way she acted, the clothes she wore, the things she said, and the food she ate . . . Isn't it ironic, Qwill, that a fast-foodie like Danielle should marry an epicure who thinks ketchup is a mortal sin?"

"They hadn't known each other long before they married," Qwilleran observed.

"She didn't mention how he lavished money on her. He seemed to have plenty. He paid cash for the Fitch house and gave her an unlimited budget to do it over . . . But now I'm worried, Qwill. She ordered fabulous custom furniture and carpets for the house. Suppose . . . *just suppose* she never comes back and the studio is stuck for the order! Some of the fabrics are a hundred dollars a yard!"

"What kind of deposit did they give you?"

Fran looked sheepish. "None, actually. We didn't ask for one. This is a small town; her husband was head of the bank; they were fantastic customers . . . When I ordered things for your barn, Qwill, did I ask for a deposit?"

"Well . . . no."

"So when we were on the plane and she was jabbering away, I was dying to know her plans, although I didn't want to ask her flat out. I thought about it hard and then took a deep breath and said, 'Danielle, this is going to be a rough

99

time for you, but it would help you adjust if you'd really get involved in the theatre club. You have talent. You should be playing a role in our next production.' You can see I was desperate, Qwill."

"People have been struck down by lightning for lesser lies."

"Well, it worked. Danielle perked up and asked what kind of role."

"I could suggest a couple," Qwilleran said unkindly.

Fran ignored the jibe. "We're scheduled to do *Hedda Gabler*, and I'm to do the title role, but I'd gladly step aside if it would convince her to stay in Pickax and finish the house."

"*And let her do Hedda?* You're losing it, Fran. You're tired. I'll go home. You go to bed and sleep it off."

"No, I mean it! I'd coach her every step of the way. She's got a phenomenal memory for prices, style numbers, and the names of fabrics. She should be able to learn lines."

"There's more to acting than learning lines. Do you want to turn a tragedy into a farce?"

Fran said, "Any port in a storm, as Dad says. Anything to keep a good customer, as Amanda says. By the time Danny-girl had tossed off her third drink, she wanted to finish the house, move in, add a swimming pool, give some parties, buy a couple of horses, and take riding lessons. She also asked about a voice coach and acting lessons. By the time we landed at Metro, she was feeling no pain. Carter Lee was waiting, and they had a tearful reunion. As soon as possible, I said good-bye and told them we looked forward to seeing them both in Pickax — soon."

Qwilleran walked home through the snow and cold, hardly noticing either. He kept stroking his frosted moustache as he pondered Fran's problem and her dubious solution. By the time he let himself into the condo, he looked like a snowman, and the hoary image frightened the Siamese.

He brushed off his outerwear and mopped up the puddles on the foyer's vinyl floor. Then he called Polly with the news.

She was equally aghast. "That tinny voice? In the role of Hedda?"

"I'm afraid so."

"And what about Carter Lee? Is he coming back? Lynette will be disappointed if he doesn't. She's dying to have her house listed on the National Register."

"Do you think it will qualify?"

"Carter Lee thinks so. And Willard Carmichael thought so." Then Polly changed the subject abruptly. "Have you heard the latest newscast?"

"No. What's happened?"

"The police have arrested a suspect in the string of robberies."

"Who?" he asked impatiently.

"The name won't be released until the arraignment."

"If I were a betting man," Qwilleran said, "I'd put my money on George Breze."

 7

"Late to bed and late to rise" was Qwilleran's motto, and he was remarkably healthy, certainly wealthy, and — if not exactly wise — he was witty. On that particular January morning at seven o'clock, he was sleeping peacefully when he was jolted awake and virtually catapulted from his bed by the crashing drums and brasses of the "Washington Post March," as if the entire U.S. Marine Band were bursting through his bedroom wall. He required a few seconds to realize where he was: on the balcony of a poorly built condominium in Indian Village, and his next-door neighbor was playing John Philip Sousa.

Before he could find Wetherby Goode's phone number, the volume was toned down. One could still hear and feel the *thrum-thrum-thrum* of the drums, but the music itself was replaced by the sound of gushing, pelting water. Wetherby Goode was taking a shower.

Only then did Qwilleran recall the news of the night before: the arrest of a robbery suspect, name withheld. He knew he could cajole Brodie into confiding the name if he went downtown to headquarters, so he dressed, fed the cats, and left the house without coffee.

His neighbor was shoveling snow instead of

waiting for the Village sidewalk blower. "Good exercise!" he shouted, puffing clouds of vapor.

"I can see that," Qwilleran said. "Good concert this morning, too, but rather short."

Wetherby paused and leaned on his shovel. "Sorry about that. I have a new Sousabox, and my cat must've rubbed her jaw against the controls. I was in the shower and didn't realize what was happening."

"That's all right. What's a Sousabox?"

"It plays fifty Sousa marches. The inventor's a friend of mine in California, and I can get you one wholesale if you're interested."

"I'll give it some serious thought," Qwilleran said. "Better finish your shoveling before it starts to snow again."

He went on his way, thinking that Wetherby was friendly and well intentioned, even though he overdid the quotations and had strange taste in music. Fifty marches! Yet, he had a cat, and that was to his credit.

There was a coffeepot at the police station, and Qwilleran helped himself before barging into Brodie's office and dropping into a chair.

"Who invited you?" The chief scowled.

"I won't stay long. I just came for coffee. Tell me who was arrested, and I'll leave. It'll probably be in the paper this afternoon and on the air at twelve."

Brodie shook his head. "You'll never believe it, Qwill. I didn't myself, but the evidence was there. When we found the loot and went to pick him up for questioning, he'd skipped town."

"*Who? Who?*" Qwilleran insisted with some irritation.

"Lenny Inchpot."

"No! What led you to Lenny?"

"Anonymous tip on the hotline, telling us to search the manager's locker at the Indian Village clubhouse. We went out there with a warrant and had to cut the padlock. And there they were — all the items reported stolen — well, not all of the stuff. Things like sunglasses, videos, gloves, you know. No money, though. And no lambskin car coat. There was even a doll that the Kemple family reported stolen not too long ago."

Qwilleran huffed into his moustache. "Can you imagine a young man like Lenny stealing a doll?"

"It was a rare one, they said."

"And is Lenny Inchpot suddenly an expert on rare dolls?" This was said tartly.

"He's a friend of the Kemples' daughter. Do you know about the family's doll collection?"

"I've heard about it." For two years or more, Qwilleran's readers had been urging him to "write up" the Kemple collection. He declined. He had written about teddy bears, but that was under duress. Under no circumstances was he prepared to write about dolls. He said, "So where did you find Lenny? You said he skipped town."

"In Duluth. He's being arraigned this morning, with a public defender."

Qwilleran smoothed his moustache. "I get a fishy feeling about this case, Andy. I'd like to use the phone on my way out."

On his way out he called his attorney, G. Allen Barter.

The youngest partner in the Hasselrich, Bennett & Barter law firm was Qwilleran's representative in all dealings with the Klingenschoen Foundation, and the two men saw eye-to-eye on many matters. Even the attorney's choice of office furniture suited Qwilleran's taste. It was a contemporary oasis in a dark jungle of aged walnut and deep red leather. And while old Mr. Hasselrich served his clients tea in his grandmother's porcelain cups, G. Allen Barter served coffee in Art Deco mugs. He had recently changed his letterhead from George A. Barter because the name was confused once too often with George A. Breze. Either way, his clients called him Bart. He was fortyish — a quiet, effective professional without pretensions.

When Qwilleran turned up in his office, Barter said, "We'll have someone at court for the arraignment, and I think we can get him released to the custody of his mother until the hearing."

Qwilleran nodded, thinking of all the courthouse personnel, from judges on down, who lunched at Lois's. He patted his moustache. "Something tells me it's a frame-up, Bart. I don't know anything about Lenny's personal life, except that his girlfriend was killed in the explosion last fall. But he could have an enemy — a rival who wants his job. It's only part-time, but it's a soft spot for a student: interesting work, good pay, flexible hours . . . Incidentally, did you read in the paper that the stolen money was replaced by an anonymous donor? The check was drawn on a Chicago bank, and the public is assuming it came from the K Fund. I know nothing about it. How about you?"

"I certainly wasn't involved."

"Any developments in the Limburger file?"

"Yes, the estate is willing to sell the hotel and the family mansion, and the K Fund is willing to buy, restoring the hotel and converting the mansion into a country inn."

"In that case, they might consider Carter Lee James for the restoration work. He's the cousin of Willard Carmichael's widow. He was here for the holidays and had a sensational idea for Pleasant Street. You may have heard about it. Everyone's hoping he'll return to implement it."

"Do you think he's good?"

"Willard recommended him, and the property-owners are impressed. It appears he's done most of his work on the East Coast. At any rate, the K Fund should check him out."

"What's his name?" Barter wrote it down.

"Meanwhile, there's something good you could do. Gus Limburger had promised to leave his German Bible and cuckoo clock to his handyman, but they weren't mentioned in his will. Someone should grab those two items and give them to the handyman, Aubrey Scotten."

"I think we can swing that," the attorney said,

making a note. "And how do your cats like living in a small condo instead of a large barn?"

"Oh, they're happy," Qwilleran said. "They enjoy listening to the plumbing noises."

When Lenny Inchpot was charged with several counts of robbery, the locals vented their emotions loudly in the supermarkets and other public places:

"I don't believe it! Somebody made a mistake! He's a good kid!"

"What'll happen to him? Will he go to jail? It'll kill his poor mother."

"Not Lois! Most likely his poor mother will go out and kill the judge with a frying pan!"

Two days later Danielle Carmichael returned to town, and the gossip was less kind:

"Nobody's seen her wearin' black."

"I'll bet he left her well fixed."

"What'll she do with that big house he bought? Open a bed-and-breakfast or something?"

"Or something! That's about the size of it."

Qwilleran checked in at the design studio to get an update from Fran Brodie.

"Yes, Danny-girl is back. I've talked to her on the phone, but I haven't seen her. The things I ordered for her house are trickling in — all contemporary, of course. That was the big quarrel between her and Willard. When I dropped her off in Detroit, she couldn't wait to dump the traditional furniture his first wife had bought. He'd had it in storage."

"How soon can she move into her house?" he asked, hoping for her early departure from Indian Village. She was too close for comfort; she would become increasingly chummy.

"Not soon. The drifts are so deep in the Hummocks, even our delivery truck couldn't get in. Besides, her lease at the Village has a few months to run. Meanwhile, she intends to work with Carter Lee. Amanda thinks they'll cut into our business, but she just likes to carp. Actually, the whole restoration project on Pleasant Street will be good for us."

"In what way?"

"When Carter Lee recommends an authentic wallcovering, window treatment, and rug, the order will be placed through our studio, which gets a designer discount. Likewise, when he suggests an antique pier mirror as a focal point, Susan Exbridge will scout for it."

"And in both cases he gets a kickback," Qwilleran presumed.

"The word is *commission*, darling," Fran corrected him loftily.

"Has he returned as yet?"

"He'll be here at the end of the week."

"And what news about *Hedda Gabler*? Are you going ahead with your insane idea?"

Fran threw him an expressive scowl she had learned from her father. "Frankly, that's why Danielle returned so soon. She attended rehearsal last night and read lines."

"And . . . ?"

Fran's scowl changed to involuntary laughter. "When the snooty Hedda says *She's left her old hat on the chair* in Danielle's rusty-gate voice, it's hard to keep a straight face."

"I warned you it would turn into a farce," Qwilleran said. "The only Ibsen drama ever played for laughs!"

"Don't panic! We'll work it out. Unfortunately, she doesn't like the man who's playing Judge Brack. She'd rather play opposite you, Qwill."

"Sure. But she's not going to play opposite me. I'm the drama critic for the paper, remember? I can't have one leg on the stage and the other in row five."

"But she's right. You'd be a perfect Brack, and you have such a commanding voice. Also, to be grossly mercenary about it, your presence in the cast would sell tickets."

"If you're chiefly interested in the box office, the K Fund will be glad to buy out the house for all nine performances."

"Forget I mentioned it," Fran said.

The four o'clock lull at Lois's Luncheonette would be an auspicious time to visit the suspect's mother, Qwilleran thought. Would she be fighting mad or pained beyond words? To his surprise, Lenny himself was the only one in sight. He was mopping the new vinyl floor, a hideous pattern of flowers and geometrics that had been donated to the lunchroom and installed by devoted customers.

"Mom's in the kitchen, prepping dinner," Lenny said. Though in work clothes, he looked more like a club manager than a mop-pusher.

"Don't disturb her," Qwilleran said. "It's you I want to see. Let's sit in a booth." He indicated a corner booth behind the cash register. "Did G. Allen Barter contact you?"

"Yeah. Do you think I need him?"

"You certainly do! Don't worry about the expense. The K Fund is interested in your case. Bart will see that you're exonerated."

"But what if I'm guilty?" the young man said with a mischievous grin.

"We'll take that chance, smart-ape! Even Brodie thinks the allegations are preposterous, but he had to follow the letter of the law. You'll notice they didn't keep you in jail or ask you to post bond. Now . . . would you like to tell me what you know? I'd like to find the real culprit, not that it's any of my business. How long have you been working at the clubhouse?"

"About six weeks. Don's a good boss. All the members are fun. It's better than desk clerk at the hotel, plus I get a nice office."

"Where was the money jar kept?"

"In my office, in a cabinet with pencils, tallies, nut dishes, and other stuff. There wasn't any lock on the cabinet, but the jar was covered with a paper bag."

"What did you think when the money was stolen?"

"I couldn't understand it. Nobody knew the jar

was there except the bridge club."

"Who else had access to your office?"

"Anybody who wanted to pay their dues or see the schedule of events — plus there were maintenance guys, cleaning crew, caterers."

"Where was your locker?" Qwilleran asked.

"In the back hall with all the other employee lockers."

"Do they have locks?"

"Padlocks are supplied, but nobody uses them. I just put my boots and jacket in there."

"Is your name on your locker?"

"Sure. They all have names."

"Why did you go to Duluth?"

"Well, I had to study for exams, you see, and in Pickax I've got too many friends who like to party, so I went to my aunt's house in Duluth. I no sooner opened my books than a couple of deputies knocked on the door. They were guys I went to school with, and they were embarrassed because they thought I really stole the stuff. I knew I hadn't . . . At least, I don't think I did," Lenny said with a wicked grin.

"Don't let your whimsical sense of humor get you into trouble," Qwilleran advised him.

A loud voice from the kitchen interrupted. "Lenny! Who's that you're gabbin' with? Get off your duff and mop that floor! Folks'll be comin' in for supper."

Lenny yelled back, "It's Mr. Q, Mom. He wants to talk about the case."

"Oh! . . . Okay . . . Give him the other mop

111

and put him to work. He can talk at the same time."

"I'm leaving," Qwilleran shouted.

"Want a doggie bag? I've got some meatballs left over from lunch."

Back in Indian Village the Siamese were sleeping in Qwilleran's reading chair. They had cushioned baskets, windowsills, and perches in their own room on the balcony. Yet, with feline perversity they preferred a man-size lounge chair with deep cushions and suede covering.

While they were waking and yawning and stretching and scratching their ears, Qwilleran phoned Don Exbridge at home and caught him in the middle of the happy hour.

"Something's screwy somewhere!" Exbridge said. "If Lenny's guilty, I'm a donkey's uncle! Come on over for a drink! Bring Polly!"

"Wish I could, but I'm working tonight," Qwilleran said. "I just want you to know G. Allen Barter is representing him."

"Great! Great! And his job will be waiting for him when it's all over."

"Have you had any applicants for it?"

"Some other students. We've taken applications, that's all. We're waiting to see which way the wind blows. The manager at the gatehouse is working two jobs."

"Well, you know, there's no telling how long Lenny will have to wait for a hearing, and I could recommend a temporary substitute who'd be perfect in the interim — an older woman, very responsible, cheerful — used to working with people. And she doesn't want to earn much money; it might affect her Social Security."

"Who is she?"

"Celia Robinson. You wouldn't be disappointed. Why don't I tell her to apply for the job?"

"She's got it! She's got it already! . . . Sure you don't want to come over for a drink?"

Feeling smug, Qwilleran hung up the phone and called Celia at her apartment in town.

"Hi, Chief!" she greeted him. "Happy New Year! Or is it too late?"

"It's never too late. Happy New Year! Happy Mother's Day!"

She screamed with laughter, a chronic overreactor to his quips.

"Seriously, Celia, have you heard about Lenny Inchpot's trouble?"

"Have I? It's all over town. His mother must be out of her mind."

"We're all concerned, and I personally suspect dirty work."

"Do I smell something cooking, Chief?" she asked eagerly.

"Just this: Lenny's position at Indian Village needs to be filled, quickly, by a temporary substitute. It's part-time, managing the social rooms at the clubhouse. I suggest you apply. Don Exbridge is expecting your call. I'll explain later. *It's your kind of job,* Celia."

"Gotcha, Chief!" she said knowingly and with

a final peal of laughter.

Two cats were watching Qwilleran closely when he replaced the receiver, as if to say, What about those meatballs? He crumbled one, and they gobbled it with gusto, spitting out the onion fastidiously. Then, while he was watching them do their ablutions, Koko deliberately walked over to Yum Yum and rapped her on the nose. She cowered.

"Koko! Stop that! Bad cat!" Qwilleran scolded as he picked up the little one and nuzzled her head under his chin. "What's that monster doing to my beautiful little girl? Why don't you hiss at him — scare the daylights out of him?"

To Koko he said, sharply, "I don't like your behavior, young man! What's wrong with you? If this continues, we'll have to find a cat shrink."

He reported the incident to Polly that evening when he went to her place for dinner. The Siamese were curled up blissfully together when he left. Polly thought Koko was frustrated by some new development in his life. It might have something to do with hormones. The veterinarian could prescribe something. Bootsie was taking pink pills.

Once a week she invited Qwilleran to what she laughingly called a "chicken dinner." The dietician at the hospital had given her seventeen low-calorie, low-cholesterol recipes for glamorizing a flattened chicken breast: with lemon and toasted almonds, with artichoke hearts and garlic, and so forth.

"Think of it as *scaloppine di pollo appetito,*" Polly suggested. To Qwilleran it was still flattened chicken breast — in fact, *half* a flattened chicken breast. He always thawed a burger for himself when he went home. On this occasion the week's special was FCB with mushrooms and walnuts.

Upon arrival, Qwilleran had first checked the whereabouts of Polly's Siamese. Now he noticed that Bootsie was watching him and crouched as if ready to spring.

Qwilleran inquired, "Why doesn't he sit comfortably on his brisket, the way other cats do?"

"He's not relaxed in your presence, dear," she explained.

"*Bootsie's* not relaxed?" he exploded. "What about Qwilleran? Did I ever pounce on his back and refuse to get off? Did I ever ambush him from underneath a table?"

"I'll put him upstairs in his room," she said, "or all three of us will have indigestion."

They had much to talk about. Qwilleran described his forthcoming book: a compilation of Moose County legends, anecdotes, and scandals, to be titled *Short and Tall Tales*. All would be collected on tape, and it might be possible to produce a recorded book, as well as a print edition. Homer Tibbitt would kick off with the story of the Dimsdale Jinx. Suggestions would be welcome.

"Try Wetherby Goode," she said. "He has stories about lake pirates that he tells to children at the library once in a while. Do you ever see him?"

"Only when he's shoveling his sidewalk. He has a cat, so he can't be too bad. It's a technocat who operates an electronic device that plays only Sousa marches."

"That reminds me, Qwill. You haven't mentioned how you like *Adriana Lecouvreur*. I've never heard it myself and don't know anything about the composer."

He had forgotten to listen to his Christmas gift, but he had read the brochure and spoke convincingly. "Francesco Cilea was born in Italy in 1866 and had already composed works at the age of nine. *Adriana* is an interesting opera with good female roles and some lush melodies. We'll listen to it together, some Sunday afternoon." He had handled that rather well but took the precaution of changing the subject. "Have you and Lynette made your annual pilgrimage to the hill?"

Lynette had a driving desire to visit the Hilltop Cemetery once every winter. The gravestones on the crest of the hill, rising from the snow and silhouetted against the sky, were a moving sight when viewed from the base of the slope. Her ancestors were among them, and one gravesite was reserved for "the last of the Duncans-by-blood."

Polly said, "I don't mind going with her. On a good day it's a beautiful sight. It would make a poignant painting . . . Incidentally, Lynette is on cloud nine; Carter Lee phoned her from Detroit. He's coming back and wants her to be cheerleader for the Pleasant Street project."

"Is this a paid position?"

"I don't think so, but Lynette enjoys working for a cause, and she's very enthusiastic about the project. He took her to dinner several times before he left, and she was the first property-owner to sign a contract . . . By the way, her birthday will be soon, and I'd like to give a party. Would you join us?"

"If you'll let me provide the champagne and birthday cake."

"That would be nice. But no candles! It's her fortieth. I'd invite Carter Lee, of course, and that would mean inviting Danielle, and that would mean inviting another man."

"How about John Bushland?" Qwilleran said. "He'll bring his camera." It occurred to him that the presence of a professional photographer might distract the photogenic young widow.

They had dined on *petti di pollo con funghi e noci* and were now having decaffeinated coffee in the living room when Qwilleran felt he was being watched again. Bootsie was staring at him between the balusters of the balcony railing.

"Oh, dear! He got out!" Polly said. "He's learned to stand on his hind legs and hang on the lever-type door handle. Does Koko do that?"

"Not yet," Qwilleran said with some disquietude. "Not yet!"

8

The first contributor to *Short and Tall Tales* was to be Homer Tibbitt, official historian of Moose County, who knew the story of the Dimsdale Jinx. The retired educator, now in his late nineties, was still researching and recording local history, and his fantastic memory made him a treasure. He might not remember where he left his glasses or what he had for breakfast, but events and personages of the distant past could be retrieved on demand. He lived with his sweet eighty-five-year-old wife in a retirement village, her responsibilities being to find his glasses, watch his diet, and drive the car — in good weather. In winter they both welcomed visitors.

"How were your holidays?" Qwilleran greeted them. "Was Santa good to you? Did he bring you a few more books?" Their apartment was cluttered with books and memorabilia.

Rhoda touched her ears prettily. "Homer gave me these garnet earrings. They were in his family."

Her husband, a bony figure sitting in a nest of cushions, was wearing a maroon shawl. "Rhoda gave me this. Gloomy color! Makes me feel like an old man."

"I knitted it," she said. "He's forgotten that he

chose the color . . . Shall I refill your hot water bottle, dear?"

While she was out of the room, Qwilleran said, "She's a lovely woman, Homer. You're lucky to have her."

"She chased me for twenty-five years before she caught me, so I'd say she's lucky to have me! What's news downtown?"

They were discussing the murder of Willard Carmichael and the arrest of Lenny Inchpot when Rhoda returned with the towel-wrapped bottle. "Terrible things are happening these days," she said, shaking her head. "What is the world coming to?"

"Terrible things have always happened everywhere," her husband said with the stoicism of age.

"Like the Dimsdale Jinx?" Qwilleran suggested, turning on the tape recorder. "What brought it about?"

"It started about a hundred years ago, when the mines were going full blast, and this was the richest county in the state. This isn't a tall tale, mind you. It's true. It isn't short either."

"Fire away, Homer. I won't ask questions. You're on your own."

The old man's account, interrupted only when his wife handed him a glass of water, was later transcribed as follows:

There was a miner named Roebuck Magley, a husky man in his late forties, who worked in

119

the Dimsdale mine. He had a wife and three sons, and they lived in one of the cottages provided for workers. Not all mine owners exploited their workers, you know. Seth Dimsdale was successful but not greedy. He saw to it that every family had a decent place to live and a plot for a vegetable garden, and he gave them the seed to plant. There was also a company doctor who looked after the families without charge.

Roebuck worked hard, and the boys went to work in the mines as soon as they finished eighth grade. Betty Magley worked hard, too, feeding her men, scrubbing their clothes, pumping water, tending the garden, and making their shirts. But somehow she always stayed pretty.

Suddenly Roebuck fell sick and died. He'd been complaining about stomach pains, and one day he came home from work, ate his supper, and dropped dead. Things like that happened in those days, and folks accepted them. Men were asphyxiated in the mines, blown to bits in explosions, or they came home and dropped dead. Nobody sued for negligence.

Roebuck's death certificate, signed by Dr. Penfield, said "Heart failure." Seth Dimsdale paid Mrs. Magley a generous sum from the insurance policy he carried on his workers, and she was grateful. She'd been ailing herself, and the company doctor was at a loss to diagnose her symptoms.

Well, about a month later her eldest son Robert died in the mineshaft of "respiratory failure," according to the death certificate, and it wasn't long before the second son, Amos, died under the same circumstances. The miners' wives flocked around Betty Magley and tried to comfort her, but there was unrest among the men. They grumbled about "bad air." One Sunday they marched to the mine office, shouting and brandishing pickaxes and shovels. Seth Dimsdale was doing all he could to maintain safe working conditions, considering the technology of the times, so he authorized a private investigation.

Both Robert and Amos had died, he learned, after eating their lunch pasties underground; Roebuck's last meal had been a large pasty in his kitchen. The community was alarmed. "Bad meat!" they said. Those tasty meat-and-potato stews wrapped in a thick lard crust were the staple diet of miners and their families.

Then something curious happened to Alfred, the youngest son. While underground, he shared his pasty with another miner whose lunch had fallen out of his pocket when he was climbing down the ladder. Soon both men were complaining of pains, nausea, and numb hands and feet. The emergency whistle blew, and the two men were hauled up the ladder in the "basket," as the rescue contraption was called.

When word reached Seth Dimsdale, he notified the prosecuting attorney in Pickax, and the court issued an order to exhume the bodies of Roebuck, Robert, and Amos. Their internal organs, sent to the toxologist at the state capital, were found to contain lethal quantities of arsenic, and Mrs. Magley was questioned by the police.

At that point, neighbors started whispering: "Could she have poisoned her own family? Where did she get the poison?" Arsenic could be used to kill insects in vegetable gardens, but people were afraid to use it. Then the neighbors remembered the doctor's visits to treat Mrs. Magley's mysterious ailment. He visited almost every day.

When Dr. Penfield was arrested, the mining community was bowled over. He was a handsome man with a splendid moustache, and he cut a fine figure in his custom-made suits and derby hats. He lived in a big house and owned one of the first automobiles. His wife was considered a snob, but Dr. Penfield had a good bedside manner and was much admired.

It turned out, however, that he was in debt for his house and car, and his visits to treat the pretty Betty Magley were more personal than professional. He was the first defendant placed on trial. Mrs. Magley sat in jail and awaited her turn.

The miners, convinced of the integrity of the doctor, rose to his support, and it was difficult to seat an unbiased jury. The trial itself lasted longer than any in local history, and when it was over, the county was broke. Twice its annual budget had been spent on the court proceedings.

The story revealed at the trial was one of greed and passion. Dr. Penfield had supplied the arsenic — for medical purposes, he said, and any overdose was caused by human error. Mrs. Magley had baked the pasties and collected the insurance money, giving half to the doctor. He was found guilty on three counts of murder and sentenced to life in prison.

Mrs. Magley was never tried for the crime because the county couldn't afford a second trial. The commissioners said it wasn't "worth the candle," as the saying went. It would be better if she just left town, quietly.

So she disappeared, along with her youngest son, the only one to survive. Seth Dimsdale retired to Ohio and also disappeared. The Dimsdale mine disappeared. The whole town of Dimsdale disappeared. It was called the Dimsdale Jinx.

When Homer finished telling his tale, Qwilleran clicked off the tape recorder and said, "Great story! Is any of this on public record?"

"Well, the *Pickax Picayune* never printed unpleasant news, but other newspapers around the state covered it," the historian said. "Those clippings are on file in the public library."

"On microfilm, thanks to the K Fund," said

Rhoda, smiling and nodding.

Homer said, "You should be able to get a transcript of the trial at the courthouse, but there was a fire some years back, and I don't know if the Penfield file was saved. Mostly, the story has been handed down by word of mouth. My relatives still talk about it and take sides, sometimes violently . . . I warn you, Qwill, never argue with a fellow whose grandfather told him the doctor was innocent!"

It had been a strenuous recital, and the old man's energy was flagging. It was time for his nap, his wife said. Qwilleran thanked him for a well-told tale and squeezed Rhoda's hand.

On the way home he drove through the scene of the crime: the ghost town called Dimsdale. The only landmark was a dilapidated diner, surrounded by weeds that choked the stone foundations of miners' cottages. Back in the woods was a slum of rusty trailer homes occupied by squatters, and a side road led to a high chain-link fence around the abandoned mineshaft. A sign said "Danger — Keep Out." A bronze plaque erected by the historical society said: SITE OF THE DIMSDALE MINE, 1872–1907.

It was January 25, and Qwilleran phoned the public library. While waiting to be connected with the chief librarian, he could visualize her in her glass cubicle on the mezzanine, reigning like a benevolent despot over the paid staff, the unpaid volunteers, and the obedient subscribers who never, never brought food, beverages, radios, or wet boots into the building.

"Polly Duncan here," she said pleasantly.

"What's today's date?" he asked, knowing she would recognize his voice.

"January twenty-fifth. Is it significant?"

"Birthday of Robert Burns. Tonight's the night! Point of no return!"

Gleefully she exclaimed, "It's Scottish Night! You're going to wear your kilt! I wish I could see you before you leave. What time is the dinner?"

"I leave at six-thirty, with trepidation," he admitted.

Polly said she would stop on her way home from work, to bolster his courage.

Qwilleran was allowing two hours to dress for Scottish Night at the men's lodge. He fed the cats early, then disappeared into his bedroom and closed the door. There he faced the unfamiliar trappings: the pleated kilt, the sporran, the flashes, the bonnet, the dubh. Bruce Scott, owner of the men's store, had told him the evening would be informal: no Prince Charlie coatees, no fur sporrans, and no fringed plaids thrown over the shoulder and anchored with a poached egg. Bruce had sold him a leather sporran and a correct pair of brogues and had given him a booklet to read.

The trick, according to the helpful text, was to develop an attitude of pride in one's hereditary Scottish attire. After all, Qwilleran's mother had been a Mackintosh, and he had seen movies in

125

which the kilt was worn by brave men skilled with the broadsword.

With this attitude firmly in place, Qwilleran strapped himself into what the dictionary called "a kind of short pleated petticoat." His kilt had been custom-tailored from eight yards of fine worsted in a rich red Mackintosh tartan. On this occasion, it would be worn with a white turtleneck and bottlegreen tweed jacket, plus matching green kilt-hose and red flashes. "Not flashers," Bruce had cautioned him. These were tabs attached to the garters that held up the kilt-hose — a small detail but considered vital by the storekeeper and the author of the booklet. The kilt itself had to end at the top of the kneecap and could not be an eighth-of-an-inch longer. The leather sporran hung from a leather belt.

Then there was the bonnet. Qwilleran's was a bottlegreen Balmoral — a round flat cap worn squarely on the forehead, with a slouchy crown pulled down rakishly to the right. It had a ribbon cockade above the left temple, a pompom on top, and two ribbons hanging down the back. According to the booklet, they could be knotted, tied in a bow, or left hanging. He cut them off and hoped no one would notice.

Studying his reflection in the full-length mirror, Qwilleran thought, Not bad! Not bad at all! Meanwhile, the Siamese were out in the hall, muttering complaints about the closed door. After one last glance in the mirror, he opened the door abruptly. Both cats levitated in fright, turned to escape, collided headlong, and streaked down the stairs with bushy tails.

When Polly arrived, she was overwhelmed with delight. "Qwill!" she cried, throwing her arms around him. "You look magnificent! So jaunty! So virile! But I do hope you're not going to catch cold in your bad knee, dear."

"No chance," he told her. "The parking lot's behind the lodge, and we duck into the rear entrance in bad weather. I won't need boots or earmuffs — just a jacket. Also, Bruce says the knee is all gristle and doesn't feel cold, as long as you're wearing good wool socks. That may be true, or he may be a good sock-salesman. You wouldn't believe what I paid for these socks!"

She walked around him and noted the straight front of the kilt — a double panel wrapped left over right. "Why isn't it pleated all around?"

"Because I don't play in a marching band and I'm not going into battle. Ask me anything. I've read the book. I know all the answers."

"What's that odd thing in your sock?"

"A knife, spelled d-u-b-h and pronounced *thoob*. I can use it to peel an orange or spread butter."

"Oh, Qwill! You're in a playful mood tonight! Do I know you well enough to ask what you wear under the kilt?"

"You do! You do indeed! And I know you well enough not to answer. It's known as the mystique of the kilt, and I'm not going to be the first to

127

destroy a centuries-old arcanum arcanorum!"

Downtown Pickax was deserted except for men in kilts or tartan trews ducking into the back door of the lodge. Qwilleran showed his knife to the doorman and was greeted by Whannell Mac-Whannell, who had invited him to be a guest. "I'll introduce you and mention your mother," he said. "What was her full name?"

"Anne Mackintosh Qwilleran."

Big Mac nodded. "Half my female relatives are named after Lady Anne. Let's go downstairs and look at the new exhibit."

The walls of the lower lounge were covered with maps, photographs of Scotland, and swatches of clan tartans. Qwilleran found the Mackintosh dress tartan, mostly red, and the Mackintosh hunting tartan, mostly green for camouflage in the woods. The majority of men were in kilts, and he felt comfortable among them.

Gil MacMurchie, the dowser, was wearing a lively Buchanan tartan. Qwilleran said to him, "I'm ready to buy your dirks, if you haven't sold them."

"They're still there." MacMurchie paused and looked down sadly. "But the one I was saving for myself was stolen."

"No! When?"

"While I was running those ads to sell my furniture and dishes and pots and pans. Strangers were traipsing through the house, some of them just nosey, and I couldn't keep an eye on all of them."

"Did you report it to the police?"

"Oh, sure, and after Lois's boy was arrested, I went to the station to see if my dirk turned up in his locker, but it wasn't there."

"How ironic," Qwilleran said, "that the thief should take the one your wife gave you."

"The hilt was silver," MacMurchie said. "The others have brass hilts."

The wail of a bagpipe summoned them to the dining hall on the upper level, where the walls were hung with antique weaponry. As soon as everyone was seated at the large round tables, the double doors were flung open, and in came the police chief in kilt, red doublet, towering feather bonnet, and white spats. A veritable giant, he walked with a slow swagger as he piped the inspiring air "Scotland the Brave." The skirling of the pipes, the swaying of the pleated kilt, and the hereditary pride of the piper made an awesome sight. He was followed by a snare drummer and seven young men in kilts and white shirts, each carrying a tray. On the first was the celebrated haggis; on each of the other six was a bottle of Scotch.

Bagpipe, haggis, and Scotch circled the room twice. Then a bottle was placed on each table, and toasts were drunk to the legendary pudding, which was sliced and served. Diners guffawed while old haggis jokes were told. "Did you know the haggis is an animal with two short legs on one side, for running around mountains?"

Then dinner was served: Forfar bridies, taters and neeps, and Pitlochry salad. Big Mac said to Qwilleran, "I hear you interviewed Gil for your column."

"Yes, but it can't run until I've seen a dowsing demonstration. When do you think snow will melt this year?"

"My guess is April. In 1982, it was all gone by March twenty-ninth, but that was a fluke. Last year the official meltdown was three-eighteen P.M. on April fourth. My backyard was the Secret Site."

Every year the *Moose County Something* invited readers to guess the exact minute when the last square inch of snow would disappear from a Secret Site, usually someone's backyard. It was considered an honor, and the property-owner was sworn to secrecy.

MacWhannell said, "I had to monitor the situation constantly near the finish time. When the last patch of snow was the size of a saucer, I phoned the paper, and they sent a reporter, photographer, notary public from city hall, and Wetherby Goode. They stood around, watching it shrink and holding a stopwatch. It disappeared at three-eighteen exactly."

Qwilleran said, "One wonders if the hot breath of the onlookers hastened the finish time."

"Not enough to make a difference. The nearest guess was four-twenty-two P.M. The winner was a carpenter from Sawdust City. He won a year's subscription to the paper and dinner for two at the Old Stone Mill."

The emcee rapped for attention. The evening would include the reading of Robert Burns's poems and the serious business of drinking toasts to Scottish heroes. First there was a moment of silence, however, in memory of Willard Carmichael, who had connections with the Stewart clan. Brodie piped "The Flowers of the Forest" as a dirge.

Then Whannell MacWhannell stood up and announced, "Tonight we honor someone who came to Pickax from Down Below and made a difference. Because of him we have better schools, a better newspaper, better health care, a better airport, and a column to read twice a week for entertainment and enlightenment. If you pay him a compliment, he'll give credit to his mother, who was a Mackintosh. It gives us great pleasure to add a name to our roll of distinguished Scots: the son of Anne Mackintosh Qwilleran!"

Qwilleran walked to the platform amid cheers in English and Gaelic. A photographer from the *Something* was taking pictures.

"Officers, members, and guests," he began. "I've long admired the Scots — with their bagpipes, kilts, and tolerance for oatmeal porridge. For hundreds of years Scottish fighting men, shepherds, and outlaws have worn the kilt and wrapped themselves in the plaid on cold nights, out on the moor. Wearing kilts they faced the muskets of English redcoats at Culloden, brandishing their swords and howling their defiance. In World War One, regiments of soldiers in tartan kilts stormed the beaches, led by intrepid pipers. They plowed through icy water, cursed the choking smoke, and fell to enemy fire, but the Scots kept on coming — screaming their battle cries and urged on by the screeching pipes. The Germans called them 'Ladies from Hell.'

"Gentlemen, I confess it has taken some heavy persuasion to get me into a kilt, but here I am, wearing the Mackintosh tartan as a tribute to Anne Mackintosh Qwilleran, a single parent who struggled heroically to raise an obstreperous male offspring. Anything I have achieved — and anything I have become — can be traced to her influence, encouragement, and devotion. In her name I accept this honor, proud to be among the Ladies from Hell!"

Brodie piped "Auld Lang Syne," and the audience stood up and sang, "We'll take a cup o' kindness yet."

Later in the evening, after circulating in the lounge and accepting congratulations, Qwilleran said to Gil MacMurchie, "If you're going home from here, I'll meet you there and write a check." In a short while he was on Pleasant Street, and Gil was admitting him to a house that was emptier than before. Qwilleran followed him to the glass-topped display table, hopping aside to avoid stepping on Cody.

"Sorry. I thought she was a black rug," he said. The dog was flat out on the floor, belly on the floorboards, and all four legs extended.

"That's her froggy-doggy trick. I don't suppose you've found a home for her, have you?"

"Not yet, but I'm working on it."

The four dirks with scabbards and brass hilts were under the glass in the curio table, along with the two brooches.

"Was the table not locked?" Qwilleran asked.

"Hasn't been locked for years! The lock's broken. The key's lost." He wrapped the dirks and brooches in newspaper while Qwilleran wrote a check for a thousand.

The Siamese recognized the sound of the car motor when he drove into the attached garage, and they knew the sound of his key in the lock. They had forgotten their original scare at the sight of the kilt and bonnet. Their greeting was positive without being effusive.

When he unwrapped his purchases on the kitchen counter, both cats jumped up to investigate the large round stones in the brooches, the brass hilts of the dirks, and the brass-mounted scabbards. Qwilleran withdrew one dirk from its scabbard, and Koko went into paroxysms of excitement over the blade, baring his fangs and flattening his ears as he moved his nose up and down the blood grooves.

9

When Qwilleran returned home after Scottish Night, there were messages on the answering machine from friends who had heard about his honor on the eleven o'clock newscast, and there were phone calls the next morning. John Bushland was one who called with congratulations.

Qwilleran said, "I saw you taking pictures at the dinner. Was that for the newspaper or the lodge?"

"Both. I'm doing a video for lodge members: Brodie playing the pipe, MacWhannell reading Burns's poetry, and everybody whooping it up."

"Did Polly call you about Lynette's birthday party?"

"Yes, and I've got an idea for a gift. See what you think . . . On New Year's Eve I got a great full-face color shot of her, talking with two guys — wine glass in hand, eyes sparkling, nice smile. The light balance was just right, and she looked young and happy."

"Who were the guys?"

"Wetherby Goode and Carter Lee James. I could blow it up and put it in a neat frame. Do you think she'd like it?"

"She'd be thrilled. Do it!" Qwilleran said.

Then Carol Lanspeak phoned congratulations

and said, "You deserve a monument on the court-house lawn, but that will come later."

"Much later, I hope," he said.

"Are you and Polly free on Sunday? I want to give a quiet little dinner for Danielle. I know it's short notice." When he hesitated, she added, "She thinks you're a superguy, and it would do her a world of good if you could be there. You always know exactly the right thing to say."

Qwilleran was thinking fast. Danielle would be at Lynette's birthday party, and one evening with Googly Eyes would be enough in one week, if not too much. He said, "You're right about the short notice, Carol. I've invited guests for Sunday and couldn't possibly cancel."

"I wouldn't ask you to do that," she said, "but we'll do it another time, won't we?"

"How is Danielle?" He thought it only civil to inquire.

"She's holding up very well, and Carter Lee is coming back, so she won't be lonely. It's important for her to do something constructive, and the lead in *Hedda Gabler* is a real challenge."

Qwilleran thought, It's a disaster waiting to happen.

"She's a quick study. I wish the whole cast could learn lines as fast." Carol was directing the play. "The main problem is that she doesn't like the actor we cast for Judge Brack. It's a personality clash."

"Who's playing Brack? George Breze? Scott Gippel? Adam Dingleberry?" Gippel weighed

135

three hundred pounds; Dingleberry was about a hundred years old; Breze was a mess.

Carol was not amused. "We have the drama and debate coach from the high school, and he's good, but he's dropping out. Danielle would rather play opposite you."

"It's out of the question." He thought, She's used to having her own way because she's gorgeous.

"I understand, Qwill. Sorry you and Polly can't be with us on Sunday."


Qwilleran had some errands to do downtown. He always did Polly's grocery-shopping on days when she was working at the library, in return for which she invited him to dinner frequently. It was one of the mutual advantages in living only three doors apart. He rolled her trash container to the curb once a week; she sewed on buttons for him; they fed each other's cats when necessary.

While downtown he stopped at the office of the *Moose County Something* to pick up a free newspaper. The day's edition had just been delivered from the printing plant, and he found the whole staff in a state of jocosity, grinning slyly and making abstruse quips. The reason soon became clear.

On the front page was a full-length photo of Qwilleran in Scottish Highland attire. He groaned. Did they have to print it four columns wide and eighteen inches high? Did they have to headline it "Lady from Hell"? The ribbing from

fellow staffers did nothing to ease his embarrassment:

"Hey Qwill, you look like an ad for Scotch!"

"Look at those knees!"

"What's that thing in his sock?"

"All he needs is a bagpipe!"

"Are you available for films and commercials,
Qwill?"

He said, "Obviously it was a slow day on the
newsbeat." He picked up an extra copy for Polly
and left the building, briefly considering a week's
vacation in Iceland. But then he drew upon the
qualities that life had bestowed upon him: the
aplomb of a journalist, the spirit of an actor, and
the confidence of the richest man in the northeast
central United States. He parked in the municipal
lot and entered Amanda's design studio through
the back door, carrying a newspaper-wrapped
package.

Fran greeted him, waving that day's edition of
the *Something*. "Qwill! Your picture on the front
page is fabulous! Marry me!"

"You'll have to wait your turn. Take a
number."

"Dad even called me about it! He was all
choked up with emotion — something that never
happens. Everyone's talking about it."

"I'm afraid so. I'm thinking of leaving the country until it blows over."

"What do you have wrapped in newspaper?"
she asked. "Fresh fish?"

He showed her the four dirks he had bought

137

and asked how to display them on the wall. "I don't want them under glass. I want instant access in case of attack by the Pickax pilferer. He, she, or it stole a dirk from Gil MacMurchie."

She unwrapped the dirks, frowned at them silently, then vanished into the stockroom, leaving Qwilleran to wander around the shop and look for a valentine gift for Polly. He found an oval jewelbox shaped from natural horn and inset with a sunburst of brass.

Fran returned from the stockroom carrying an antique pine picture frame, a simple rectangle of wide flat boards mitered at the corners and waxed to a mellow golden brown. She said, "This was the base for an old ornate frame of gilded gesso, which was badly chipped. We stripped it down to the pine and gave it this nice finish. We can put a backing in it for mounting the dirks and then devise clamps or clips for holding them."

"Perfect! You're so clever, Fran."

"The bill will go out in the mail tomorrow."

"How's the play going?"

"Not splendidly. Danielle's become a temperamental star. We lost a good Judge Brack because of her. She wants someone exciting for the role, since they have so many scenes together." Fran looked at Qwilleran hopefully, and he could see where the discussion was leading.

He said, "Couldn't Larry play the judge?"

"He's playing Tesman."

"How about your friend Prelligate?"

"He's doing Lovborg."

"Why not switch Larry to the judge, let Prelligate do Tesman, and bring in Derek Cuttlebrink for Lovborg?"

"You're bonkers, Qwill. Derek is almost seven feet tall. It would be a joke."

"Derek playing Lovborg is no funnier than Danielle playing Hedda."

"Forget Derek!" she said with finality.

Qwilleran persisted. "In *Macbeth* he crumpled his figure so that he looked a foot shorter. That might work well for Lovborg, who has a crumpled reputation, so to speak. Furthermore, Derek is a popular actor, and you wouldn't have to worry about ticket sales. His groupies would attend every performance, and the K Fund wouldn't have to bail you out."

Fran rolled her eyes in exasperation. "Go away, Qwill. Just leave your dirks and go away! Leave the country! You need a change of climate."

Obediently he started for the back door, then returned. "Do you happen to know the family with the famous doll collection?"

"Of course I know the Kemples. I worked with Vivian Kemple on their house. It's on Pleasant Street. She and her husband are both involved in rare dolls."

"May I use your phone?" he asked, adding dryly, "You can add the charge to my bill."

A man with a particularly loud voice answered, and Qwilleran identified himself.

"Sure! We've met at the Boosters Club, Qwill. I'm Ernie Kemple." He was the Boosters' official back-slapper and glad-hander, greeting members at every meeting.

"I'm calling about your doll collection, Ernie, as a possibility for the 'Qwill Pen' column."

"Well, now . . . we don't like publicity. You know what happened to the Chisholm sisters' teddy bears."

"That was a freak situation," Qwilleran said.

"Yeah, but we had a doll stolen recently — not worth a lot in dollars but highly collectible. Makes you stop and think, you know . . . Tell you what: Come and see the collection for your own enjoyment. It's art; it's history; it's an investment."

"Thank you. I'll accept the invitation." It was a break for Qwilleran. He could satisfy his curiosity without having to write about . . . *dolls*.

"Tell you what," Kemple said. "Come over now, and I'll rustle up some refreshments. My wife's out-of-town, and I'm waiting for three o'clock so I can pick up my grandson from school. I retired January One. Sold Kemple Life and Accident to the Brady brothers."

"I'll be right there," Qwilleran said.

Pleasant Street looked particularly pleasant that afternoon. A new fall of snow had frosted the lacy wood trim on the houses, and the whole street was an avenue of white ruffles. The Kemple house, more attractive than most, was painted in two shades of taupe, reflecting Fran Brodie's educated taste.

"A most attractive house," Qwilleran said to

Ernie Kemple when he was admitted. Like the exterior, the rooms showed the hand of a professional designer. Traditional furniture was arranged in a friendly contemporary manner; colors dared to depart from the historically correct; old paintings and engravings were hung with imagination. And there was not a single doll in sight!

Kemple replied in a booming voice that would make crystal chandeliers quiver. "You like it? I think it's pretty good myself. Comfortable, you know . . . But now my wife thinks maybe we should let Carter Lee James restore it to nineteenth-century authenticity. He and his assistant went through the house, making notes. But heck! We just spent a bundle with Amanda's studio, and I hate to see it go down the drain. Vivian — that's my wife — says everybody on the street is going along with James. It's supposed to increase the value of the property, and maybe give us a tax break. What do you think, Qwill? This James fellow presents a convincing case. Of course, he's not doing it for nothing! But he seems to be knowledgeable, and people like him. What's your opinion?"

"I haven't heard his pitch firsthand, but Lynette Duncan is sold on him," Qwilleran said.

"The question is: Suppose we stick to our guns. Would we want to be the only holdout in the neighborhood? . . . Well, why are we standing here? Let's go in the kitchen and have some cake and coffee. I have a sweet tooth, and the Scottish bakers has this Queen Mum's cake that's unbeat-

141

able, if you like chocolate."

Qwilleran sat at the kitchen table and looked at a group of framed photos on a side wall. "Is the curly-haired blond boy your grandson? You don't look old enough to have grandchildren."

"Well, thanks for the compliment. Yes, that's my little Bobbie. My daughter's divorced and living with us, and she works part-time, so Vivian and I get pressed into service as baby-sitters. And Qwill, I'm here to tell you it's the greatest thing that ever happened to a retired insurance agent! I have granddaughters, too, but they're in Arizona. That's where Vivian is now, visiting our son."

The kitchen was old-fashioned in its large size and high ceiling but updated in its cabinetry, appliances, and decorating. Slick surfaces made Kemple's great voice reverberate and made Qwilleran wince. "Have you ever been on the stage, Ernie?"

"Sure! I belonged to the theatre club for years. I played Sheridan Whiteside in *The Man Who Came to Dinner*. I left the club when we started doing a lot of traveling . . . Do you drink regular or decaf? We've got both. I grind the beans fresh."

"Regular," Qwilleran requested and waited for the racket of the grinder to stop before saying, "The club is casting a play right now that has a perfect role for you. Are you familiar with *Hedda Gabler*?"

"Is that the one where a woman is so wrapped up in her house that she loses her husband?"

142

"You're thinking of *Craig's Wife*, by George Kelly. This is Ibsen's drama about another self-centered woman who destroys one man and falls under the power of another. The role of Judge Brack is made to order for you, and I happen to know they're looking for an actor powerful enough to carry it. How do you look in a moustache?"

"Sure, I could handle that role, and I have the time now. The moustache is no problem. I've lived with spirit gum before."

"You'd be playing opposite a very striking young woman who's new in this area."

"Is that so?" Kemple said with increased interest. "Who's directing?"

"Carol Lanspeak."

"Oh, she's good! Not only talented but organized. I think I'll take your suggestion and surprise Vivian when she comes home. She's always telling me I could play Madison Square Garden without a mike."

"Are you both natives of Moose County?"

"No, we came up here from Down Below twenty years ago, because it seemed like a good place to raise kids. Also because I liked to hunt. I had mounted heads all over the place — my office, too. Then suddenly I turned off. I brought down a six-point buck one day, only wounded, and when I went to finish him off, he looked up at me with sad eyes. It was like a knife in my heart! I never went hunting again. Even got rid of the trophies."

The two men applied themselves, almost reverently, to the Queen Mum's cake, and there was little conversation for a while.

"How did you get interested in dolls?" Qwilleran asked then.

"When I gave up hunting, I needed a new hobby. History was my minor in college, and Vivian was getting into classic dolls, so I started researching historic dollmakers in England, France, and Germany — almost a hundred of them. It's good for a couple to have a hobby they can share, and it's good to be learning something."

"What did Vivian collect before classic dolls?"

"Primitives. Old Moose County dolls that the pioneers made for their kids. Carved and painted wood, stuffed flour sacks, all that type of thing."

Qwilleran remarked that he had yet to see a doll on the premises.

"All upstairs. In glass cases."

"Under lock and key?"

"Never thought it necessary, but now . . ." Kemple shrugged.

Qwilleran pointed to another photo in the wall grouping: a pretty young blond woman. "Your daughter?"

"Yes, that's Tracy, around the time she was married."

"She looks familiar."

"You've seen her at the Old Stone Mill. She works lunches there, dinners at the Boulder House Inn. She's a waitress. *Server* is what they

144

want to be called now. She could have had a nice job in the insurance office, but she likes meeting people, and she likes those big tips! And believe me, she gets them! She has a nice personality. . . . More coffee? Or do you want to see the dolls?"

Upstairs in the six-bedroom house there were three rooms outfitted with museum-type cases. The first room contained primitives made between 1850 and 1912. One doll consisted of thread spools strung together so that the arms and legs moved. Another was carved from the crotch of a small tree, with the forked branches for legs. A stuffed stocking had crudely stitched features: crossed eyes, crooked nose, upside-down mouth.

"Ugly," Kemple said, "but every one was loved by some little kid."

"Who has access to these rooms?" Qwilleran asked.

"Personal friends, serious collectors, and groups we belong to — that's all. During the holidays we had Vivian's Sunday-school class and then the historical society. In our will we're leaving the primitives to the Goodwinter Farm Museum. The classics will be sold to put our grandkids through college. They're appreciating in value all the time."

"I'd like to see the classics."

Dazzling was the word for the two rooms displaying the china, porcelain, wax, bisque, and papier-mâché beauties. Twelve to twenty inches tall, they had pretty faces, real hair, and lavish

145

costumes. There were hoop skirts, bustles, elaborate hats, muffs, parasols, kid boots, tiny gloves, and intricate jewelry. Rich fabrics were trimmed with lace, embroidery, ruffles, buttons, and ribbons.

Kemple pointed out French fashion "ladies," character dolls, brides, and pudgy infants. Flirty dolls with "googly" eyes that moved from side to side reminded Qwilleran of Danielle; he had always suspected she was not quite real.

Ever the historian, Kemple pointed out that the older dolls had small heads, long arms, and a look of surprise. Then came plump cheeks, soulful eyes with lashes, and tiny pursed lips. Parted lips showing tiny teeth were a later development.

Qwilleran was fascinated by certain facts about the wax dolls. Some had human hair set in the wax head with a hot needle, hair by hair. Wax had a tendency to melt or crack, and kids had been known to bite off a piece and chew it like gum.

"Little cannibals!" Qwilleran said. He listened patiently as Kemple discussed patent dates, dollmakers' logos, and the construction of jointed and unjointed dolls. Then he asked about the doll that had been stolen. It was carved and painted wood, eight inches tall, and very old. The paint was badly worn, and it was thought to have come from a native American village on the banks of the Ittibittiwassee River. It might have been more of a talisman than a toy.

"It was the first that ever disappeared from our

collection," Kemple said. Then he lowered his voice to a rumble. "It was found in Lenny Inchpot's possession, you know."

"In his locker," Qwilleran corrected him, "while he was out-of-town. Police had to cut the padlock, yet Lenny says he never locked it, and I believe him. I've asked my own attorney to take the case. It's my opinion that he was framed."

Kemple looked relieved. "Glad to hear that. Tell your attorney I'll go as a character witness at the hearing if he wants me to. That boy's been in this house hundreds of times. He was Tracy's boyfriend when they were in high school. He had a reputation as a prankster, but he wouldn't do anything like stealing from people."

"Aren't we all pranksters at that age?"

"Yes, but his were clever. Let me tell you about one. Everybody knew the mayor was having an affair with a woman who worked at the post office. One night Lenny painted big yellow footprints on the pavement, leading from the city hall to the post office. The cop on the nightbeat saw him doing it, but it was such a good joke he looked the other way. It was the kind of paint that washes off, and fortunately it didn't rain till the whole town had seen it. That was our Lenny! Vivian and I considered him a future son-in-law."

"What happened?"

"Tracy eloped with a football player from Sawdust City. She's impulsive. It didn't last, and she and Bobbie came home to live with us. Then Lenny's girlfriend was killed, and he started coming to the house again."

"How did Tracy react to his arrest?"

"She was troubled, I could tell, but she wouldn't talk to me. She'll talk to her mother, though. I'll be glad when Vivian gets home." He paused to reflect on family secrets. "You see, Tracy's always one to go for the main chance, and now she's set her sights on Carter Lee James. My fatherly instinct is flashing red. I don't want her to be disappointed again. It seems to me that all the women are flipping over him."

"Understandably," Qwilleran said. "He has a likable personality, good looks, and a glamorous profession."

"That's for sure, and my daughter is a beautiful young woman. James has wined and dined her a few times, and her hopes are up. She comes home late with stars in her eyes. What can I say? She's a grown woman. She wants a husband, a father for Bobbie, and a home of her own. Nothing wrong with that."

"Not to digress, but . . . how does she feel about the Pleasant Street project?"

"Oh, she's all for it! She says it'll make our neighborhood world-famous. I'm not sure that prospect appeals to me . . . But look! Why am I burdening you with my problems?"

"No burden. No burden at all," Qwilleran said. "I can put myself in your shoes. I know exactly how you feel." He had an interviewer's talent for empathy, and often it was genuine.

Driving home from Pleasant Street, he was glad

he had no parental responsibilities. It was mid-afternoon, and it had been a day of diffused activity, little of which really concerned him. It was his congenital curiosity that involved him in the problems of others. What he needed now was a good shower, a dish of ice cream, and an absorbing book.

The Siamese were sleeping soundly. Only when he opened the refrigerator door did they wake and report to the kitchen for a lick of French vanilla. After that, Yum Yum ran around in joyful circles, but Koko read Qwilleran's mind. That cat knew it was booktime and stood on his hind legs at the hutch cupboard and sniffed titles.

There were favorites brought from the barn, recent purchases from Eddington Smith, and gifts from friends who knew Qwilleran's fondness for old books. Koko's nose traveled up and down each spine, moving from one to the other until it finally stopped, like the planchette on a Ouija board. It stopped at *Ossian and the Ossianic Literature*, the book written by A. Nutt.

Qwilleran thought, Is he expressing an uncomplimentary opinion about me? Or does he really want to hear about ancient Gaelic poetry?

Although not in the mood for a scholarly study of a centuries-old mystery, Qwilleran gave it a try. He read aloud, and after a while all three of them were asleep in the big lounge chair.

# 10

By the end of January, Qwilleran had several leads for *Short and Tall Tales*, and one that particularly appealed to him was the story of Hilda the Clipper. It was funny, old-timers said, and yet it was sad. She was an eccentric woman who had terrorized the entire town of Brrr seventy years before. Brrr, so named because it was the coldest spot in the county, was a summer resort town situated on a promontory overlooking the big lake. In winter it resembled an iceberg in the North Atlantic.

The person said to know the details of the Hilda saga was Gary Pratt, proprietor of the Black Bear Café in Brrr, and Qwilleran drove out to see him one day. The noon rush was over, but one could still order a bearburger — not related to *Ursus americanus* but simply the best ground beef sandwich in the county.

The café was in a hotel on the highest point in town; a sign on the roof, visible for miles, said: ROOMS . . . FOOD . . . BOOZE. A kind of poetry in the internal vowels made it memorable, and it had been there as long as anyone could remember, guiding trawlers and pleasure boats into harbor.

Affectionately known as the Hotel Booze, the

plain, boxlike structure dated back to the rough-tough days of mining and lumbering. Gary Pratt had inherited it along with its debts and code violations. Wisely he had preserved its dilapidated appearance, which appealed to boaters and commercial fishermen, while making just enough repairs to satisfy the county license bureau.

He leaned on the bar while Qwilleran sat on a wobbly barstool, eating a bearburger. Gary was a big bear of a man, having a lumbering gait and a shaggy black mop of hair, with beard to match. "Glad you agreed to be grand marshal of the Ice Festival, Qwill."

"I wasn't aware I'd agreed," Qwilleran muttered between bites. "Who else is in the parade?"

"The queen, wrapped in synthetic polar-bear skins and riding in a horse-drawn sleigh. Dogsleds drawn by packs of huskies. A fleet of motorbikes with riders in polar-bear costumes. Two high-school bands on flatbeds. Eight floats celebrating winter sports. And torch bearers on cross-country skis."

Qwilleran refrained from making the cranky remarks that came to mind. The festival, after all, was going to be good for the county, and hundreds of go-getters were working hard to make it a success. Besides, the sandwich he was eating was courtesy of the house.

"Tell me about your book," Gary said. "What's the idea?"

"A collection of stories and legends about the early days of Moose County, to be published by the K Fund and sold in gift shops. Proceeds will go to the historical museum. How do you happen to know about Hilda?"

"My father and grandfather told the story so many times, I learned it by heart. Are you gonna record it?"

"Yes. Let's go to your office, where it's quieter." The following account was later transcribed:

My grandfather used to tell about this eccentric old woman in Brrr who had everybody terrorized. This was about seventy years ago, you understand. She always walked around town with a pair of hedge clippers, pointing them at people and going *click-click* with the blades. Behind her back they laughed and called her Hilda the Clipper, but the same people were very nervous when she was around.

The thing of it was, nobody knew if she was just an oddball or was really smart enough to beat the system. In stores she picked up anything she wanted without paying a cent. She broke all the town ordinances and got away with it. Once in a while a cop or the sheriff would question her from a safe distance, and she said she was taking her hedge clippers to be sharpened. She didn't have a hedge. She lived in a tar-paper shack with a mangy dog. No electricity, no running water. My grandfather had a farmhouse across the road, and Hilda's shack was on his property. She lived there rent-free, brought water in a pail from his handpump, and helped herself to firewood from his woodpile in winter.

One night, right after Halloween, the Reverend Mr. Wimsey from the church here was driving home from a prayer meeting at Squunk Corners. It was a cold night, and cars didn't have heaters then. His model T didn't even have side curtains, so he was dressed warm. He was chugging along the country road, probably twenty miles an hour, when he saw somebody in the darkness ahead, trudging down the middle of the dirt road, and wearing a bathrobe and bedroom slippers. She was carrying hedge clippers.

Mr. Wimsey knew her well. She'd been a member of his flock until he suggested she quit bringing the clippers to services. Then she gave up going to church and was kind of hostile. Still, he couldn't leave her out there to catch her death of cold. Nowadays you'd just call the sheriff, but there were no car radios then, and no cell phones. So he pulled up and asked where she was going.

"To see my friend," she said in a gravelly voice.

"Would you like a ride, Hilda?"

She gave him a mean look and then said, "Seein' as how it's a cold night . . ." She climbed in the car and sat with the clippers on her lap and both hands on the handles.

Mr. Wimsey told Grandpa he gulped a couple of times and asked where her friend lived.

"Over yonder." She pointed across a corn-field.

"It's late to go visiting," he said. "Wouldn't you rather I should take you home?"

"I told you where I be wantin' to go," she shouted, as if he was deaf, and she gave the clippers a *click-click*.

"That's all right, Hilda. Do you know how to get there?"

"It's over yonder." She pointed to the left.

At the next road he turned left and drove for about a mile without seeing anything like a house. He asked what the house looked like.

"I'll know it when we get there!" *Click-click.*

"What road is it on? Do you know?"

"It don't have a name." *Click-click.*

"What's the name of your friend?"

"None o' yer business! Just take me there."

She was shivering, and he stopped the car and started taking off his coat. "Let me put my coat around you, Hilda."

"Don't you get fresh with me!" she shouted, pushing him away and going *click-click*.

Mr. Wimsey kept on driving and thinking what to do. He drove past a sheep pasture, a quarry, and dark farmhouses with barking dogs. The lights of Brrr glowed in the distance, but if he steered in that direction, she went into a snit and clicked the clippers angrily.

Finally he had an inspiration. "We're running out of fuel!" he said in an anxious voice. "We'll be stranded out here! We'll freeze to death! I have to go into town to buy some gasoline!"

It was the first time in his life, he told Grandpa, that he'd ever told a lie, and he prayed silently for forgiveness. He also prayed the trick would work. Hilda didn't object. Luckily she was getting drowsy, probably in the first stages of hypothermia. Mr. Wimsey found a country store and went in to use their crank telephone.

In two minutes a sheriff's deputy drove up on a motorcycle. "Mr. Wimsey! You old rascal!" he said to the preacher. "We've been looking all over for the Clipper! Better talk fast, or I'll have to arrest you for kidnapping!"

What happened, you see: Hilda's dog had been howling for hours, and Grandpa called the sheriff.

"Great story!" Qwilleran said. "Is there a sequel? What happened to Hilda?"

"Well, for her own protection the county put her in a foster home, and she had to surrender her hedge clippers. The whole town breathed a lot easier."

"How long had they tolerated her threats?"

"For years! People were long-suffering in those days. They were used to the hardships of pioneer living. Their motto was: Shut up and make do! Is life better in the Electronic Age, Qwill? Sometimes I think I was born too late. My mother lives Down Below, and one night she had dinner in a neighborhood restaurant. The computer was

155

down, and not a single employee could add up a dinner check! Geez! I'm only thirty-five, but I feel like a dinosaur because I can add and subtract."

"Don't lose the skill," Qwilleran advised. "Computers may not be here to stay."

"Let's go back in the bar and get something to drink. I'm dry," Gary suggested. "And I want to ask you about something." He poured coffee for Qwilleran and beer for himself, and then said, "A guy came in here a couple of weeks ago and said he was a restoration consultant from Down Below, doing a lot of work in Pickax. He said this hotel could be a gold mine if I restored it and got it on the National Register, but it would have to be authentic. Well, the thing of it is: My customers like it the way it is — grungy! However, I just told him I couldn't afford it."

"What kind of money was he talking about?" Qwilleran asked.

"Twenty thousand up front for his services, plus whatever the contractor would charge for doing the work. Do you know anything about this guy?"

"Carter Lee James. Willard Carmichael spoke highly of him. He's doing over Pleasant Street as a historic neighborhood — or that's what the plans are."

"How come I haven't read anything in the paper?"

"The project is only now getting under way. He didn't want any premature publicity."

"He's a nice guy, very friendly and down to

earth. He had his assistant with him, and she was a real babe."

Qwilleran said, "She's his cousin, and she's Willard's widow."

"Oh . . . yeah . . . yeah. Too bad about Willard. I met him at the Boosters Club. He was all excited about the Ice Festival. You say they're cousins? I bought them a drink when they were here, and they sat in that corner booth. They didn't act like cousins, if you know what I mean."

"She flirts with everyone," Qwilleran said. "She'd flirt with John Wayne's horse!" Then he asked Gary what he thought about Lenny Inchpot's arrest.

"They're nuts! He's about as guilty as you and me! I know Lenny. He belongs to the Pedal Club. Won the silver in the Labor Day race!"

"I'm sure he'll get off. G. Allen Barter is taking his case. Then what? One wonders if the police have any other leads."

Driving home, Qwilleran realized how much he missed his late-night get-togethers with Chief Brodie at the apple barn, when suspicions were aired and official secrets were leaked over Scotch and Squunk water.

Even before he unlocked his front door, he knew there was a message on the answering machine. Koko was announcing the fact with yowls and body-bumps against the door panels. Given the condo's quality of construction, it was doubtful how much battering the door could take.

157

The message was from Celia Robinson, requesting him to call her at the clubhouse before five-thirty, her quitting time. She had a little treat for him and the cats and would drop it off on the way home.

He phoned immediately. "Visitors bearing treats are always welcome. Do you know where we are? Building Five on River Lane. Park in the driveway of Unit Four."

At five-thirty-three her bright red car pulled in, looking brighter and redder against the maze of snowbanks.

Always jolly, she greeted Qwilleran in a flurry of contagious happiness. "Here's some goat cheese, a thank-you for steering me to this wonderful job! I only wish it were permanent . . . Hello, kitties! . . . I saw your picture on the front page and cut it out. I'm going to frame it. I bought an extra copy to send to Clayton." She walked into the living room and flopped into the deep cushions of the sofa, facing the frozen riverbank. "This is a lot smaller than the barn, but you've got more of a view. And some new furniture! I never saw a coffee table like this!"

"It's an old pine woodbox that had four or five coats of paint. Fran Brodie stripped it down to the wood and waxed it."

"Some people are so clever! It sure is pretty. What do you keep inside?"

"Old magazines. Would you like a mug of hot cider, Celia?"

"No, thanks. I have to go home and cook. Mr.

O'Dell is coming to supper. Clayton thinks we should get married. What do you think, Chief?"

"Never mind what I think," Qwilleran said. "What does Mr. O'Dell think? Has he been consulted?"

Celia screamed with laughter. "He hasn't said anything, but I know he's interested. He has a house. I'd hate to leave my apartment. It's so central."

"What are your priorities, Celia? Love or location?"

She laughed again, uproariously. "I might have known you'd say that! . . . Well, what I want to tell you: I've found a home for the little black dog that Clayton liked. He couldn't take it home; it would only make trouble with his stepmother. What's the dog's name?"

"Cody. A female schnauzer. Who wants to adopt her?"

"A nice young man from the Split Rail Goat Farm. He came to the clubhouse today to give a talk to the Daffy Diggers — that's a garden club."

"I know Mitch Ogilvie very well," Qwilleran said. "Also his partner, Kristi. Cody will be happy with them."

Confidentially Celia said, "They're thinking of getting married. I hope they do. He's such a nice young man!"

"Are you implying that all nice young men make good husbands? I'm a nice middle-aged man, but you don't see me galloping down the aisle."

"Oh, lawsy!" She laughed. "I put my foot in it again! Anyway, Mr. Ogilvie said he'd give what's-her-name a good home."

"Good! I'll pick up what's-her-name myself and deliver her to the farm." As the wordplay sent her into a spasm of hilarity, he added, "Now tell me about your job, Celia."

"Well, I collect members' dues and schedule parties and help the caterers and supervise the janitors."

"Has there been any talk about Lenny Inchpot?"

"Plenty! Nobody thinks he's guilty, except for one man who thinks Lenny cracked up after his girlfriend was killed in the explosion. Is there anything I can do about the Lenny case, Chief?" Being an avid reader of detective and espionage fiction, Celia relished her role as secret agent.

"Just keep your eyes and ears open," Qwilleran suggested. "Bear in mind that Lenny may have been framed, and the person who stole the bridge club's money may have rigged Lenny's locker. Who's the man who said he'd cracked up?"

"I don't know. He's around a lot. Want me to find out who he is?"

"Yes. Do that. As soon as possible."

"Okay, Chief. And now I've really got to go home and cook. We're having spaghetti."

Qwilleran politely averted his eyes as she struggled to get out of the deep sofa.

When he went to the MacMurchie house the

next morning, he was met at the door by a smiling Scot and a bouncing schnauzer, yipping for joy. Her travel luggage was assembled in the foyer: a carton contained her comb and brush, leashes, dishes, a supply of dried food, and some old socks. MacMurchie said, "The food is a combination of rice and lamb that she seems to prefer, but she also likes popcorn and bananas. The horse blanket is her bed. The socks are her toys, knotted together in pairs. On TV she likes National Geographic programs and dog-food commercials."

Qwilleran said, "It looks as if you're ready to move out yourself. What will happen to the house then?"

"The restoration won't start until after spring thaw, but that's all right. By that time more property-owners will have signed up, and there'll be a saving on labor costs. The work will be done by an out-of-town contractor. He specializes in restoration."

"That won't make the local construction industry happy," Qwilleran said.

"It makes sense, though. The job's too big for the little fellers around here. XYZ Enterprises could handle it, but Carter Lee James isn't impressed by the kind of work they do. He's been staying, you know, in one of their apartment buildings."

"I know exactly what he means, Gil. I live in the Village, too."

Cody was listening, pancaked on the floor in

her froggy-doggy pose.

"On your feet, young lady," Qwilleran ordered. "We're going for a ride."

On the way to the country, Cody rode up front in the passenger seat, standing on her hind legs and watching the snowy landscape whiz past. The Split Rail Farm was in the Hummocks, where drifts swirled in grotesque configurations and made familiar landmarks unrecognizable. The split rail fence that gave the goat farm its name had disappeared under the hummocks of snow thrown up by county plows, and the long drive-way was a narrow white canyon. As for the Victorian farmhouse with its menacing tower, it looked surreal against the white background. Strangest of all was the silence.

Mitch Ogilvie, looking bucolic in his rough beard and heavy stormwear, came from a low sprawling barn to meet them. A few years before, he had been a fastidiously groomed and properly suited desk clerk at the Pickax Hotel. After that he was the casual but neat manager of the Farm Museum. Now he was the cheesemaker on a goat farm.

"Kristi's milking," he said, "but she told me to say hello. She's all excited about getting the pooch. What's his name?"

"Cody is a she. You'll like her," Qwilleran said. He carried her into the house, saying, "Here we are! Good dog! Nice new home!"

Mitch piled her luggage in the middle of the kitchen floor. "Let her explore," he said. "We'll

162

have some cheese and crackers while she decides if she wants to live here. I wonder how she feels about goat cheese."

"In my humble opinion, Mitch, any dog who eats popcorn and bananas won't balk at goat cheese."

They drank coffee and sampled several cheeses and listened for canine noises in other parts of the house. Occasionally there would be a musical moaning as Cody talked to herself about some questionable discovery.

After a while Qwilleran asked about the procedure in getting the house on the National Register. Built by a Civil War hero, it was the only edifice in Moose County to have official historic recognition. A bronze plaque in the driveway testified to the honor.

"There was a lot of red tape," Mitch replied, "and Kristi and I have a lot of sweat equity invested in it. Luckily we had the experts from the K Fund advising us. There was one government printout *six yards long* that really threw me for a loop. To me it was all gobbledygook . . . Why do you ask, Qwill? Are you going to try and get your barn registered?"

"No, it's been irreversibly modernized, but there's a whole neighborhood in Pickax that hopes to be registered, and I wondered about the procedure. Do you still have the six-yard printout? I wouldn't mind reading it."

"Sure. I'll dig it out for you. With your sense of humor you might have some fun with it in the

'Qwill Pen' column."

Cody, having okayed the premises, returned to the kitchen where her lares and penates were still in the middle of the floor. Mitch found her dishes and put out water and food for her.

"She'll be happy here," Qwilleran said as he put on jacket, hat, and gloves. "Take care of her; she comes from a good Scottish household. And tell Kristi I was sorry to miss her, but goats come before guests."

It was Qwilleran's responsibility to pick up the champagne and birthday cake for Lynette's party. In ordering the cake from the Scottish bakery, he had requested a Scots theme, and he expected the usual three-layer confection with a thistle design in pink and green icing. His reaction, when he picked it up, was: Ye gods! It was a foot-square sheet cake frosted in an all-over *plaid* in red, blue, green, and yellow; a skewer was stuck in the middle, flying a paper flag with an indecipherable message.

"That's 'Happy Birthday' in Gaelic," the baker said proudly. "It's the first I've ever done like this. Do you like it?"

"It's absolutely . . . unique!" he said with a gulp of dismay, as he wondered what Polly would say. She might have another heart attack.

"I'll wrap the flag in a bit of wax paper. You can stick it in the cake when you get home."

Polly was having her hair done at Brenda's, and he delivered the cake to her condo, letting himself in with his own key and explaining to Bootsie the legitimacy of his errand. He had been given instructions to leave it in the refrigerator, the only catproof vault in the house, and he took the precaution of taping a sign to the front of the appliance: OPEN DOOR WITH CARE! WILD CAKE INSIDE!

Lynette's birthday party lacked effervescence, despite the bubbles in the champagne that Qwilleran poured. The hostess worried about the prime rib she was roasting in a new and untested oven. The bereaved widow was resolutely glum. The guest of honor seemed nervous; did she fear her age would be revealed? Background music might have relieved the tension, but the stereo was out-of-order.

According to Moose County custom, the right-hand end of the sofa was reserved for the guest of honor. Carter Lee sat at the other end, wearing one of his monogrammed shirts. Lynette looked as if she had dressed to dance the Highland fling: pleated green tartan, black velvet jacket, and ghillies with long laces wound about her white-stockinged legs.

They said all that could be said about the weather. Carter Lee had no desire to talk shop. Qwilleran's skill as an interviewer failed him; his questions produced no interesting answers. To fill the silences, Bushy hopped around with his camera, taking candids.

When Qwilleran suggested that Lynette open

her gifts, she said firmly, "No! After dinner!" Fortunately the roast beef was superb; the Yorkshire pudding was properly puffy, and Lynette thought the plaid birthday cake was stupendous.

For coffee and cordials the diners moved back into the living room, and Lynette opened her gifts: violet sachets from Polly, a silver "poached egg" from Qwilleran, Bushy's framed photo, a bottle of wine from Danielle, and the smallest of small boxes from Carter Lee.

It was obviously a ring. Was that why Lynette had been self-conscious and Carter Lee had seemed unnaturally shy? When he slipped the ring on her left hand, Polly gasped audibly at the size of the diamond. Danielle merely tapped the floor with her uncommonly high-heeled shoe. Bushy took another picture or two. Qwilleran opened another bottle of champagne.

Then the couple answered questions: Yes, they had set the date . . . No, there would be no announcement in the paper until after the ceremony . . . Yes, it would be soon, because they were honeymooning in New Orleans and wanted to be there for Mardi Gras. . . . No, it would not be a church wedding — just a small affair at the Indian Village clubhouse . . . Yes, that's where they had met, across a bridge table.

After the guests had left, Qwilleran's first question to Polly was: "Did you know anything about this little bombshell?" He was helping her clear away the party clutter.

"Not an inkling! They haven't known each other very long. I hope she knows what she's doing."

"I thought she was deeply involved at the church. Why no church wedding?" he asked.

"I can guess why," Polly said. "I was in her wedding party twenty years ago when she was left waiting at the church — literally. She was in her grandmother's satin gown with yards of veil. She was carrying white roses and violets. Six attendants were in violet taffeta. The church was filled with wedding guests. But the groom and grooms-man didn't arrive. Someone telephoned the hotel; they had left, so they must be on the way. The organist started playing voluntaries to reassure the fidgety guests. Someone called the police to inquire if there had been an accident. We waited in the anteroom, and waited, and waited. Lynette started looking pale, then she turned the color of our dresses and passed out. The groom never showed up."

"That was a brutal thing to do," Qwilleran said. "What was wrong with the guy?"

"He was a local boy from a good family, but he was afraid of marriage and afraid to break it off. His family was mortified."

"What happened to him? Did he ever show his face?"

"He joined the armed services and lost touch with everyone. Lynette was hospitalized. The worst part was returning the hundreds of wedding presents!"

Qwilleran said, "So we can assume that's why she doesn't want an item in the paper until after the ceremony."

"It appears so, doesn't it?" Polly agreed. "Danielle seemed less than happy about her cousin's engagement, it seemed to me."

"Someone should tell her she's not losing a cousin; she's gaining a cousin-in-law." Then, after a moment's reflection, he added, "Do you suppose Lynette is going to get her revenge by jilting Carter Lee?"

"Oh, Qwill! How can you be so cynical? She'd never do a thing like that!"

## 11

The morning after Lynette's birthday party and the surprising engagement announcement, Qwilleran was wakened by what he feared was a pounding heartbeat, but it was the *thrum-thrum-thrum* of Wetherby Goode's wake-up music on the Sousabox. The volume was low enough to eliminate all but the percussion, which reverberated along the steel beam running the length of Building Five. A brochure listing fifty Sousa marches, with dates, had been stuck behind Qwilleran's door handle by his friendly neighbor, but whether the morning selection was the "U.S. Field Artillery March" (1917) or "Pet of the Petticoats" (1883), one could not tell.

The Siamese, too, were awake and could hear and feel the *thrum-thrum-thrum.* Koko, waiting for his breakfast, sat on his haunches and slapped the carpet with his tail in time with the percussion.

A remarkable cat, Qwilleran thought; his tail was becoming more eloquent all the time. He fed them, brushed them, and joined them in a little active recreation. Although the day was cold, the sun was bright, streaming in the living room window and reviving the lone housefly that had come with the condo and was spending the winter in

Unit Four, Building Five. In the game they played, Qwilleran stood with folded newspaper, ready to swat; the cats leaped and made futile passes and crashed into each other as the fly swooped playfully around the two-story living room. He had been living with them long enough to have a name, Mosca, and none of his pursuers really wanted to catch him.

For his own breakfast, Qwilleran had two sweet rolls from the freezer and several cups of coffee from the computerized coffeemaker. Then he got an early start on his column for February 1:

> January is the jet lag of December; March wishes it were April, but February is its own month — noble in its peaceful whiteness, the depths of its snowdrifts, and the thickness of its ice. February is unique in its number of days. February is the only month that can be pronounced four different ways. It's the birthdate of presidents and the month of lovers. Let us all praise . . .

His typing was interrupted by the telephone, and he heard Celia Robinson's voice saying with unusual crispness, "Mr. Qwilleran, this is your accountant's office. The numbers you requested are two, eighteen, five, twenty-six, five. Repeat: two, eighteen, five, twenty-six, five."

"Thank you for your prompt assistance," he said.

It was exactly as he had guessed. The code

spelled B-R-E-Z-E. It was scoundrely George Breze who suggested that Lenny Inchpot had "cracked up." According to conventional wisdom in Moose County, it was Old Gallbladder himself who was cracked — or crooked. Breze-bashing was a favorite pastime in the coffee shops, partly in fun and partly in earnest. He was suspected of everything, yet was never charged with anything, leading critics to believe that corrupting government officials was one of his crimes. Where did he get his dough, they wondered. On Sandpit Road he rented trucks, leased mini-storage units, ran a do-it-yourself car wash that was always out of detergent, cannibalized junk cars, and sold odds and ends of seasonal merchandise, such as rusty, bent, secondhand snow shovels.

Qwilleran returned to his typewriter. There was much to be said about February. It was second only to December as the favorite month of the greeting card industry. Commercially, valentines had an edge over year-end holiday greetings, which specialized in goodwill; valentines could be sentimental, passionate, flattering, comic, or insulting — something for everyone. Qwilleran described his own seven-year valentine feud that began in high school:

In my sophomore year there was a girl in Mrs. Fisheye's English Comp class who was brainy and aggressively disagreeable. The problem was that we were rivals for Top Dog status in the class. That year I received an anonymous homemade valentine that I knew came from her. A large red folder had these words printed on the cover. "Roses are red, violets are blue, and this is how I feel about you." Inside was one word — BORED! — along with a repulsive magazine photo of a yawning dog. I said nothing but saved it and mailed it back to her the following February, anonymously. In our senior year it returned to me, somewhat dog-eared but still anonymous. The charade continued annually all through college. Then I left Chicago, and that was the end of our silent feud. I don't remember the girl's name, but I think she really liked me.

As Qwilleran typed, both cats were on his writing table: Yum Yum sitting on her brisket and enjoying the vibration transmitted through the wooden surface. Koko, the more cerebral of the two, watched the type bars jump and the carriage lurch, as if he were inventing a better way. Suddenly his ears alerted, and he looked toward the phone. A few moments later, it rang.

Qwilleran expected Polly to phone her day's grocery list. Instead, it was Lynette. "I had a wonderful time last night! Thank you again for that lovely brooch. I'll wear it to pin my clan sash on my wedding day."

"I'm glad you like it," he murmured.

"And the *plaid cake* was so clever! Polly said you brought it. Was it your idea?"

"I'm afraid I can't take the credit," he said tactfully.

"Now Carter Lee and I have a big favor to ask. Would you mind if we dropped by for a few minutes?"

"Not at all. Come at five o'clock and have a glass of wine."

After that, Qwilleran drove to Pickax to hand in his copy and have lunch at the Spoonery. He hoped also to see Brodie about Lenny's case, but the police chief was attending a law enforcement meeting. He attended quite a few of those, and Qwilleran wondered if they were held in ice fishing shanties on the frozen lake.

The Spoonery was a downtown lunchroom specializing in soups; it was the brainchild of Lori Bamba, an ambitious young woman who was always trying something new. Qwilleran sat at the counter and ordered the Asian hot and sour sausage soup. "How's Nick?" he asked Lori. "I never see him any more."

"He's spending such long hours at the turkey farm, I hardly see him myself, but he's happy not to be working at the prison."

"For both your sakes, I'm glad he cut loose from that job. And how's the soup business?"

"I'm learning," she said with a good-natured shrug. "There's more demand for tomato rice and chicken noodle than for eggplant peanut."

"This, my friend, is Pickax," he reminded her.

"Do the kitties feel at home in Indian Village?" Lori had five of her own and was his mentor in affairs of the cat.

"Home is where the food is. Feed them at the appointed hour, and they'll be happy anywhere. There's one odd development, though. Our next-door neighbor plays Sousa marches, and not only does Koko beat time with the music, but he's started whacking the floor at other times."

"Does he swish his tail from side to side?"

"Definitely! Right, left — bam, bam — right, left!"

Lori said seriously, "That's a danger signal. Does he direct his anger at Yum Yum?"

"Yes, and at me, too! He's trying to tell me something, and I'm not getting it. He's exasperated. Cats! They can drive you crazy . . . This soup is great, Lori."

"Thanks. May I quote you? All I need to do is say, 'Mr. Q likes it,' and there'll be a run on Asian hot and sour sausage soup."

From there he went to the design studio to pick up his dirks. "Superb job of framing!" he told Fran Brodie. "My compliments!"

"Where'll you hang them?"

"In the foyer, over the chest of drawers."

"Don't hang them too high," she cautioned. "Men of your height tend to hang wall decorations too high. It's the Giraffe syndrome." Then her manner changed from flip to confidential. "I heard a fantastic rumor this morning. Lynette is getting married at long last! And to Carter Lee James, if you can believe it!"

"It just proves there's hope for you, Fran," he

said, knowing how to tease her.

"Yes, but how many Carter Lee Jameses are there to go around?" she retorted.

"Where did you hear the rumor?"

"One of my good customers called me. Do you think it's true? Lynette's older than he is, you know. He might be marrying her for the Duncan money."

"That's an unkind remark. She has a lot of good qualities, and they're both interested in old houses — and bridge. I hear they're excellent players."

"I'm surprised Danielle didn't tell me — if it's true."

"How's the play going?" he asked, smoothly changing the subject.

"Good news! We were able to get Ernie Kemple for Judge Brack, and it's perfect casting, although his booming voice and Danielle's tinny one sound like a duet for tuba and piccolo. You should come to rehearsal some night and have a few laughs. She calls him J.B. You know the line where Hedda points General Gabler's pistol and says: *I'm going to shoot you, Judge Brack*. Well, Danielle gave a little wiggle and said, 'I'm gonna shoot you, J.B.' We all broke up!"

Qwilleran tamped his moustache. "If you want my opinion, Fran, this play will never make it to opening night." On the way out of the studio he asked casually, "Is your dad an ice fisherman?"

"No, he's not much of a sportsman. A little

duck hunting in the fall, that's all. Why do you ask?"

"Just wondered . . . Has he said anything lately about the Willard Carmichael murder?"

"Not recently. When it first happened he said it would never be solved unless a suspect in another street crime confessed in a bid for leniency."

On the way home Qwilleran thought about Lenny Inchpot and George Breze. He needed to confer with Celia Robinson — but how and where? Her bright red car parked in front of his condo twice in quick succession would arouse the curiosity of neighbors, Polly included. Gossip was a way of life in Pickax, although it was called "sharing information." Rumors traveled on the Pickax grapevine with the speed of light. When Qwilleran was living at the barn, his location was secluded; even so, Andy Brodie had observed a red car entering the woods that screened the barn from Main Street. With all of this in mind, Qwilleran found it wise to brief Celia by mail, as he had done when they worked together on the Florida investigation . . . As soon as he arrived home, he typed the following communication:

(For your eyes only. Memorize, shred, and flush.)
TO: Agent 0013½
FROM: Q
MISSION: Operation Winter Breeze
ASSIGNMENT: To tail the subject identi-

fied in your report. Code name: Red Cap. Introduce yourself as Lenny's replacement. Play the friendly club hostess. Find out why Red Cap spends so much time in the TV lounge when he could be selling rusty snow shovels on Sandpit Road. Be charming. If he offers to buy you a drink, accept. You can pour it in the plastic ferns when he isn't looking. Bear in mind that Red Cap *may be* the Pickax Pilferer, and he *may be* covering up by falsely accusing Lenny. When mission is accomplished, phone headquarters to set up a rendezvous in the fresh produce department at Toodle's Market.

Toodle's Market was the perfect venue for a clandestine meeting. Strangers commonly exchanged opinions on the best oranges for juice, the best way to cook beets, or the best buy in wine. Furthermore, food demonstrators created a party atmosphere by handing out samples of cheese spread or olive butter, and there were little paper cups of coffee available. One could easily talk with the opposite sex without causing a traffic jam in the telephone system.

To deliver the briefing to Celia's mailbox at the gatehouse, Qwilleran strapped on his snowshoes — or "webs" as they were called by the real buffs — and he trekked through the woods over a fresh fall of snow, trudging with wide-legged stance and long strides, keeping a slow and steady pace with a slightly rolling gait. He found it tranquilizing.

At the gatehouse, he found a certain esthetic satisfaction in unstrapping the webs and sticking their tails in the snowbank.

As five o'clock approached, Qwilleran gave the Siamese an early dinner and instructions on how to behave during the visit of the happy couple. "No flying around! No knocking things down! No domestic quarrels!" They acted as if they understood, regarding him soberly, although actually they were just digesting their food.

The guests drove up promptly at five, Carter Lee driving Willard's Land Rover. In the foyer, they removed their boots and hung scarfs and coats on the clothes tree, which Lynette admired at length. It was a square column of brass seven feet tall, with angular hooks of cast brass at varying levels.

"It's Art Deco, old but not antique," Qwilleran said. "Fran found it in Chicago. It came from the office of an old law firm."

The visitors hung their hats on the top hooks: one fluffy white angora knit, and one Russian-style toque of black fur. Then they walked into the living room and remarked about the fine wintery view and the beautiful cats.

"This one is Koko, and that one is Yum Yum," said Lynette, who had fed them one weekend in Qwilleran's absence. She extended a hand familiarly for them to sniff, but with typical feline perversity they ignored her and went to Carter Lee.

"Don't take it personally," the host explained to her. "They always consider it their duty to check out a newcomer."

The newcomer said, "My mother, who lives in Paris, has a Siamese called Theoria Dominys du Manoir des Ombreuses. Dodo, for short."

Lynette said, "We're going to France in May. Carter Lee speaks French fluently, and I'm going to brush up what I learned in high school. *Le crayon est sur la table.*"

"For starters, then, how about a glass of merlot or pinot noir?" Qwilleran suggested. Red was Moose County's wine of choice in cold weather.

While he was pouring, they took the best seats in the house: the deep-cushioned sofa sheltered somewhat by the overhanging balcony and in full command of the view. The waning daylight was prolonged by the brilliant whiteness of the riverbank and the frozen river below.

"To all appearances, it's frozen solid," Qwilleran said, "but when I'm snowshoeing and all is silent, I can hear a faint trickle of water under the ice. The cats can hear it all the time. They sit in the window, listening."

The starry-eyed bride-to-be said, "We plan to have a summer place . . . don't we, honey? Either on the Ittibittiwassee or Rocky Burn." He nodded and smiled, looking quietly contented.

Amiable small talk continued for a while. Sitting apart on the sofa, the couple held hands across the center cushion and exchanged fond glances occasionally. Then, as if by hand signal,

179

Lynette said, "We'd be grateful, Qwill, if you and Polly would stand up for us at our wedding. Polly is willing."

"Of course! I'm honored to be asked. What's the date?"

"A week from Tuesday. It's scheduled so we can honeymoon during Mardi Gras."

Carter Lee added, "We have a reservation that starts Wednesday, at an inn near the French Quarter."

"New Orleans is an exciting place for a wedding trip," Qwilleran murmured.

Lynette said blithely, waving the hand with the dazzling diamond, "There's an old superstition: 'Marry on Tuesday, many a bluesday.' But I'm not worried. The ceremony will be here in the clubhouse, with the pastor of our church officiating. Then there'll be a simple reception for about forty —"

"But we'd like you and Polly," Carter Lee interrupted, "to be our guests for dinner at the Boulder House Inn. We're staying there overnight and leaving on the shuttle flight Wednesday morning. The inn has limo service to the airport."

"It'll be a Scottish wedding, Qwill," Lynette said. "I'll wear a sash in my clan tartan over a white dress and fasten it with the silver brooch you gave me. Polly will wear her floor-length kilt and a clan sash. Then there are several Scottish customs, like a wreath of flowers in my hair and a silver coin in my shoe — for luck. At the reception Polly will break the traditional oatcake over my head."

Qwilleran said, "You can buy oatcakes at the Scottish bakery, but silver coins haven't been struck since the 1960s."

"I'll cheat. I'll put a thin dime in my shoe. Carter Lee has to leave his left shoelace untied during the ceremony."

"I'll cheat, too," Carter Lee said. "I'll wear evening pumps."

"Yes, he'll be in dinner clothes," Lynette said, "but we're counting on you, Qwill, to wear full Highland dress."

He nodded his agreement, having received innumerable compliments on his Scottish Night debut.

"Since I'm marrying out of my clan, I'm supposed to keep my maiden name. Once a Duncan, always a Duncan . . . But you don't mind, do you, honey?"

Her fiancé squeezed her hand and smiled indulgently. They were being so coyly sentimental that Qwilleran shuddered inwardly. Coy sentimentality was beyond his frame of reference. Furthermore, he had a dinner date, and they had said they would drop in for a few minutes; they had been there more than an hour. He should never have served them a second glass of wine. In an effort to jog them loose from their prenuptial euphoria, he changed the subject, saying somberly, "Carter Lee, how is your cousin? Is she — ? Is she — ?"

"She's holding up," he replied. "She'd like to marry again, and that's a healthy sign. She should go on with her life. She has so much to give. I hate to see it go to waste, don't you, Qwill?"

Before Qwilleran could formulate an appropriate reply to a debatable question, all three of them were unnerved by a sudden fracas in the foyer: snarling, thumping, hissing, growling. He jumped up and rushed to the scene. The two cats were fighting over the Russian fur hat, rolling in it and kicking it — and each other — with hind legs like steel pistons.

"Stop that!" Qwilleran thundered, and the two culprits streaked away in opposite directions. "My apologies!" he said to Carter Lee.

"No problem. I'll just give it a good shake."

They drove away in the Land Rover, and Qwilleran went to dinner at Polly's, but not before giving the Siamese a treat and saying, "You rascals!"

## 12

Qwilleran's life that winter was a jigsaw puzzle of work, social events, reading, daily snowshoeing, telephone calls, and the exigencies of domesticity with two Siamese cats. Once a week the pieces fell into place when he spent a predictable weekend with Polly Duncan. He could count on contentment and stimulation in equal quantities, plus at least one set-to with Bootsie. The weekend following Lynette's birthday party, something went wrong, however. It started with broiled whitefish and broccoli at her place on Saturday evening and ended with Sunday dinner at the Palomino Paddock, a five-star restaurant in Lockmaster County.

Over the whitefish Qwilleran said, "If Lynette thinks she can keep her wedding sub rosa until after the fact, she's living in a fool's paradise. I saw Fran Brodie today, and already she'd heard the news from a customer."

Polly said, "It's the newspaper publicity she wants to avoid. Her friends are being invited informally by phone, and they understand she doesn't want them to talk about it."

"Of course they understand, but will they keep their traps shut? This county is inhabited entirely by blabbermouths."

"Qwill, dear, you're so cynical."

"I've decided why Danielle was so moody at last night's party. Willard had arranged to take her to Mardi Gras, and it's his hotel reservation that's now being used by Carter Lee for his honeymoon, so Danielle is left out . . . unless Lynette jilts him, in which case he can take Danielle."

"It's not a matter for levity," Polly said in gentle rebuke. "Lynette's intensely committed to this marriage. She's resigned from her job at the clinic, and she's transferring her property to joint ownership."

"So you think it's safe to go ahead and buy a wedding gift? If we'd known sooner, they could have had a black female schnauzer."

"It's really a problem, deciding what to give them. She has a houseful of heirloom silver, porcelain, and art."

Qwilleran said, "We could commission a portrait artist to paint the two of them together in front of their gingerbread house — like Grant Wood's *American Gothic* but without the pitchfork. There's a guy in Lockmaster who does portraits, and he's quite good."

Polly liked the idea enormously.

During their time together they talked about this and that. She said, "You're enjoying your snowshoes, aren't you? I see you shoeing around the Village in your orange padded vest and orange hat."

"That's so rabbit hunters won't mistake me for a snowshoe hare . . . Have you done anything about getting your stereo repaired?"

"I've called Lucky Electronics three times."

"When you call Lucky, you're lucky if he shows up, and if he comes to look at your problem, he has to order a new part, and if it ever arrives and he installs it, you're lucky if it works. We should buy you a new rig, state-of-the-art."

Then they talked about the library. "We have a problem with the new water-saving commode in the restroom," Polly said. "It flushes with a crash and a roar that resounds throughout the building. The clerks giggle; the subscribers are alarmed; and I'm embarrassed, but the plumber says there's no way out — it's the law!"

On the way home from Lockmaster on Sunday evening, Qwilleran made a big mistake. He asked, "Have you had any luck in finding Bootsie a companion?"

"At last! My friend in Lockmaster is having a litter, and she's promised me first choice."

"Be careful what you call your new kitten. T. S. Eliot says the name you give your cat can affect his self-esteem, or words to that effect. It may be that Bootsie doesn't like his name."

"What do you mean?" she asked tartly.

"You have to admit that Bootsie is hardly an appropriate name for a noble, aristocratic animal like a Siamese. If it's causing him to doubt his self-worth, that could account for his bad disposition."

Polly bristled. "He's very sweet and loving when we're alone."

"But you have to lock him up when you have company. Does that sound like a well-adjusted pet?"

"You're the only one who can't get along with him!" Polly said belligerently. "I think you and your theories are absurd, and that goes for T. S. Eliot, too."

Qwilleran was unaware that one should never question a person's choice of name for a pet, no matter how intimate the friendship. Unwittingly he had crossed the line. "Sorry I mentioned it, Polly. I didn't mean to upset you."

"Well, I'm very much upset, and I find this entire conversation unconscionable. Just drop me at the front door. I have a headache."

He did as she requested, and she was gone without another word. He had never witnessed such an outburst from this intelligent, reasonable woman.

The Siamese realized he was disturbed, and they kept their distance, regarding him anxiously. Without speaking to them, he got into a lounge robe and bedroom slippers and scooped a dish of ice cream for himself. Snow was falling lightly. The daylight was fading. Sprawled in his big chair with feet propped on the ottoman, he wondered, Now what? Should I call and apologize? Will she come to her senses? What did I say? How did it start?

Suddenly the doorbell rang urgently and repeatedly. He swung his feet to the floor and hurried to open the door. Standing in the snow was a little birdlike woman with no coat, no boots, merely a shawl over her gray hair and around her thin shoulders.

"Please help!" she cried. "Our cat's trapped! She'll kill herself!" She pointed down the row of condos.

"Right away!" He pulled a jacket off the clothes tree and followed her through the snow in his bedroom slippers. She was one of the retired schoolteachers in Unit Two.

Their golden Persian had fallen behind the laundry equipment and was entangled in the works, struggling frantically, squealing piteously, and in danger of strangling.

"Stand back!" he said. "I'll pull the washer out. She'll be all right." Speaking reassuringly to the terrified animal, he extricated her and handed her to the small woman who had come to his door.

"Poor Pinky! Poor Pinky!" she sobbed, hugging and kissing her pet.

The other sister, a taller woman but equally thin, said emotionally, "How can we thank you, Mr. Qwilleran?" Then she saw him standing in a puddle of melting snow on the vinyl floor. "My heavens! Look at you! No shoes! You poor man! You must be frozen! . . . Jenny! Bring towels! . . . What can we do, Mr. Qwilleran?"

"Just give me a towel and throw my slippers in the dryer," he said, "and a cup of hot coffee wouldn't hurt." The aroma of coffee was drifting from the kitchen.

"Would you like some brandy in it? Come and sit down . . . Jenny, where's the heating pad? And bring the blue quilt!"

Pinky had disappeared, no doubt dismayed by the half-clad male intruder who now sat in her favorite chair, wrapped in the blue quilt, with bare feet bundled in a heating pad, while the two women fluttered about, worrying and trying to help.

They introduced themselves as Ruth and Jenny Cavendish. "We have two cats, and we know you have a pair of Siamese," Ruth said. "We read about them in your excellent column."

Jenny presented Pinky's partner, another golden Persian, named Quinky. "Actually, the names are Propinquity and Equanimity."

"Ideal names for cats!" he declared. This adventure, he thought, is going to pay off; already ideas were crowding his head. He gave his keys to Ruth, who brought his boots from the foyer of Unit Four, and his slippers were returned to him, warm and dry.

The sisters insisted they would be eternally grateful.

About the idea spawned by the adventure: He would write a trenchant treatise on the specialized art of naming cats (Polly, take note!) and would invite readers to mail in the names of their own cherished felines. As a columnist, Qwilleran was not averse to letting subscribers do his work for him. Reader participation, it was called. He knew

188

Arch Riker would say, "Not another cat column! Please!" Let him scoff! Riker was not yoked with the responsibility of penning a thousand entertaining, informative, well-chosen words twice a week. For starters, Qwilleran made a list of well-named cats of his acquaintance:

Toulouse, a black-and-white stray adopted by an artist.

Wrigley, a native of Chicago, now living in Pickax.

Winston, the bookstore longhair, who resembled an elder statesman.

Agatha and Christie, two kittens abandoned in the parking lot of the library.

Magnificat, who lived at the Old Stone Church.

Beethoven, a white cat born deaf.

Holy Terror, the pet of a retired pastor and his wife.

Then he developed some of his pet ideas: Oriental breeds react favorably to names with an Eastern connotation, like Beau Thai and Chairman Meow. Others like important titles that bolster their self-esteem, like Sir Albert Whitepaws, Lady Ik Ik, or Samantha Featherbottom, even though these honorifics are used only in formal introductions; nicknames are acceptable for everyday use. A cat who dislikes his name may develop behavior problems, which are corrected when his name is changed from Peanuts to Aristocat. In three days a cat named Booby will adjust to the proud, Roman senatorial name of Brutus.

When deftly organized and couched in Qwilleranian prose, the ideas made a commendable "Qwill Pen" column, which concluded with the following:

Who are your cats? Write their names on a postcard and mail it to "Cat Poll" at the *Moose County Something*. The names may be clever, ordinary, bawdy, sentimental, silly, or scatalogical. This is not a contest! There are no prizes!

When Qwilleran handed in his copy at the newspaper, Junior Goodwinter said, "We've been swamped with phone calls from readers, wanting to know the four ways to pronounce February." He scanned the new copy in bemused silence until he reached the final paragraph. "Oh boy! Wait till the *Lockmaster Ledger* sees this! They'll think we've gone bananas. You say *no prizes!* You'll never get results without offering a reward. How many postcards do you expect to get?"

"A few," Qwilleran said with a shrug. "The point of the column is to get people thinking and talking."

The paper was on the street at mid-afternoon. That evening he received a phone call from a voice that was soft, gentle, and low. "Qwill, are you on speaking terms with me?"

"No, but I'm on listening terms," he said gently. "I've missed your soothing voice."

"Forgive me for being so peevish. I've always

been touchy about Bootsie's name, I'm afraid. I don't know why. You're not the only one who's objected to it."

Qwilleran knew why. In naming her cat, she had made a bad choice, and she knew it, but she resented having it pointed out.

Polly said, "But your column gave me an idea. Do you really think Bootsie would adjust to a new name in three days? I'm thinking of calling him Brutus. *This was the noblest Roman of them all!*"

There were other calls that evening, one in the grating voice that made his blood curdle. "Hi, Qwill. This is Danielle. I've seen you out hiking on your snowshoes."

"It's cheap transportation," he said.

"How would you like to hike over here some afternoon and run lines with me, and maybe you could give me some advice."

"Thank you for the invitation, but I'm a working stiff, and my days are fully scheduled," he said, adding quickly, "How are the rehearsals going?"

"Oh, they're fun —"

"That's good. I wish I had time to chat, Danielle, but I have a houseful of guests here. Will you excuse me?"

"Dammit!" he said to Koko after hanging up. The cat was sitting on the table, slapping it with his tail — right, left, right, left.

The next call was more welcome, being the brisk voice that Celia Robinson used for under-

191

cover communication:

"Mr. Qwilleran, this is Mrs. Robinson. I'm going to *Toodle's Market* tomorrow morning. They have a good buy on *apples,* and I know you eat a lot of *apples.* I'll pick up a bagful for you, if you want me to. I'm going at ten o'clock before they're all picked over."

"I'll appreciate that. Very thoughtful of you," he said.

At ten o'clock the next morning he found her in the fresh produce department at Toodle's Market, inspecting apples for bruises and wormholes.

Carrying the store's green plastic shopping basket, he sidled up to her and said loudly, *"Do you think these are good eating apples?"*

*"They're Jonathans, a nice all-purpose apple."* Then she added under her breath, "Had a long talk with Red Cap."

*"Winesaps are what I really like."*

*"I think they're out of season . . .* I've got the tape in my handbag."

Another customer joined them. "Aren't you Mr. Q? I think your column is just wonderful!"

"Thank you," he said as he loaded his basket with apples.

"I always clip it and send it to my daughter in Idaho."

"That's pleasant to hear." He moved away in slow motion, following Celia to the oranges. *"How can you tell if these are good juicers?"*

*"I always look for thin skins . . .* Meet me at the deli counter."

They separated, then met again where Qwilleran was buying sliced turkey breast for the cats and some Greek olives for himself. Celia was eating cheese spread on a cracker. She slipped him something in a paper napkin and then disappeared in the crowd. It was the tape.

What he heard when he played Celia's recording impressed him as a boy-meets-girl script for over-sixties. Her friendly voice alternated with a hoarse male twang:

"Are you Mr. Breze? Hi! I'm Celia Robinson from the manager's office."

"Howdy! Sit down. Have a drink."

"How do you like this weather? Pretty cold, isn't it?"

"No good for the rheumatiz!"

"That's a nice-looking shirt you're wearing. I like to see a man in a plaid shirt."

"Wife give it to me eight years ago. 'Bout ready to be washed. Heh heh heh."

(Female laughter.) "Oh, Mr. Breze! You're so funny!"

"Call me George. You're a nice-lookin' woman. You married?"

"I'm a widow and a grandmother."

"Have a slug o' whiskey. I'm divorced. Wife run off with a hoe-down fiddler."

"Is that why you're living in the Village?"

"Yep. Gotta house on Sandpit Road — too big for just me. Know anybody with ninety thou to throw away?"

"Ninety thousand! It must be quite a fine house."

"Well, the roof don't leak. If I find me another woman, I'll keep the house and fix it up. There's a feller what says I can get money from the guv'ment to fix it up. Showed me some pitchers, what it'd look like. Mighty purty pitchers."

"That sounds too good to be true, doesn't it? Who is this man?"

"Young feller. Lives here in the Village. Don't know his name . . . Have a snort. I'm havin' another. What's your drink?"

"Thanks, but I never drink on the job."

"Don't go away. Be right back. (Pause.) Well, here's mud in yer eye! What's yer name?"

"Celia Robinson. I'm substituting for Lenny Inchpot while he's away. Do you know him?"

"Sure. He got thrown in jail for stealin'."

"But people tell me he's a very honest young man. He's going to college part-time."

"That don't make him honest. They found the goods on 'im, di'n't they?"

"I wonder who tipped off the police to look in Lenny's locker."

"Warn't me!"

"Do you know what kinds of things were stolen?"

"Nope. Di'n't say on the radio. Maybe it

said in the paper. Don't read the paper."

"Why not, Mr. Breze? It's a very good one."

"Call me George. It's a waste o' time readin' the paper. I'm a successful business-man. I don't need to read. I can hire people to read and write."

"Are you telling me you can't read, Mr. Breze? . . . George?"

"Could if I felt like learnin'. Never took the time. Too busy makin' money. Plenty o' people can read and write, but they're broke."

"What kind of business are you in . . . George?"

"Any goldurned thing that'll make money. Wanna job? Can you cook?"

(Click)

When the tape clicked off, Qwilleran huffed into his moustache. It was the old duffer he had tried to interview during the mayoralty campaign — the candidate who made news by polling only two votes. His house was an ugly, square, two-story barracks with a hip roof and a tall brick chimney rising from its center. Local wags said it looked like a plumber's plunger. A sad piece of real estate, it had no trees or shrubs, no grass, no window shutters, not even any paint. Breze him-self was either pathetically naive or arrogantly ignorant.

Koko had been listening and making gurgling

noises that sounded sympathetic, and Qwilleran suddenly felt sorry for Old Gallbladder. He had suspected the despised fellow on the basis of prejudice, not evidence. In fact, the moustache that was the source of Qwilleran's hunches had been entirely dormant during Operation Winter Breeze . . . So, if Breze didn't steal the goods and rig Lenny's locker and tip off the police, who did?

# 13

It was the weekend before the wedding, and Qwilleran and Polly were together again. As a peace offering he gave her the jewel box of polished horn and brass that he had been saving for February 14. For her valentine he had ordered a state-of-the-art stereo from a catalog.

Polly said one evening, "I always thought Lynette and Wetherby Goode might get together. She admires his whimsical weathercasting style, and they both play bridge, and he presents a good appearance, although slightly heavy-set."

Qwilleran thought Wetherby's emcee personality might be too exuberant as a steady diet. "Carter Lee is laid-back, sophisticated, a perfect gentleman. Wetherby is the 'Stars and Stripes Forever'; Carter Lee is Pachelbel's *Canon*."

"Did you know, Qwill, that Wetherby's real name is Joe Bunker?"

"That being the case, he was wise to change it," Qwilleran said sagely.

The Tuesday-night wedding took place in the social hall of the clubhouse. A white runner on the red carpet led to the fireplace, which blazed festively. Before it, a white-draped table held red and white carnations in a brass bowl and red candles in tall brass holders. A Valentine wedding, the guests said; so romantic! They stood on either side of the runner: chiefly Lynette's friends from the bridge club, the church, and the medical clinic, plus the Rikers and the Lanspeaks and John Bushland with his camera. Many of the men were in kilts; the women wore clan sashes draped from shoulder to hip.

When the recorded music — Scottish tunes for flute and dulcimer — suddenly stopped, the guests turned toward the entrance. The double door opened, and Andrew Brodie in bagpiper's regalia piped the wedding party down the white aisle with the traditional strains of "Highland Wedding." First came the officiating clergyman, then the groom and groomsman and — after a few suspenseful moments — the bride and her attendant.

Lynette's clan sash, predominantly green, was a column of brilliant color fastened on her shoulder and cascading down the front and back of her long white dinner dress. She wore a wreath of stephanotis in her hair. The same green tartan figured in Polly's evening skirt and clan sash, worn with a white silk blouse. Qwilleran was resplendent in full Highland kit. Against the Duncan green and Mackintosh red, the groom's black dinner clothes looked ominously somber.

"He looks like a waiter," Riker later confided to Qwilleran.

The ceremony was brief and flawless. There

were no sentimental tears — only happiness — as the fire crackled on the hearth and the words were said. Then Brodie piped the triumphal "Scotland the Brave" and led the wedding party and guests to the dining hall. An oatcake was broken over the bride's head, and she made the first cut in the wedding cake with a dirk.

Champagne was poured and toasts were said and guests kissed the bride. Danielle was the first to kiss her cousin. "Give me a big hug," she said.

Even Qwilleran was kissed by many of the women including, of all people, Amanda Goodwinter. "This is turning into an orgy," he said to her.

"You said it!" she muttered. "Did you see how the Carmichael woman bussed her cousin? I hope Lynette knows what she's doing. It's bad luck to marry on Tuesday or marry in green."

"Don't worry," Qwilleran said. "With a silver coin in her shoe and oatcake crumbs in her hair, she's home safe."

Carter Lee was his usual charming self, flashing his winning smile at the guests in between fond glances at his bride. She was brimming with the joy she had lost twenty years before. When Brodie played a lively tune, she hoisted her skirt and danced the Highland fling.

Mac MacWhannell said to Qwilleran, "Too bad she didn't marry a Scot. Know anything about his genealogy?"

"No, but James is a good British name. You

know: King James . . . P. D. James . . . and all those others."

"When they're back from their honeymoon," Big Mac promised, "we'll invite him to join the genealogy club." And then he said, "That was an interesting column on naming cats. We have two gray ones, Misty and Foggy, and our daughter in New Hampshire has a kitten called Arpeggio. It runs up and down the piano keys."

"The things you hear when you don't have a pencil!" Qwilleran said. "Send the names in on a postcard."

"No!" Arch Riker protested. "No more postcards! The mailroom is swamped! What are we supposed to do with them all?"

Mildred said, "My grandkids have a tomcat called Alvis Parsley. He likes rock and roll."

"I believe they tune in to a rhythmic beat," said the choir leader from the church. "Ours sits on the piano with her tail swinging to the music. We call her Metro, short for metronome."

Everyone joined the game. Everyone knew an aptly named cat: a tom named Catsanova; a shrimp addict called Stir Fry; a pair of Burmese known as Ping and Pong.

"Send postcards!" Qwilleran reminded them.

Polly said to him, "You've opened a Pandora's box. Is it going to be a blessing or a curse?"

When the piper swung into a strathspey, it was a signal that the newlyweds were leaving. Qwilleran, who was driving the getaway car, fished the car keys from his sporran and asked

Riker to bring his van to the clubhouse door.

En route to Boulder House Inn, the couple in the backseat raved about the gift from the couple in the front seat, little knowing how close they had come to getting a schnauzer. Carter Lee said they would schedule a sitting with the portraitist as soon as they returned. Polly hoped they would have good weather in New Orleans. Lynette hoped not to gain any weight.

As for the driver, his moustache was giving him some uneasiness. Champagne had flowed freely at the reception, and he was probably the only one who was totally sober. He kept thinking about the X-rated kiss that Danielle had bestowed on the groom . . . and about the hints that they were not really cousins . . . and about the hasty marriage that was a topic of local gossip.

The Boulder House Inn perched on a cliff overlooking the frozen lake and was indeed built of boulders, some as big as bathtubs, piled one on top of another. Snow accented every ledge, lintel, sill, and crevice. Indoors, some of the floors were chiseled from the huge flat rock that made the foundation of the building. Four-foot split logs blazed in the cavernous fireplace, around which guests gathered after dinner to listen to the innkeeper's stories.

Silas Dingwall was like the innkeeper in a medieval woodcut: short, rotund, leather-aproned, and jolly. Smiling and flinging his arms wide in welcome, he ushered the wedding party to the best table in the dining room. The centerpiece

201

was a profusion of red carnations, white ribbons, and white wedding bells of plastic foam. A wine cooler stood ready, chilling a bottle of champagne, courtesy of the house.

"May I open it?" he asked.

The cork escaped from the bottleneck with a gentle *pffft!* and he poured with a flourish, while lavishing felicitations on the bridal pair. He ended by saying, "I'll be your wine steward tonight, and Tracy will be your server."

Involuntarily Qwilleran's hand went to his upper lip as he saw the innkeeper speak to a pretty young blond woman. He saw Dingwall gesture toward their table. He saw her nod.

Lynette and Carter Lee were drinking an intimate toast to each other, with arms linked and eyes shining, when the blond server approached the table. She took a few brisk steps, wearing a hospitable smile, then slowed to a sleepwalker's pace as her smile turned to shock. "Oh, my God!" she cried and ran blindly from the dining room, bumping into chairs and lurching through the swinging doors to the kitchen.

There was silence among the diners. Then hysterical screams came from the kitchen, and the innkeeper rushed through the swinging doors.

"Well!" Polly said. "What was that all about?"

Lynette was bewildered. Carter Lee seemed poised. Qwilleran looked wise. He thought he knew what it was all about.

The innkeeper, red-faced, bustled up to the

table. "I'm sorry," he said. "Tracy is not well. Barbara will be your server."

After the wedding dinner, Qwilleran and Polly chose to drive back to Pickax without waiting for the storytelling hour around the fireplace. She had to work the next day, and he was less than comfortable with the situation as he perceived it. But he was "best man," and he had made the best of it.

While the two sisters-in-law embraced with tears of joy, the two men shook hands, and Carter Lee thanked his best man for being witness to the ceremony.

"It's the third time I've performed this role," Qwilleran said, "and it's the first time I've done it without dropping the ring, so that bodes well!"

Before leaving, he told Silas Dingwall about *Short and Tall Tales* and made an appointment for the next day to record "something hair-raising, mysterious, or otherwise sensational." The innkeeper promised him a good one.

On the way home, no mention was made of the waitress's outburst. Polly told him he was the handsomest man at the wedding; he told her she looked younger than the bride. Both agreed that Lynette looked beatific.

"So you see, you were wrong about her jilting him, Qwill."

"First time in my life I've ever been wrong," he said with a facetious nonchalance that he did not really feel.

On the way to Boulder House Inn, the day after the wedding, Qwilleran reviewed the incident of the previous evening. The server's name was Tracy; she was a pretty blond; she was obviously Ernie Kemple's daughter, who had been wined and dined by Carter Lee James. Her father knew she was gullible; he feared she would be hurt again. Now Qwilleran was wondering what kind of husband Lynette had acquired. He was a suave young man who was enchanting local women, including Polly. She remarked about his engaging ways. He was being called charming, gallant, gentlemanly. What else was he?

Arriving at the inn, Qwilleran was greeted effusively by Silas Dingwall, who was excited about being "in a book." He said, "We'll go in the office, where it's quiet."

"And first tell me something about yourself," Qwilleran said.

Over coffee he learned that Dingwall was descended from the survivors of a shipwreck more than a century before. All his life he had been fascinated by tales handed down through the generations.

"There were ghost stories, murder mysteries, rum-running thrillers and you-name-it. My favorite is the Mystery of Dank Hollow, a true story about a young fisherman who was also a new bridegroom. It happened, maybe, a hundred and thirty years ago when Trawnto was a little fishing village. Want to hear it?"

"I certainly do. Just tell it straight through. I won't interrupt."

As eventually transcribed, the story went like this:

One day a young fisherman by the name of Wallace Reekie, who lived in the village here, went to his brother's funeral in a town twenty miles away. He didn't have a horse, so he set out on foot at daybreak and told his new bride he'd be home at nightfall. Folks didn't like to travel that road after dark because there was a dangerous dip in it. Mists rose up and hid the path, you see, and it was easy to make a wrong turn and walk into the bog. They called it Dank Hollow.

At the funeral, Wallace helped carry his brother's casket to the burial place in the woods, and on the way he tripped over a tree root. There was an old Scottish superstition: Stumble while carrying a corpse, and you'll be the next to go into the grave. It must have troubled Wallace, because he drank too much at the wake and was late in leaving for home. His relatives wanted him to stay over, but he was afraid his young wife would worry. He took a nap before leaving, though, and got a late start.

It was a five-hour trek, and when he didn't show up by nightfall, like he'd said, his wife sat up all night, praying. It was just turning daylight when she was horrified to see her husband staggering into the dooryard of their little hut. Before he could say a word, he collapsed on the ground. She screamed for help, and a neighbor's boy ran for the doctor. He came galloping on horseback and did what he could. They also called the pastor of the church. He put his ear to the dying man's lips and listened to his last babbling words, but for some reason he never told what he heard.

From then on, folks dreaded the Dank Hollow after dark. It was not only because of the mists and the bog but because of Wallace's mysterious death. That happened way back, of course. By 1930, when a paved road bypassed the Hollow, the incident was mostly forgotten. And then, in 1970, the pastor's descendents gave his diary to the Trawnto Historical Society. That's when the whole story came to light:

Wallace had reached the Dank Hollow after dark and was feeling his way cautiously along the path, when he was terrified to see a line of shadowy beings coming toward him out of the bog. One of them was his brother, who had just been buried. They beckoned Wallace to join their ghostly procession, and that was the last thing the poor man remembered. How he had found his way home in his delirium was hard to explain.

The pastor had written in his diary: "Only the prayers of his wife and his great love for her could have guided him." And then he added a strange thing: "When Wallace collapsed in his dooryard, all his clothes were inside out."

"Whew!" Qwilleran said when the story ended. "Is Dank Hollow still there?"

"No, they filled it in a few years ago and built condominiums. I'm not superstitious, but I'd sure think twice before buying one. When will your book be published?"

"As soon as I've collected a sufficient number of yarns. I might have space for one of your rum-running tales at a later date, if you'd be good enough to —"

"I'd be honored! . . . More coffee?"

While drinking his second cup of coffee, Qwilleran asked, "What happened to the server who was supposed to wait on our table last night?"

"Tracy? Well, she's a good worker, and pretty, and has a nice way with customers, but she's a very impulsive type. She suddenly rushed into the kitchen as if she'd seen a ghost. She was hysterical, and my wife took her into our private quarters so the guests wouldn't be disturbed. We didn't know what kind of seizure it was, so we called 911. We also called her home, and her father came and got her. It turned out that the gentleman who just got married was supposed to be her boyfriend. Can you beat that?"

"It's been the stuff of Greek tragedy, opera,

and novels for centuries," Qwilleran said. "The villain usually gets stabbed."

"She has a little boy, you know, and that might be why she lost out. An elegant young man like Mr. James might not want to take on a ready-made family."

Especially, Qwilleran thought, when the alternative is a woman with property and inherited wealth.

From the Boulder House Inn, Qwilleran drove to the Pickax community hall, where the Boosters Club was having its weekly luncheon. Ernie Kemple would be there as official greeter, and Qwilleran wanted to have a few words with him. There would be a fast lunch and an even faster business meeting, and then the members would hurry back to their stores and offices.

Kemple was welcoming them at the door with his usual hearty banter, but Qwilleran detected an undertone of anxiety. He said, "Ernie, let's talk after the meeting." He wanted to brace him for the newspaper coverage of the wedding. But first he had to stand in line for his soup-and-sandwich platter, which he carried to one of the long institutional tables. He sat next to Wetherby Goode and across from Hixie Rice.

"Bean soup again! Ham and cheese again!" the weatherman complained. "I thought the lunches would have more class after they let you gals join."

"Don't worry," she said. "Next week it'll be

208

fruit salad and melba toast."

During the business session it was she who gave the update on the Ice Festival:

• Contestants coming from eight states, including Alaska.

• Prizes valued at a quarter-million, donated by business firms and well-wishers.

• Seven colleges sending student-artists to the ice sculpture competition.

• Snow-moving equipment in three counties on stand-by, ready to build the rinks, race tracks, and snow barriers.

• Hospitality tents leaving Minneapolis by truck on Monday.

• Fifteen thousand polar-bear buttons already delivered.

• Jim Qwilleran lined up as grand marshal of the torchlight parade.

• Volunteers needed for hospitality tents and traffic control.

"Need any indoor volunteers?" Wetherby Goode called out. "I can't stand the cold."

After the applause and the grand rush for the exit, Qwilleran and Ernie Kemple stayed behind. "How goes it?" Qwilleran asked in a warmly sympathetic tone.

"Tracy's in the hospital. She tried to OD. Vivian's flying home from Arizona. That Carter Lee James is a heel! He's been trying to use Tracy to get us to sign up for his project. Last night she found out in the cruelest way. She was assigned to wait on his table at the Boulder House. It turned out to be his wedding party! He'd married the Duncan woman, who has a house on our street."

"I know," Qwilleran said. "I was there, and I just want to tip you off; there'll be a big spread on the wedding in today's paper."

"Oh, God! I'll be glad when Vivian gets home. She's coming in on the five o'clock shuttle. Tracy won't talk to me. I'd warned her, but she wouldn't listen, so now she hates me because I was right. Can't win!"

"They have to make their own mistakes," Qwilleran murmured as if he were an expert on parenting.

"You don't know how hard it is," Kemple said, "to stand by and see them go over the cliff. This is her second disappointment. She should've stayed with Lenny. She'll never get him back now . . . but here I am, dumping my woes on you again."

"Don't apologize," Qwilleran said. "I'm really concerned."

He was, too. There were increasing tremors on his upper lips, and Koko had been staring at him and slapping the floor vehemently with his tail.

## 14

After the Boosters' luncheon, Qwilleran killed time until three o'clock, reading out-of-town newspapers at the public library. He was waiting for a chance to talk to Lenny Inchpot at his mother's restaurant. At three o'clock he bought a copy of the *Something* and took it with him to Lois's Luncheonette, where he dawdled over apple pie and the local news. The wedding was handled as a photo feature with a minimum of text:

### VALENTINE WEDDING
### IN THE VILLAGE

Lynette Duncan of Pickax and Carter Lee James of New York City were united in marriage Tuesday evening in a Scottish wedding at the Indian Village clubhouse. Witnesses for the couple were Polly Duncan and James Qwilleran. The Reverend Wesley Forbush officiated.

The photos were credited to John Bushland: a close-up of the bride and groom; the wedding party in front of the fireplace; the oatcake ritual; the bride making the first cut in the wedding cake with a Scottish dirk; and a group shot of guests in tartans and Brodie with his bagpipe.

When the last customer had left and the Closed sign was hung in the window, Lenny started mopping the floor. Qwilleran went to the kitchen pass-through and shouted at Lois, "Permission requested to speak to the mop-jockey on matters of vital importance."

"Go ahead," she yelled back, "but make it snappy. He's got work to do."

"Park the mop, Lenny, and sit down for a few minutes," Qwilleran said. "Did you hear that Tracy Kemple's in the hospital?"

"No! What happened?"

"Nervous breakdown. Have you seen today's paper?" He opened it to the wedding page. "The bridegroom is Carter Lee James."

"Oh-oh!" Lenny said with a gulp. "Tracy thought she was on the inside track with that guy. I guess it was wishful thinking."

Or, Qwilleran thought, deliberate misrepresentation. "Do you know how she met him?"

"Sure. He was trying to sell the Kemples on signing up for his big project. It meant paying a lot of money up front, and Ernie wasn't keen on the deal. To me, Carter Lee sounded like a sharpie, but Tracy was impressed by the houses he'd had published in magazines . . . You know, Mr. Q, I've been suspicious of strangers ever since that smooth talker with a bunch of flowers blew up the hotel last year. Where I made my mistake with Tracy — I told her I thought Carter Lee was a phoney. That was a dumb thing to do. I

212

should've kept my big mouth shut. All it did was make her mad, and she told me to get lost . . . That's the story. Now what?"

"It's for you to decide. For starters, you might call Ernie and sympathize with him. He's feeling down."

"Yeah, I could do that. I always got along with Ernie."

"He's willing to appear at your hearing as a character witness. So am I."

"Honest? That's great, Mr. Q! And thanks for lining up Mr. Barter. He's a super guy!"

"Okay. See you in court."

When Qwilleran left the lunchroom, Lenny was swishing the mop around like a sleepwalker.

"Get with it!" his mother screamed. "Folks'll be comin' in before the floor's clean!"

Before going home, Qwilleran bought six copies of the *Something* for Polly to give Lynette on her return. He dropped them off at the library.

"Did you know Carter Lee is from New York?" he asked.

"I know only that he's worked in eastern cities. Lynette says his portfolio of past projects is thrilling. I'd like to see it."

"So would I," he said.

"I'm expecting you to come for another chicken dinner tonight. We've had seven of the recipes so far; only ten to go."

"I can hardly wait," he said ambiguously. "Any excitement at the library today? Any loud voices? Any wet boots?"

"You wouldn't believe it, Qwill! The clerks and volunteers talk about nothing but the naming of cats! I told them Bootsie is now Brutus, and his companion will be named Catta, which is said to be Latin for the female of the species. My assistant has three cats: Oedipuss, Octopuss, and Platypuss. And the silver tabby who sleeps in the window of Scottie's men's shop is Haggis Mac-Tavish."

Soon Moose County would have something else to talk about.

Late that same afternoon, Qwilleran was pulling into his driveway, and Wetherby Goode was pulling out. The weatherman tooted his horn lightly and lowered the window. "Got a minute, Qwill?"

There was an element of anxiety in the question that made Qwilleran say, "Sure. Want to come in?"

When Wetherby saw the Siamese, who were being politely inquisitive, he said, "You've got two top-of-the-line cats here. Mine's an orange tiger called Jet Stream, slight pun intended. He answers to Jet-boy."

"Care for a drink, Wetherby?"

"No, thanks. I'm on my way to the station. Call me Joe. That's my real name."

"Well, sit down, Joe, and tell me what's eating you."

He sat on the edge of a chair. "What did you think about the Ice Festival update at the luncheon?"

214

"I'd say they've done a superlative job of organization and promotion. I'm not keen on being grand marshal, but I hope it's a popular and financial success."

"So do I, but — I hate to say this, Qwill — there's a warming trend in the offing. A *real* warming trend!"

"It can't last more than a couple of days. This is February!"

"The weather's been weird all over the globe. An unseasonable and prolonged warm spell is not only possible but inevitable — that plus warm rain! Do you realize what it'll do to the Ice Festival? A premature thaw could wipe out the profits expected by local business firms, not to mention disappointing thousands of people in three counties! After I give the long-range forecast tonight, I may have to leave town. Don't they always shoot the messenger who brings bad news? A meteorologist's lot, like that of a policeman, is not a happy one. Listeners expect forecasts to be perfect, but they don't care about warm fronts and cold air pockets. They only want to know which jacket to wear and whether to close the car windows . . . Well, anyway, I felt like unloading the bad news on somebody. Thanks for listening."

When Wetherby left, Qwilleran went to his office alcove to read the day's mail and have another look at the wedding photos in the *Something*, only to find that someone . . . someone had thrown up a hairball on the newspaper. Both cats

215

crouched nearby, waiting for him to make the discovery.

"I don't know which of you did this," he said, "but I consider it a new low! A breach of etiquette!"

Yum Yum squeezed her eyes, and Koko acted as if he'd lost his hearing.

While dressing to have dinner at Polly's (flattened chicken breast with ripe olives, garbanzos, and sun-dried tomatoes), Qwilleran received another annoying phone call from Danielle. Impudently she said, "Hi, snookums! Wanna come out to play tonight?"

Stiffly he replied, "*Whom* are you calling? We have no small dogs by that name at this number."

"Qwill, this is Danielle," she said with the shrillness that jarred his nerves.

"I would never have guessed."

"Oh, you're a big kidder! My cousin's away on his honeymoon, and I don't have anybody to play with. Why don't you come on over for drinks and dinner? I'll thaw something."

"The invitation is almost irresistible," he said, "but I have a previous engagement."

The brief but irritating exchange made the prospect of flattened chicken breast a gustatory delight. For the walk to Polly's, he left his hat and gloves at home. The temperature was incredibly mild, and the sidewalk — instead of being dusted with white — was black with wetness.

"You're not wearing your hat!" Polly greeted him.

"It seems to be a little warmer tonight," he said, without revealing his privileged information.

"I've just found out the difference between friendly snow and unfriendly snow," she said with enthusiasm. Polly collected scraps of information as avidly as the Kemples collected dolls. "Flurries and snow showers are friendly; blizzards and snow squalls are unfriendly. Do you find that interesting?"

"Very," he replied, thinking of the forthcoming thaw. "How's Brutus?"

"I think he's pleased with his new name."

"Have you heard from Lynette?"

"No, I'm sure she has other things on her mind," Polly said. "But Mildred called about the gourmet club. They're skipping the February meeting as a token of respect for Willard — a moment of silence, so to speak."

"That's appropriate. I'll go along with that."

"Have you heard how Danielle is doing in the play?"

"Only that tickets for all performances are selling fast. It's my theory that Pickax audiences will eagerly pay money to see the widow of a murdered man."

"How ghoulish!" Polly said with a shudder.

After dinner — it was the best recipe so far — they listened to the tapes Qwilleran had recorded for *Tall Tales*. He said, "Koko has heard them twice, and each time he yowls at 'The Dimsdale

217

Jinx.' Either he's uncomfortable with Homer Tibbitt's high-pitched voice, or he knows what pasties are all about."

"Brutus loves pasties," Polly said over her shoulder as she went to answer the phone. "Lynette! We were just talking about you! Qwill's here. Wait a minute . . . Qwill, would you take this phone? I'll pick up the one on the balcony."

"How's New Orleans?" he said to the caller.

"Warm and wonderful!" Lynette talked fast and excitedly. "We're staying at a charming old inn. Our room has a four-poster bed and a fireplace. Breakfast is brought up on a huge tray: croissants, fabulous preserves, and delicious hot chocolate!"

"Be careful with that hot chocolate!" Polly warned, slipping into the conversation.

"You should see the French Quarter and the lacy wrought-iron balconies! So romantic! The coffee is strange; Carter Lee says they put chicory in it. But my favorite is the Creole gumbo. It's seasoned with something called filé powder. I'm going to buy some, so I can make it when I get home." She hardly stopped for breath. "Everything is different here. When they drink a toast, they say, 'Here's to a short life and a merry one!' The parades start Saturday. I can hardly wait!"

"Go easy on the Sazeracs," Qwilleran advised.

"I'm so happy!" she said, almost tearfully. "Carter Lee is just wonderful! Everything is perfect!"

"Well!" said Polly when the conversation ended.

"I get the impression she likes New Orleans," Qwilleran remarked.

"I'm so happy for her!"

At the end of the evening, as he sloshed home through the deepening puddles, he thought about Lynette and her new life. She had quit her job at the medical clinic and would assist her husband in a public relations capacity, promoting restoration. She had the qualifications. She knew everyone in town, and her enthusiasm for Carter Lee's accomplishments was boundless. Qwilleran had a great curiosity about the portfolio of his work that everyone praised so highly. Even Old Gallbladder had referred to the "mighty purty pitchers." Breze was no arbiter of historic design, but he might afford a way to borrow the portfolio in Carter Lee's absence.

When Qwilleran arrived home, he typed a briefing for Celia:

Mission: Operation Winter Breeze
Assignment: To lay hands on the book of "mighty purty pitchers" belonging to Carter Lee James. Start by giving Red Cap some of your homemade brownies, to prove you can cook. Let him know that you've seen his house on Sandpit Road and think it would be worth a lot of money if fixed up a little. Say you're interested in decorating and

would like to see the book of pictures . . .
Then contact Danielle Carmichael on Woodland Trail and ask to borrow it for Mr. Breze,
who is extremely eager to have his house
restored. When mission is completed, signal
headquarters.

The next morning Qwilleran deposited Celia's
briefing in her mailbox at the gatehouse. Snowshoeing was out of the question. The temperature
was in the unbelievable fifties, and a steady rain
was turning the white landscape into a porous
gray blanket. Walkways and pavements hemmed
in by the shrinking snowbanks were becoming
canals. In the mailroom the sudden thaw was the
sole topic of conversation:

"What does this do to the Ice Festival?"

"The fuzzy caterpillars were right after all. They
predicted a mild winter."

"Yeah, but their timing was off — by about ten
weeks."

"How much of this can the storm sewers
take?"

Qwilleran took his mail home to open, throwing most of the communications into his Procrastination File — a small drawer in the hutch
cabinet. One was a letter from Celia's grandson,
enclosing snapshots of the dowser and a transcript
of a tape recording. The other was an invitation
to an opening-night party at Danielle's apartment
— just a cozy little afterglow. RSVP.

When the telephone rang, he was pleased to

hear the good radio voice of his next-door neigh-bor:

"Qwill, things are getting pretty sloppy out there, but we have to eat, and they say the road to Kennebeck is not too bad. Are you free? Are you hungry? Would you like to go to Tipsy's?"

"I always like to go to Tipsy's, rain or shine, with friend or foe," said Qwilleran.

"Let's take my van. It's bigger and makes bigger roostertails."

"Apparently no one has shot the messenger as yet."

"Not yet! But the promoters of the Ice Festival are monitoring the ice from hour to hour . . . !"

# 15

The two men splashed down River Lane in Wetherby Goode's van. "Some weather!" the weatherman said.

"How did the landscape liquefy so fast?" Qwilleran asked.

"Warm rain. Like pouring hot tea on ice cubes."

"The county's gone from a beautiful swan to an ugly duckling overnight."

"And it's going to get uglier," Wetherby predicted. *The rain, it raineth every day.*"

"Is the Ice Festival doomed?"

"I'm not predicting. I'm not even opening my mouth. All I can say is: The fuzzy caterpillars knew something we didn't know. The parking lot at the Dimsdale Diner is under water, and the people in Shantytown are being evacuated. They're afraid the old mine may cave in."

"How about the Buckshot mine on our road?"

"The situation's not so dangerous. The Dimsdale mine, you see, is in a fork between two rivers, the Ittibittiwassee and the Rocky Burn."

Qwilleran said, "Our river seemed to be rushing faster and making more noise, but I don't see much rise in the water level. In any case, I suppose the bank is high enough to protect us. And we have all those cats in Building Five; if they can predict an earthquake, they should be able to predict a simple flood."

"The only bad thing would be if a freak wave in the lake sent a surge up the river. It might reach Sawdust City, but it wouldn't reach us. You don't need to give your cats swimming lessons yet."

"The schools will have to close if the buses can't get through the mud on the back roads. Perhaps we should lay in a supply of emergency foods. My barn was prepared for power outages — with canned goods, a camp stove, bottled water, and batteries — but I have nothing here. I should buy for Polly, too."

Wetherby said, "We can shop at the Kennebeck Market after lunch, if there's anything left."

"I suggest we shop before lunch," Qwilleran countered.

The town of Kennebeck was situated on a hummock, and Tipsy's Tavern was high and dry on the summit. The restaurant had started in a small log cabin in the 1930s, named after the owner's cat. Now it was a sprawling roadhouse of log construction, with dining rooms on several levels. In one of them hung an oil portrait of the celebrated white cat with black markings. The food was simple and hearty; rustic informality prevailed; and the servers were older women who called customers by their first names and knew what they liked to drink.

After a Squnk water and a bourbon had been brought to the table, Qwilleran said to his companion, "I suppose you're a native, Joe."

"A native of Lockmaster County. I came from a town called Horseradish."

"In jest, I suppose."

"You think so? Look it up on the map," Wetherby said. "It's on the lakeshore. Not many people realize it was once the horseradish capital of the Midwest. That was back in the nineteenth century, of course, long before Lockmaster County became fashionable horse country. If there's any connection, I can't figure it out. What's happened to Horseradish — it's all summer homes and country inns now. Some of my relatives still live there."

"What brought you to Moose County, Joe?"

"Well, after college I worked in television Down Below, and then I had a mid-life crisis ahead of schedule and decided to come back up north. My first thought was Lockmaster City, but then I saw what was happening to Pickax City, and I liked what I saw. So here I am, with Jet-boy. Before him I had another orange cat called Leon, with a head as big as a grapefruit, no neck, and a disposition like a lemon. We were a pair, let me tell you! But that was Down Below. My disposition improved after I came home."

Qwilleran asked the logical question. "What happened to Leon?"

"He stayed with my ex-wife. He probably reminds her of me . . . What are you ordering? I always get the steak sandwich on an onion roll." Then he started talking about Lynette. "She shocked the whole bridge club by marrying so fast, after being on the shelf so long."

"Do you know she's one of your greatest fans, Joe? She goes around quoting your daily quips: *The north wind doth blow, and we shall have snow.* She's impressed!"

"Too bad I didn't know that!" Wetherby puffed out his chest. "What do you know about her husband?"

"Not much. I was invited to be best man because I own a kilt."

"Yeah, I think I was invited to the reception because I play cocktail piano."

"Willard Carmichael told me that Carter Lee's a highly regarded professional Down Below and could do great things for Pickax. Did you know Willard?"

"Only around the bridge table, but he seemed like a good egg. I hated what happened to him."

The steak sandwiches were served, and Qwilleran pushed the condiment tray across the tabletop, saying, "Horseradish?" Then he asked, "Does your hometown have any local yarns or legends that make good telling? I'm working on a collection for a proposed book. So far, I have stories from Dimsdale, Brrr, and Trawnto Beach."

"I have a great-uncle in Horseradish who could tell you some doozies. The town had a problem with lake pirates in the old days. It was the chief port for the whole county, and pirates would board the cargo ships and make their victims walk the plank. Bodies were always being washed up on the beach with hands tied behind their backs. They were buried, but the poor souls couldn't rest in peace, so Horseradish had a lot of ghosts. People were kept awake by the moaning and door-slamming and cold drafts . . . Is that the kind of thing you're interested in?"

"Keep right on going."

"One day a man came into town riding on a mule, and he said he had the power to de-haunt houses."

Qwilleran said, "That would make a good movie, if it hasn't already been done."

"Don't laugh! This really happened! People gave him money, and he went to work in the attics, throwing sand around and chanting mumbo jumbo. Then he suddenly disappeared, along with some of their treasures."

"How about the ghosts? Did they disappear, too?"

"No one really knows. The victims of the scam were too embarrassed to talk about it . . . Sorry I don't have more details."

"I'd like to meet your great-uncle, Joe. I'd like to go to Horseradish with my tape recorder. Would he be willing to talk?"

"Talk! You couldn't shut him up! Take plenty of tape. He's a great old fellow. And by the way, he's got a big gray cat called Long John Silver."

Qwilleran was pleased to find another lead for

*Tall Tales*. He enjoyed his steak sandwich. He found Wetherby to be good company. He liked his enthusiasm and candor. It occurred to Qwilleran that a weatherman from Horseradish might have been a more suitable match for Lynette than a restoration consultant from New York.

On the way back to Indian Village, the driver was busy maneuvering the van through puddles, but at one point he turned to his passenger and said, "I shouldn't ask you this, since you were best man at the wedding —"

"I told you why I was there," Qwilleran said. "I hardly know the groom. Go ahead and ask."

"Were you surprised at the match between Lynette and Carter Lee? Was Polly surprised?"

"I won't presume to answer for Polly. They're sisters-in-law, and she was glad to see Lynette so happy. But . . . yes, I was surprised — as much as a veteran journalist is ever surprised."

"The reason I ask: I observed Carter Lee at the bridge club. The way he buttered her up was marvelous to behold. And it worked."

" 'All's fair in love and war,' they say."

"Maybe, but I'm inclined to think of him as a fortune hunter. Although Lynette has a job and never puts on airs, we all know she inherited the whole Duncan estate. And it seems to me they got married pretty fast. 'Marry in haste; repent at leisure,' as the saying goes."

"Someone should have told me that twenty years ago," Qwilleran said.

"In case you don't know, Qwill, there's another fortune hunter in the woods, and she's got her sights on you!"

"Danielle?" Qwilleran dismissed her with a shrug. "She's a little flaky. Believe me, Joe, I've learned how to deal with Lorelei Lee types. They come in all shapes, sizes, and model numbers. I appreciate your concern, though . . . Does Danielle still show up at the bridge club?"

"Hardly ever, which is okay with us; she's a terrible player. She's busy rehearsing a play. Can you imagine? She's doing the lead in *Hedda Gabler!*"

"I can't imagine," Qwilleran said quietly.

On Saturday morning another businesslike call from "the accountant's office" informed him that the "documents" he had requested were being delivered to the gatehouse at Indian Village. To pick them up he drove his van carefully through flooded lanes, between shrinking snowbanks, under gray skies that were dumping even more water on the soggy terrain. *The rain, it raineth every day* had been the weatherman's morning adage, not a comforting one.

The clerk in the mailroom handed him a large flat package wrapped in white tissue and tied with red ribbon. "It looks like a valentine," she said. "Maybe it's a big chocolate heart."

At home the Siamese played with the ribbons while Qwilleran read the accompanying note from Celia:

Dear Chief,

No problem! I didn't even have to give Red Cap any brownies. He said okay, so I called the lady and she let me pick it up. My! She's a strange one! Let me know if there's anything else I can do. Just had a letter from Clayton. He wants to know how you liked his snapshots.

Celia

Qwilleran had not even glanced at Clayton's photos; they were in the Procrastination File. As for the famous Carter Lee James portfolio, it was a leather-bound scrapbook of color photographs under plastic: interiors and exteriors of old houses. They were all apparently authentic and obviously expensive. Before he could peruse them critically, the phone rang again, and he heard the booming voice of the retired insurance agent:

"Qwill, this is Ernie. Ernie Kemple. Is your condo still high and dry?"

"So far, so good. Any flooding on Pleasant Street?"

"No, knock on wood. Every house has a sump pump working overtime."

"How's Tracy?"

Kemple lowered his voice to a gruff rumble. "Do you happen to be coming downtown? I know the driving's bad, but . . . I don't want to talk on the phone."

Qwilleran said, "I could be lured downtown if someone wanted to have lunch at Onoosh's."

"I can meet you there anytime."

"I'll leave right away."

Ittibittiwassee Road, being a major county thoroughfare, was passable. Even so, Qwilleran silently thanked Scott Gippel for selling him a vehicle with a high axle, as the wheels swished through large puddles and small floods, spraying roostertails. Crossing the bridge, he stopped to observe the water level. It was higher than usual but still well below the concrete bridge-bed. Many bridges on back roads were submerged with only their railings visible, according to WPKX.

He tuned in the hourly newsbreak: "Six inches of rain fell in one hour at the official checkpoint in Brrr. Many paved secondary roads are under five inches of water, and the sheriff's department warns motorists to stay on main highways whenever possible. In the Black Creek valley, volunteer fire fighters are going from door to door, warning families to move to higher ground. Emergency shelters are being set up in schools and churches."

Traffic was sparse for a Saturday, and there were few pedestrians downtown. Qwilleran and Kemple were the only customers at Onoosh's.

Her partner waited on them. "We told our girls to stay home. Onoosh is alone in the kitchen," he said.

She waved at them from the pass-through.

Qwilleran ordered stuffed grape leaves and tabbouleh. Kemple decided on falafel in a pita pocket.

"You asked about Tracy," he said, still speaking in his confidential rumble. "Her mother's home now and knows how to handle her. They can communicate."

"Did Tracy see the wedding story in the paper?"

"Not until she calmed down, but now she has an entirely new take on the situation. She feels guilty."

"How do you explain that?"

"You remember the little doll of ours that was found in Lenny's locker; we'd reported it stolen . . . Well, the drama unfolds! Scene One: Tracy had given it as a good-luck token to Carter Lee, without our knowledge. Scene Two: She and Lenny had a falling out, and in the heat of battle he said Carter Lee was a phoney. Scene Three: She's just confessed to my wife that she repeated Lenny's slur to Carter Lee."

"Why?" Qwilleran asked.

"It was on one of her glamorous dates with the big city dude. They were drinking margaritas at the Palomino Paddock. She was high. She didn't know what she was doing."

"Interesting," Qwilleran mused, touching his moustache.

"When the doll turned up in Lenny's locker, she was afraid to come forward. It would spoil her chances with Carter Lee. But now she hates him, and she's filled with remorse for what happened to Lenny. She wants to go to his hearing and tell the judge the truth."

"This gets complicated, Ernie. In coming to

the defense of the one, she's accusing the other. If he planted the doll in Lenny's locker, one can assume he also planted the video, sunglasses, etc. And that implies he stole them. He may be a cad and a user, but is he a petty thief? He's a professional man with standing in the community; does he go around snitching sunglasses? Does it mean he also stole the bridge club's money — and his own coat at the New Year's Eve party? Before Tracy does anything, she should consult G. Allen Barter."

Kemple, who had been hunched over the table, leaned back in his chair and drew a deep breath. "That's why I wanted to bounce it off you, Qwill. That's a good idea."

"Another thing, Ernie: I hate to say this, but is it possible that Tracy is lying to get revenge on Carter Lee?"

"I admit I thought of that, Qwill. You know, my daughter used to be a sweet, innocent girl, but she got off the track, and circumstances have changed her."

"If it's true that she's lying, she could be in deep trouble. Yes . . . you'd better talk to Bart in a hurry."

"I appreciate your interest and your advice, Qwill." He reached for the check. "This lunch is on me, and I'll even throw in a little carved and painted wooden doll for a good-luck token."

"Keep it!" Qwilleran said. "I've got all the good luck I can use . . . By the way, how are the rehearsals for *Hedda Gabler*?"

Kemple's guffaw rattled the beaded fringe on the hanging lights overhead. "I call the play *Hedda Cauliflower*. Danielle isn't playing Hedda; she's playing Adelaide in *Guys and Dolls*. And I'm not playing Judge Brack; I'm playing the villain in *The Drunkard*. You should come to a rehearsal, just for laughs. Trouble is, I feel sorry for Carol. Fran Brodie, too. They're working so hard! Why did they ever give that role to Danielle?"

"Good question," Qwilleran said.

As he drove out Ittibittiwassee Road, Qwilleran was plagued by other questions: Was Carter Lee indeed the petty thief who had annoyed townfolk in December? If so, what was his motivation? Would a man of his professional standing stoop to stealing used clothing intended for the needy? Was the petit larceny a rehearsal for the grand larceny in the Village clubhouse? A sum estimated at two thousand dollars had been taken from the money jar. As for the lambskin coat reported stolen on New Year's Eve, Qwilleran had seen its like in catalogs, priced at fifteen hundred. But then he had seen Carter Lee wearing a similar, if not identical, coat when he and Lynette made their impromptu visit. Was it the same coat, or had he bought a new one? If the same, had he recovered it, or had it never really been stolen?

Nothing made much sense until Qwilleran arrived home. The Siamese met him at the door, prowling restlessly. It was too early for their dinner. They were bored. No birds, no falling leaves, no dancing snowflakes. They needed action.

In one drawer of the hutch cabinet there were cat toys galore: things that bounced, rattled, rolled, glittered, or smelled like catnip. Yum Yum could entertain herself for hours with one of these, batting it under the sofa, then pawing it out again. Koko, on the other hand, was too worldly-wise for such kittenish amusements. He preferred the stimulation of the chase, and he sat on his haunches gazing speculatively into the upper reaches of the living room.

"Okay, where's Mosca?" Qwilleran said, folding a newspaper and whacking his left palm.

They waited. The cat gazed upward hopefully; the man whacked his palm. Their pet housefly was conspicuously absent, and a sickening thought occurred to Qwilleran. There was a possibility that Koko had caught him and eaten him. "Disgusting!" he said as he tossed his folded newspaper into the wastebasket.

Yum Yum was on the hutch cabinet, scratching at the wrong drawer. He rapped on the front of the toy drawer. "No! No! Over here!" It made no difference; with catly persistence she pawed the wrong drawer.

"Cats!" he said, rolling his eyes in exasperation. To convince her, he jerked open the drawer and showed her the Procrastination File. In her nearsighted way she studied the letters, sealed envelopes, brochures, and clippings for a long minute, then jumped down and went to the kitchen for a drink of water.

It was a reminder to Qwilleran, however, to look at Clayton's photos: candids of the dowser, close-ups of the forked stick, shots of Cody, and one of Carter Lee measuring the mantel with a tapeline and Danielle making notes. Also in the envelope was the transcript of Clayton's tape recording. Much of the dialogue duplicated Qwilleran's tape, but there was an unexpected interlude:

| | |
|---|---|
| Man: | Refinish floor. Strip and refinish five-foot varnished mantel. Repaper room in Victorian design . . . Am I going too fast for you, Danny? . . . Replace two panes in breakfront with crowned glass . . . Hello there! Who are you? |
| Clayton: | I'm visiting my grandma. Mind if I take some pictures to show my mom when I get home? |
| Man: | On the double! We're working here . . . Danny, where were we? |
| Woman: | (shrilly) With crowned glass. |
| Man: | Replace chandelier with gaslight fixture. |
| Woman: | Chuck, did you see those daggers in the hall? |
| Man: | What about them? |
| Woman: | One has a lion on the handle. |
| Man: | Do you like it? |
| Woman: | It's my sign. Leo. |
| Man: | Well . . . |

| Woman; | Do you think I could? |
|---|---|
| Man: | He'll never miss it . . . Hey, what is it you want now, kid? |
| Clayton: | Is this your dog? |
| Man: | Get him out of here! Both of you, evaporate! |
| Clayton: | C'mon, pup. C'mon. |

Qwilleran read no further. The stolen dirk had not turned up in Lenny's locker, but Danielle had given one like it to Lynette as a wedding gift. The hilt was a lion rampant . . . Now he thought he had figured it out: Danielle was a kleptomaniac, stealing at random all over town when she first moved to Pickax. Did Willard know? Did he have the anonymous check sent from a Chicago bank to cover the theft? Did Carter Lee know her weakness and humor her? The theft of his lambskin coat on New Year's Eve may have been a playful prank, a family joke. Did she steal his good-luck doll and plant it in Lenny's locker along with the other things? Was it a *woman* who phoned the tip to the police hotline? That was one clue that could be checked.

## 16

By Saturday evening the pretty little bubbling brooks and picturesque gurgling streams of Moose County had become raging torrents, over-flowing their banks, inundating farmlands and forests. Wooded areas were so thoroughly soaked that shallow-rooted trees toppled across highways, adding to the hazard of driving. Some were washed downstream along with timbers from wrecked bridges, creating temporary dams that caused even more flooding.

As Qwilleran dressed for dinner with Polly, he tuned in the WPKX news update and heard: "The sheriff's helicopter, searching for stranded motorists in isolated areas, rescued a family of five in the Plumley Mill area an hour ago. Several vehicles are completely submerged at the fish camp west of Mooseville."

Polly called to see if driving would be too bad. They had a reservation at the Old Stone Mill. She said, "We closed the library at noon today and won't open Monday. The schools will be closed."

Qwilleran said, "I called the restaurant about their parking lot; no problem. And I called the sheriff about the highways; the access road to the Mill is . . . accessible."

The restaurant had been converted from an old grist mill; the picturesque waterwheel, almost twenty feet high, was still there, although the millstream had long since run dry. They were ushered to their favorite table and approached by their favorite server, Derek Cuttlebrink, a towering six-feet-eight.

"Hi! Guess what!" he said even before announcing the evening specials. "We may get our millstream back again. It was a branch of the Rocky Burn that dried up in the Forties. Now the Rocky Burn is running so high, it could bust right through here and start the millwheel turning again!"

"Where would the water go from here?" Qwilleran asked.

"Through No Man's Gully and into the Ittibittiwassee . . . What'll it be? One dry sherry and one Squunk with a twist?"

As he loped toward the bar on his long legs, Polly said quietly, "I'm glad Derek is buckling down to some kind of life. Meeting that girl has been good for him." At various times he had wanted to be a cop, an actor, a career busboy, or just a bum. Now he was enrolled in Restaurant Management at MCCC.

Returning with the drinks, he said, "Now for the bad news. I'm not supposed to talk about this, but the Ice Festival biggies are having a secret emergency meeting in the private dining room downstairs. It doesn't look good."

In between the friendly overtures of the attentive server, the two diners managed to discuss automation for the library, the newspaper's editorial on illiteracy, the new Brutus, and Herman Melville's obsession with good and evil.

Polly said, "I have a feeling Lynette will phone again tonight. She'll have been to the parades. Have you heard if Carter Lee is getting the commission to restore the hotel and the Limburger mansion?"

"The K Fund hasn't decided. Like the mills of God, they grind slowly." He felt as if he were living a double life. He could talk to his tablemate about his Fauré recordings and the Rikers' new car but not about his disturbing suspicions. He avoided mention of Danielle and the silver-hilted dirk, the doll found in Lenny's locker, Wetherby's opinion of Carter Lee, and his own devious scheme to get a look at Carter Lee's portfolio. Polly would only worry. Besides, Qwilleran's conclusions were based on hunches, hearsay, and idle gossip.

After poached salmon with leek sauce for her and pork tenderloin with black currants for him, they returned to Indian Village in time to receive Lynette's phone call.

"We were wondering about you," Polly said, signaling to Qwilleran to pick up the balcony phone. "What have you been doing today?"

Lynette sounded tired. "We went to the parades on Canal Street. You'd never believe the floats, music, costumes, and masks! They throw strings of beads from the floats into the crowd.

239

Then there's the partying in the streets — jostling, screaming, drinking, and goodness knows what else! Some people take their clothes off! It's wild!"

Qwilleran asked, "Are you still doing justice to the food?"

"Oh, hello, Qwill. Well, my tummy doesn't feel too good today; that Cajun stuff is awfully spicy. Carter Lee's gone out to buy some kind of remedy."

"Be careful with shellfish," Polly admonished. "You know how you sometimes react."

With a noticeable sigh, Lynette said, "Three more days of Carnival, then everything stops and we go home. I'll be glad to see Pickax again."

Afterward Polly said to Qwilleran, "It's overindulgence that's disagreeing with her."

"Or overexcitement," he said. "Going from Moose County to Mardi Gras in a few air hours is like taking a few thousand volts of electricity."

All together it was a successful weekend of reading aloud at her place, listening to music at his place, arguing about Jane Austen, doing all the things they enjoyed. Through it all Brutus behaved like a noble Roman. "See? I told you so!" That was what Qwilleran wanted to say, but he held his tongue. Even the breakfast omelette was made with real eggs and real cheese; no substitutes.

It was late Sunday afternoon when Qwilleran finally returned to Unit Four. Yum Yum was happily engaged with a crocheted mouse from the toy drawer, but Koko was nervous and unfocused. He prowled aimlessly, sniffed numerous invisible spots, jumped on and off the coffee table, peered at the ceiling.

"If you're looking for Mosca, he doesn't live here any more," Qwilleran told him. "You can't eat your cake and have it, too."

Whatever was bothering the cat was bothering him as well. All the concerns suppressed during the last twenty-four hours were resurfacing. Dejectedly he sprawled in his big chair and listened to the rain — more rain! — pattering on the deck and splashing on the windows. Indoors there was only the sound of Yum Yum scurrying after her prey and Koko murmuring to himself. Now he was on the coffee table, examining the leather-bound scrapbook; he was a fiend for leather!

On an impulse, Qwilleran leaped out of his chair and went to the telephone to look up a number. She lived in the Village. She had opinions. She was hard-headed and not afraid to speak her mind. Sometimes she could be a little crazy. She was perfect! He knew she would be home. She was not one to go splashing around flooded highways except for financial gain, and this was Sunday.

The throaty voice that answered had an added note of impatience. "Yes? Now what, dammit."

In his most mellifluous tone he said, "Amanda, this is one of your admiring constituents and a frequent customer of your studio."

"Oh! It's you! You scoundrel!" she said. "I

thought it was the city attorney again. He's been calling me all day. There's a class-action suit against Pickax on account of the flooding. The stupid voters keep voting down millage to improve the storm sewers, but they forget that when it rains. Arrrgh!"

"You have my sympathy, Amanda. It's generous of you to keep serving on the council as you do." What he thought was: You keep running for re-election because it's good for your design business.

"So what's your complaint?"

"No complaint. Only a request for three minutes of your valuable time. Do you mind if I drive over? And would you be offended if I brought a pint of very fine brandy?"

A few minutes later she admitted him to her condo, which was piled to the ceiling with furnishings from the old Goodwinter mansion.

"Be my valentine!" he said, handing her a bottle tied with red streamers from Celia's package. She would never notice that they were punctured with fang marks.

"Pretty good stuff," she said, looking at the label. "Sure you can afford it? . . . Sit down, if you can find a place. Throw those magazines on the floor. Care for a drink?"

"Not this time, thanks. I just want you to look at this scrapbook."

She accepted it questioningly and scowled at the color photos. "Is this your new hobby? Cutting out pictures from magazines?"

"What you're looking at," he replied, "is the portfolio Carter Lee James shows to prospective clients. I borrowed it without his knowledge."

"Does he pretend he did all these restoration jobs?"

"Clients get the impression that he did."

"Well, I get the impression he's a royal fakeroo! You notice they're not identified — who or where — and look at this one! A Queen Anne Victorian. It was done by a friend of mine down south, and her name isn't Carter Lee James! I've been in this house! I recognize the gasolier, the stencils on the ceiling, the parlor set! Why, I even know the bear rug in front of the fireplace!"

Qwilleran was aware she had resented Carter Lee from the beginning. "Have you done any business as a result of his recommendations, Amanda?"

"Not a penny! Two council members live on Pleasant Street. They've each paid him twenty thousand up front. How come my clients never pay me up front?"

"He's a professional charmer. You should try being more sweet-natured."

"Arrrgh! I noticed there hasn't been any publicity on Pleasant Street in your paper. How d'you explain that?"

"He doesn't want publicity until the whole neighborhood is signed up. Lynette Duncan will be promoting it for him when they return from their honeymoon."

"Poor girl! She should have stayed single!"

When Qwilleran drove into his own driveway, his neighbor rushed out of Unit Three, waving an envelope. Qwilleran lowered the car window.

"This letter belongs to you," Wetherby said. "It was in my mailbox. I just picked up my Saturday delivery. Sorry it's a day late."

"Thanks. No problem." It was a manila envelope from Hasselrich, Bennett & Barter, often bad news and always a nuisance. "Would you like to come in for a drink — and a long talk about precipitation and warm fronts?"

"I'll take the drink. Wait till I feed the cat."

When Wetherby arrived and was pulling off his boots, Qwilleran asked, "Bourbon?" They filed into the kitchen: host, guest, male cat, female cat — in that order.

"Do you like these closet doors?" Wetherby asked, indicating the lightweight louvered bifolds. A wall of them covered the broom closet, laundry alcove, and pantry. "Jet-boy opens them with his nose. He's learned exactly where to push to make them buckle. When I come home, every door in the house is ajar."

"I think Don Exbridge got a special deal on bi-folds," Qwilleran said. "They're in every room and hall in the house!"

"Not only that, but they have springs that squawk like a strangled chicken, usually when Jet-boy is making his rounds at night."

"Let's not discuss this in front of the Siamese," Qwilleran said. "They'll get ideas."

They carried their drinks into the living room and discussed the latest news: After an all-night crisis meeting, the promoters of the Ice Festival were forced to cancel the event. It was a tortured decision, but snow was turning to water, and ice was turning to slush. Ice-fishing shanties were falling through into the lake. It meant disappointment for all, loss of business for many, and embarrassment for the community.

Qwilleran said, "The newspaper is committed to covering expenses, but I feel sorry for Hixie Rice. It was her brainchild. Still, she's indomitable. Even now she's probably devising a brilliant way to utilize fifteen thousand polar-bear buttons."

"Want to hear some really surprising news?" Wetherby said with enthusiasm. "The bridge club found out who sent the anonymous check to cover the two-thousand-dollar theft."

"Who?" Qwilleran asked, expecting it to be Willard Carmichael.

"A nice little lady who lives in the Village and doesn't even play bridge. She's from an old family and gives a lot to charity. Sarah Plensdorf."

"I know her! How did you find out?"

"That's the best part. Her accountant is Mac MacWhannell, who's a guest-member of the bridge club. In doing her tax return he found a two-thousand-dollar item paid to the bridge club. Mac said the item was actually a tax-deductible donation to the Youth Center."

"Good for Big Mac!" Qwilleran said. "May I

refresh your drink?"

When he returned, Yum Yum was sitting on the visitor's lap, doing her amorous act: purring, rubbing, and gazing soulfully into his eyes.

"Nice cat," Wetherby said. "Are you still getting postcards with cat names? I know a girl in Horseradish who calls her cats Allegro and Adagio. One's lively; the other's quiet. What are you going to do with the postcards?"

"I envision a large bonfire in the newspaper parking lot."

"Has anyone had a postcard from the honeymooners?"

"I don't know. Lynette called Polly last night and is eager to come home. She's going to work with Carter Lee, promoting restoration jobs around the county."

Wetherby said, "I hope, for her sake, his project is on the up-and-up."

"You have doubts?"

"I'm a professional doubter. Plenty of suckers in Pickax seem to have twenty thousand to gamble. I suppose that's not much if you consider the total value of the property in today's market, but what do they get for their investment?"

"Expert advice, supervision of the work, and access to the National Register."

Wetherby was on his way to a dinner party, and after he had left, Qwilleran pulled out the government print-out borrowed from Mitch Ogilvie. Unfolded and spread on the floor, it did indeed measure six yards. He read it all, frequently tapping his moustache and sometimes shooing Koko away.

Next he opened the manila envelope from the law office, saw the papers to be signed, grunted an objection, and tossed them into the Procrastination File. He was in no mood for tedious work. He fed the cats, made a sandwich for himself, and determined to spend the evening on his Melville project. It would take his mind off the can of worms that had been opened when Willard Carmichael came to town. Many peculiar things had happened since then. Tomorrow he would go to see Brodie and lay it all out: weird incidents, suspicious developments, hearsay, his own qualms, and even Koko's recent idiosyncrasies. Meanwhile, he would read.

Qwilleran was reading the Melville novels in chronological order, hoping to trace the author's development. First, there were the adventure tales, then a comic potboiler, then the advent of symbolism in *Moby-Dick*, then the creeping pessimism and cynicism. Koko was equally fascinated by the books; he knew a good binding when he smelled one! But the cat had his own ideas about the reading sequence. Qwilleran was ready to start volume seven, a story about a writer, titled *Pierre*; Koko wanted him to read volume ten, pushing it off the shelf with his nose. "Thanks, but no thanks," Qwilleran told him as he opened volume seven. The cat lashed his tail like a bad loser.

At eleven o'clock the Siamese had their bedtime treat. Then the three of them trooped to the balcony, and Qwilleran continued reading in his bedroom. It was about one-thirty when his phone rang — an ungodly hour for anyone to call in Moose County.

His apprehension turned to anger when he heard the voice that he loathed. "Qwill, this is Danielle. I just got a call from Carter Lee. He's terribly worried, and —"

"What's wrong?" Qwilleran interrupted gruffly as he felt the unwelcome sensation on his upper lip.

"It's about Lynette. She's real sick. He thought it was too late to call Polly, so —"

"How ill is she?" he demanded.

"She's in the hospital. He took her to Emergency."

"Which hospital? Do you know? There must be several."

"He didn't tell me. If he calls back —"

"Did he tell you the nature of the illness?"

"It's her stomach."

"Do you have a phone number for your cousin?"

"Well, he was calling from the hospital, and I guess he's still there. If he calls back —"

"How about the inn where they've been staying?" Qwilleran asked impatiently.

"He never told me the name of it."

"Great!" he said with edgy sarcasm. "Let me know if you hear anything further, at any hour of the day or night. And now hang up so I can do some investigating."

Qwilleran sat with his hand on the cradled receiver as he planned his next call. He would not disturb Polly; it would serve no purpose and would only keep her awake all night. He remembered Lynette's last phone call: the spicy food, the upset stomach, the remedy that Carter Lee had gone out to buy. Had it worsened her condition? Or did it make her feel good enough to go out and mingle with the mob and eat God-knows-what?

He thought of calling Dr. Diane, but first he phoned the night desk of the New Orleans newspaper and identified himself as a reporter for the *Milwaukee Journal*; it sounded more legitimate than the *Moose County Something*. He said his editor wanted him to track down an emergency case — a Milwaukee citizen attending Mardi Gras. He said he needed names and phone numbers of hospitals.

"On the fax?"

"No. I'll hold."

A minute later a night deskman was reading off the information.

"Thanks. Sorry to bother you," Qwilleran said. "My editor is a bleepin' tyrant."

"Aren't they all? How's the weather in Milwaukee?"

"Not as good as in New Orleans."

"Hope you find your case. The ER in every hospital's busy tonight."

Only then did Qwilleran call Dr. Diane — with

249

apologies — and tell her the story. He said, "If I call the hospital, they won't even talk to me. As the personal physician of a prominent Pickax citizen, you can ask the right questions. I have the phone numbers of all the medical facilities. Can you do it? Can you locate her and find out her condition?"

"Of course. I'll be glad to do it." Diane had the neighborliness of a Lanspeak. "It could be something routine, like an allergy. I'll call you when I have something definite."

Qwilleran stretched out on his bed and waited. He had lost interest in reading. He may have dozed, because he suddenly found himself catapulted out of bed by a roar and clatter overhead. Enormous hailstones were pounding the roof and bouncing off the deck. They bothered the Siamese, too, who complained until they were admitted to his own bedroom. They were quiet then, except for one violent outburst from Koko for no apparent reason.

It was four-thirty before the phone rang. Dr. Diane's voice was ominously solemn. "I found her, Qwill. She was in critical condition. I called the hospital several times, at intervals, and . . ."

"She's gone?" Qwilleran gasped.

"She died an hour ago."

"What was given as the cause?"

"Gastrointestinal complications, aggravated by alcohol abuse."

"No!" he said. It was impossible, he thought. She had hardly sipped her champagne at her

250

birthday party, and she never touched hard liquor. Had Carter Lee coaxed her to try a Sazerac or some other exotic drink? . . . Then he remembered Koko's anguished howling about an hour before.

"Qwill! Are you still there?"

"I'm here, Diane. I don't know what to say. How am I going to break the news to Polly?"

"Would you like me to do it?"

"Thanks, but I think I should handle it — but not until her normal wake-up hour. I'll go to her house and tell her in person . . . Yes, that's the best way. Diane, you have no idea how much we appreciate your cooperation."

"That's what I'm here for," she said.

After hanging up, he paced the floor and tried to sort out his reactions. He was shocked by the suddenness of it all . . . saddened by the loss of a young, productive, generous, well-loved daughter of Pickax . . . overcome with sympathy for Polly, who was losing her last link with "family" . . . and he was angry, too. It was not yet five o'clock, but he called Danielle's number. The line was busy. He continued pacing the floor, and Koko watched with the anxious look that can widen a cat's eyes. Who but Carter Lee could be calling her at this hour? After a few minutes he tried the number again and heard another busy signal. What could they be saying to each other that would take so long? Or did she have the phone off the hook? He went downstairs to start the coffeemaker and then called again.

When her number started ringing, he was in a mood to shout at her: Where's your cousin? Why is he so secretive about his whereabouts? Have you been talking to him? Your line's been busy for an hour! What have you been saying to each other, for God's sake?

When she answered in her ridiculous voice, he said calmly, "Danielle, I've just heard the terrible news. We've lost Lynette. Did Carter Lee call and tell you?"

"Yes, just now. How did you find out?"

"Our local doctor was in touch with the New Orleans hospital."

"Isn't it awful? My cousin's a basket case. I was trying to buck him up."

"I'd like to call him and express my sympathy. I'm sure any kind words will help at a time like this. Did you get his phone number at the inn?"

"He's checked out already! He's coming home. I told him to get here before the airport shuts down. He's flying in today. He said he'd leave as soon as he made all the arrangements."

"I'd be glad to meet the five o'clock shuttle —"

"He wants me to pick him up. There are some things he wants to tell me. Before she died, Lynette told him to carry on the work. He wants to make Pleasant Street kind of a memorial to her."

"Did he say anything about funeral arrangements? There's a beautiful place where four generations of Duncans have been laid to rest, and the last gravesite has been waiting for the last Duncan. Does he know about it?"

"I don't know," she said.

"Important funerals for important people are a Pickax tradition."

"He didn't say anything about that."

"I see. Well, call me if there's anything I can do."

"He told me to break the news to Polly, but I don't know how."

"That's all been taken care of," Qwilleran said hastily and untruthfully. "You don't need to worry about it."

Fortified by this assortment of half-truths and white lies, Qwilleran squared his shoulders, planned his day, drank his coffee, fed the cats, brushed their fur, showered and shaved, and waited for seven o'clock.

At that hour he called the Riker residence, and Mildred said Arch was in the shower.

"Tell him to grab a towel and rush to the phone. This is important!"

Riker came on the line grumbling but curious.

Qwilleran said, "Save today's front page for a major newsbreak."

"It'd better be good," Arch said. "I'm standing here dripping."

"It's not good. It's bad. We've just heard from New Orleans. Lynette was rushed to the hospital last night, and she died this morning."

"What! What did you say? . . . What happened to her?"

"Gastrointestinal complications. Dr. Diane talked to the hospital down there."

"In other words, food poisoning," Riker said cynically. "They don't call it that in the City of Gastronomy. Do you have any details?"

"Only that she phoned Polly a couple of times and said the food was too rich and spicy for her."

"How can we reach Carter Lee?"

"He's flying back. Danielle will meet the five o'clock shuttle."

"I hope WPKX doesn't get wind of it. I'd like to have a clean newsbreak for once."

"Right! . . . Now go back to your shower, Arch. I hope you're not dripping on Mildred's new carpet."

That was easy. Breaking the news to Polly would be tough.

# 17

"Okay if I come over for a few minutes?" Qwilleran asked Polly on the phone. "I have something to discuss."

"Would you like breakfast?" she offered. "The library's closed today. I have time."

"No, thanks. I have a column to finish."

On the way there he considered his approach: how to lead up to the bad news in some non-frightening way.

She met him at the door, looking keenly interested but not anxious.

"Let's sit on the sofa," he said. "I have a confession to make." They went into the living room, and he took her hand fondly. "I've been guilty of trying to save you from worry and loss of sleep, and in doing so, I've not kept you fully informed."

"Is that such a transgression?" she asked lightly.

"Well . . . maybe. When Lynette called Saturday night, she complained of a stomach upset. It was worse than she thought. Carter Lee had to take her to the hospital."

"Oh dear!" she said in alarm. "How did you find out?"

"He called Danielle and asked her to notify us. It was after one A.M., too late to bother you, so I called Dr. Diane and enlisted her help. She called the hospital and found Lynette in critical condition with gastrointestinal complications. Diane kept calling for updates during the night, and the last time she was given the bad news."

"Oh, Qwill! What are you telling me?" Polly cried with her hands to her cheeks.

"She died about three-thirty this morning."

Polly groaned. "She was only forty! She was healthy! Is there something else they're not telling us?"

"I don't know." He had no intention of mentioning alcohol abuse now; that would come later. "You can lose your mind trying to figure it out," he said gently, hoping to steer her away from his own growing suspicions. "Just remember how happy she was in her last few weeks, and what a kind, helpful person she's been all her life."

"You're right," Polly said, taking a deep breath. "After her shattering disappointment twenty years ago, she never wallowed in self-pity but went on doing things for others and enjoying life, but . . ." Her voice wavered. "I can't talk about it now, Qwill. I need to be left alone for a while."

There was a call on his answering machine when he returned. He phoned Dr. Diane at her office.

"I had a suspicion about something," she said, "so I came to the office early to pull Lynette's file. She had signed a living will, bequeathing her eyes and body tissues for transplantation. I called the hospital, and they'd not been advised that she was an organ donor. The body had been released to a mortuary as authorized by the next of kin. I called the mortuary. It was too late even for an autopsy. They said the next of kin had signed for cremation!"

Qwilleran said, "That's not what Lynette wanted at all! Even I know that she wanted to be buried at Hilltop in the Duncan plot — with a full funeral, like her brother's."

"Apparently her husband wasn't aware of any of this," Diane said.

He thought, It's not usually discussed on honeymoons. What he said was: "Diane, I've broken the news to Polly, and she asked to be left alone for a while, but this new development is something that I think you should discuss with her."

"I'll be glad to," she said. "I don't know exactly how or when, but I'll work something out. My parents will be devastated when they hear about this."

"A lot of people will be."

"Where is her husband? I wonder."

"Flying home today. I plan to call him this evening. Perhaps I can get his explanation. Meanwhile, there'll be a front-page story in today's paper."

Qwilleran needed sleep. Two or three hours would tide him over, with his answering machine fielding calls. By ten-thirty he was awake and ready to go. He had a column to write, but the topic he had planned seemed inappropriate. It was to be a dissertation on breakfast cereal, pro and con, yesterday and today, hot and cold, with and without raisins. He phoned Polly.

"How are you feeling?" he asked kindly.

She replied wearily, like one who has survived a crying jag. "I feel more in control now. Is there something I should be doing? I'm no longer next of kin, am I? Diane phoned me. None of Lynette's last wishes have been respected. Perhaps he didn't know."

"There is something you could do, Polly, that would be very useful. Help me write a column about the Lynette that everyone remembers: dancing the Highland fling, visiting patients at the hospital, winning bridge tournaments, hostessing at the church bazaar, making her winter pilgrimage to Hilltop, tracing her ancestors back to the eleventh century."

"I could do that," she said. "I'd have to think about it, though."

"Think fast. I'm on deadline. I'll be over with my tape recorder at one o'clock."

He knew it would do her good to participate in something constructive. For him it was an easy way to grind out a column in a hurry. As it evolved, her reminiscences were so interesting, and Polly was so well-spoken, that he had nothing to do but transcribe them on his typewriter. All interviews, he thought, should be such a cinch!

While he was transcribing, there was action on

258

the hutch cabinet, Yum Yum scratching at the toy drawer, Koko pawing the other. It was the first time he had taken an interest in that particular part of the cabinet, and Qwilleran felt a twinge on his upper lip that led him to investigate. The Procrastination File contained all kinds of clutter, but on top of the pile was the manila envelope from the attorneys. Taking time out from his typing to examine the contents, he found what he expected: papers to be signed and mailed in the enclosed envelope. Bart always made it easy for him, but it could be done later, and he tossed everything back into the drawer.

"Yow-ow-ow!" came a scolding command from Koko, who was sitting on the cabinet and punishing it with his tail. It signified urgency.

Qwilleran was prompted to take a closer look at the documents and Bart's hand-scribbled instructions.

Qwill — Don't neglect to initial paragraphs G, K, and M. Mail soon as possible . . . Leaving for St. Paul while airport still open. Back Wednesday to discuss CLJ's credentials. K Fund investigators find no connection whatever with preservation/restoration field . . . May have to swim home. — Bart

Qwilleran phoned the Pickax police station and asked the chief, "When do you quit today?"

"Four o'clock."

"Don't leave! I'll be there. It's important."

259

When Qwilleran went to the newspaper office to hand in his copy, he picked up the Monday edition with the front page news story, illustrated with file photos.

The young managing editor was gloating. "For once we broke the news before WPKX. I don't know how we kept it from leaking."

"My column's a follow-up," Qwilleran said. "Polly gets all the credit." He took a few extra copies of the Monday paper for her. It was the lead story:

LAST DUNCAN DIES AT 40

Lynette Duncan of Pickax, the county's last Duncan-by-blood, died this morning at the age of 40, less than a week after her marriage to Carter Lee James. The couple were honeymooning in New Orleans when she succumbed to "gastrointestinal complications," according to the death certificate. She is survived by her husband, who was at her bedside in her last hours, and by her sister-in-law, Polly Duncan, widow of William Wallace Duncan.

Following Scottish custom, Ms. Duncan retained her maiden name when she married out of her clan. She was intensely proud of her heritage, representing the fourth generation of a family who migrated to Moose County in the 1850s and prospered as merchants. Their gravesites in the Hilltop Cemetery adjoin the meditation garden originated by the Duncan family as a place of solace for all mourners of the community.

After being graduated from Pickax High School, Ms. Duncan attended the Lockmaster Business Academy and embarked on a career in accounting. For the last five years she has been employed by the Goodwinter Medical Clinic, handling patients' health insurance claims.

Upon the death of her brother, Cameron, a year ago, she inherited the Duncan homestead on Pleasant Street and was the first homeowner to enlist in the Pleasant Street restoration project.

Community service was a way of life for Ms. Duncan, who was honored last year after serving a total of ten thousand hours of volunteer work at the hospital, public library, historical museum, and other facilities. She was an active member of the Old Stone Church.

"She was a selfless, compassionate woman," said the Rev. Wesley Forbush, "always willing to help, and never stinting of her time."

Mayor Gregory Blythe said, "She was a role model for the community and will be missed even by those who never met her."

At the time of her death Ms. Duncan was president of the Pickax Bridge Club, which she helped to found, and treasurer of the Moose County Genealogy Society.

Funeral arrangements have not been announced.

As Qwilleran finished reading the news account, two thoughts occurred to him: Lynette would be appalled to have her age printed in the headline . . . and Mayor Blythe was one of the few persons she totally disliked. Then he wondered: How will Ernie Kemple's daughter react when she finds Carter Lee is back in the running as a bachelor? Will she still come forward in Lenny Inchpot's defense? Is it too late *not to come forward?* She has confessed her complicity to her mother, but she cannot have confessed to G. Allen Barter; he left for St. Paul Friday. There was still time to retract her confession; she could tell her mother she lied in an insane fit of revenge . . . All of this was brainstorming on Qwilleran's part. *To be continued,* he told himself, as he sloshed through the puddles to city hall.

Brodie was waiting for him, with the *Moose County Something* on his desk. "Terrible news!" he said, tapping the front page. In the Pickax hierarchy, the Brodies had always been respecters of the Duncans, and he had piped at Lynette's wedding. "How must her new husband feel?"

"We'll soon find out," Qwilleran said. "He'll be here when the shuttle splashes down at five o'clock."

"I'll pipe at the funeral if he wants me to. I piped for Cameron's funeral. More than fifty cars went to the cemetery. Is the body being shipped in today? The airport's closing down."

"Her husband opted for cremation."

"What! Did I hear you right? When Cameron died, Lynette told me there was one more gravesite waiting for her. She said she'd be proud to join her ancestors on the hill. She was sentimental where her clan was concerned . . . Nice lady!"

"She can still have her funeral," Qwilleran said, "starting with a memorial service at the church, a procession of cars to the cemetery, and interment of her ashes on the hill with the traditional ceremony." He could tell by the chief's silence that he was not quite sold on the idea.

Finally Brodie said, "You must know the James fellow pretty well; you were his best man. Why wouldn't he comply with her wishes?"

"Do you think it's something that's discussed in the first week of marriage?" So far, Qwilleran had been going with the flow; now he changed course. "I don't know Carter Lee James at all! I was pressed into service at Lynette's request. Willard Carmichael first invited him up here for the holidays because his wife was homesick; they claimed to be cousins. The three of them met Lynette at the bridge club, and she invited them to see her house. That was the beginning of the Pleasant Street project, as it's called."

"I've heard about it," Brodie said, "but there hasn't been anything in the paper."

"It's been growing by word of mouth, which Carter Lee says is the healthy way to go. Property-owners pay him twenty thousand up front for consulting services, supervision of the actual work, and the possibility of being nominated for the National Register of Historic Places. Everyone who signs up is enthusiastic — and those who don't are virtually blackballed by their neighbors. The guy has a winning personality and a manner that inspires confidence."

The chief nodded. "I talked to him at the wedding. Seemed like a decent fellow."

"I even suggested that the K Fund hire him to restore the hotel and the Limburger mansion . . . and that's when the wings fell off! They checked his credentials and came up with *zilch*. Yet he claims to have restored important landmarks all over the eastern seaboard. I've seen the portfolio he shows to prospective clients, and I doubt whether it's legitimate. I also know the procedures for getting on the National Register, and no restoration consultant can guarantee his clients anything. He can only raise their hopes."

Brodie's scowl intensified as he listened. "Sounds like a scam, all right. The prosecutor should get in on this."

"Not too fast, Andy. On Wednesday, Bart Barter comes home and can tell us more about the K Fund's investigation. And tomorrow afternoon I want to set a little trap for Carter Lee, just to see how he reacts. I'll get back to you with the results — tomorrow about this same time."

"Good luck," Brodie growled without enthusiasm. Then he allowed himself a chuckle. "What does your smart cat think about this guy?"

"Well, Koko got hold of his fur hat once and was trying to kill it, if that means anything. To a cat, it's always open season on fur and feathers."

After his conference with Brodie, he waited until a suitable hour before phoning the Carmichael apartment. Danielle answered, saying that her cousin had arrived but was a wreck; he'd been without sleep for almost forty-eight hours; he was now sleeping and couldn't be disturbed.

"That's all right," Qwilleran said. "I wanted only to express my sympathy and invite the two of you for a business discussion tomorrow — and some refreshment. He might find it heartening to hear about two major restoration projects that could use his expertise. Do you think he's willing to take on something big — at a time like this?"

"He is! I know he is! What time tomorrow?"

"How about two-thirty? I'm in the last unit in Building Five. He's been here before . . . And what do you both like to drink?"

"Margaritas," she said promptly.

After that masquerade of goodwill and hospitality, Qwilleran planned — with an element of elation — how to snare his prey. For bait he would use a few drinks, a lot of sympathy, and a spurious business deal. Then he would spring the trap! There was a possibility that Carter Lee would be smooth enough, slick enough, to elude it. Although he had told the theatre club he had no acting ability, he was — in Qwilleran's book

— the Olivier, the Gielgud, the Alec Guiness of the confidence game.

It might or might not be a coincidence that volume ten on the Melville shelf — the one that riveted Koko's attention — was *The Confidence-Man.* The cat was also greatly attracted to A. Nutt's scholarly disquisition on the Ossian *hoax!* Qwilleran realized now that he should have taken the cat's eccentricities more seriously.

His immediate task was to prepare the trap. His idea, not yet fully developed, was to tell his listeners about *Short and Tall Tales* and play "The Dank Hollow" for them. After that, he would play a tall tale of his own — about a scam that victimized Pickax a hundred years ago. It would be so transparently analogous to the Pleasant Street project that the listeners would be uneasy. At least, he supposed, Danielle would be uneasy, even if her "cousin" kept his cool. Now, all Qwilleran had to do was to compose this tricky, sticky bit of fiction.

When he sat down at his typewriter, however, the events of the last twenty-four hours crowded his mind. To clear it he needed a drastic change of thought. What would it be? He looked at Koko; the cat looked at him. Opera, the man thought.

"Yow!" said Koko.

*Adriana Lecouvreur*, the man thought.

"Yow!" said Koko.

It was the compact disc album that Polly had given him for Christmas; he had never played it.

Somewhat guiltily, he slipped the first disc into the player and stretched out in his lounge chair, with his crossed legs on an ottoman and a mug of coffee in his hand.

The first act was a bustling scene backstage at the Comedie Français, with theatre personnel and their visitors fretting, plotting, and flirting. Koko sat nearby, comfortable on his brisket, but Yum Yum had disappeared. No opera-lover, she!

The music was lush; the voices were stirring. In the story, taking place in 1730, a glamorous actress and a spiteful princess were rivals for the love of a nobleman. It was a tale of intrigue, passion, deceit, and revenge. It involved a pawned necklace, a bunch of violets, a lost bracelet. Koko fidgeted from time to time. Qwilleran was following the libretto in English, but the cat was hearing it in Italian. As if he knew what it was all about, he made sounds of disapproval as the tension mounted. In the last act, as Adriana was dying in the arms of her lover, Koko howled as if his body would turn inside out.

"You spoiled the finale," Qwilleran chided him afterward, as Yum Yum crawled out from her secret hiding place.

Yet, it was not an ordinary yowl; it was a hollow, tortured wail! Qwilleran replayed the fourth act, jumping tracks to the death scene: Adriana receiving the box of dead violets, thinking them a cruel message from a lost lover, burying her face sorrowfully in the wilted flowers, not knowing they came from the princess, not knowing they were poisoned. Koko howled again. He had made the same anguished response to "The Dimsdale Jinx" when the pasties were mentioned — the poisoned pasties.

# 18

After hearing Koko's response to the opera, Qwilleran sat down at his typewriter with grim purpose. Gone was his prankish cat-and-mouse approach to setting a trap for a con man. This was a different ballgame, he told himself; no more softball; now it was hardball! Koko's reaction to the poisoned violets confirmed a cynical journalist's suspicions. It also explained the increasing disturbance on his upper lip.

In the coffee houses the local jokers liked to say, "If you want to murder your wife, do it Down Below, and you can get away with it." With hindsight, Qwilleran now found recent events painfully obvious: the hurried wedding; the transfer of property to joint ownership; the swift cremation without autopsy; the secrecy about Carter Lee's whereabouts after the death, precluding interference from anyone in Pickax.

Yet was there any actual proof that he had poisoned her? The howling of a cat — hundreds of miles away — at the moment of death was hardly admissible evidence or even grounds for arrest. Koko's electrifying cry at the mention of poison was equally thin evidence. His supranormal powers of detection and communication were known to Qwilleran, but would

269

anyone else believe them?

Of one thing he was sure: At the slightest hint that their game was up, Carter Lee and his so-called cousin would disappear, taking their fake IDs and the money from twenty trusting property-owners and any amount of loot from the Duncan house.

Qwilleran called the police chief at home. "Andy, sorry to bother you. The case we discussed is more serious than I imagined. I'm going ahead with the entrapment, but I want you to stand by. Anything can happen!"

Then he sat down at his typewriter and pounded out two or three hundred words to implement his scheme. At one point the flash of headlights turning into the adjoining driveway prompted him to telephone Wetherby. Solemnly he said, "Joe, did you hear the news from New Orleans?"

"I did! I did! And I'm mad as hell! This should never have happened! I feel like kicking a door down!"

"Well, I'm going to kick that door down, and I need your help."

"What can I do?"

"Give me fifteen minutes more at my typewriter, then come over here."

Qwilleran finished writing his tall tale and had a bourbon ready for Wetherby when he arrived. "Sit down, Joe, and I'll explain." He waited until his guest had taken a sip. "Both you and I had suspicions about Carter Lee, of one kind or another, and I've been led to believe they weren't far off base. I intend to confront him in a devious way, just to see how he reacts."

"Where is he?"

"His intention was to return home before the airport shut down, and he's now at Danielle's apartment." Qwilleran described his scheme and ripped the tall tale out of the typewriter. "Read this."

Wetherby read it with astonishment. "Is any of this true?"

"Not a word."

"That last line is pretty strong stuff. How do you plan to present it?"

"It'll be on tape, like the other yarns I've collected, and I'd like it to be read by a voice other than my own."

"Want me to do it? Let me read it once aloud with a dead mike." When he reached the last line, Koko howled. "Was that applause or criticism?" Wetherby asked.

Qwilleran grabbed both cats. "We don't want any sound effects on the tape." He carried them upstairs and shut them in their apartment.

"Will they stay there? Jet-boy knows how to operate the door handles."

"So far, they haven't figured it out, but I'm keeping my fingers crossed."

After the recording was completed and played back, Wetherby said he wouldn't mind witnessing the confrontation. "I could hide in a closet."

"You wouldn't fit. They're hardly deep enough

for a coat hanger. Better to be concealed in the bedroom upstairs, with the door ajar. They'll be here at two-thirty."

"I'll be here at two. Shall I bring my handgun?"

"Whatever makes you comfortable . . . And one more favor, Joe. Do you happen to have any tequila?"

"No. Sorry. Only bourbon."

Late that evening WPKX broadcast a flash-flood warning. The dam on the Rocky Burn had been breached by rushing water and constant battering by tree trunks, boulders, and other debris, and the Rocky Burn was now pouring billions of gallons into the old riverbed, through No Man's Gully and into the Ittibittiwassee. The giant waterwheel at the Old Stone Mill, dry and weakened after years of disuse, had been wrecked and the timbers swept downstream.

Immediately Don Exbridge and his staff started phoning residents, assuring them there was no need for evacuation under present conditions, but the situation was being monitored by the Disaster Commission. The manager's office would be open all night to answer questions, and the clubhouse was available as a shelter for anyone desiring company in the emergency. In the event that evacuation became advisable, the siren at the gatehouse would sound and state troopers would be on hand.

Qwilleran phoned Polly. She and the Cavendish sisters planned to sit up together. "Interesting women," she said. "They're natives of Moose County, but their teaching careers have taken them all over the country. What do you think of Don's handling of the emergency?"

"He does that better than he builds condos," Qwilleran said. He himself retired to his bedroom but slept half-dressed. His valuables and basic clothing were in his luggage near the front door, along with the cats' carrier and their essentials. In the emergency he left the doors open to both balcony rooms, and sometime during the night two furry bodies climbed into his bed and were not discovered until morning.

It was the roar of the water that caused him to wake. The river was turbulent but not dangerously high — as yet. Now and then a tree sailed past like a galleon with sails furled. Over his morning coffee, Qwilleran recalled how convincingly Carter Lee had postponed publicity on his endeavors and how artfully he had introduced their post-honeymoon plans. They would sit for their portraits, work together on restoration projects, visit his mother in France, buy a summer place on Purple Point . . . and Lynette innocently anticipated all of it.

The first mission of the day was to find ingredients for margaritas. In his lean years, Qwilleran had moonlighted as a bartender; in this, the affluent period of his life, he took pride in his well-stocked bar and ability to mix a variety of drinks. He was not prepared, however, for margaritas. He had only salt for the rim of the glasses.

Using the phone he confirmed his fear that the liquor store in Pickax was closed, along with every other establishment. The clubhouse bar was locked because the barkeeper was marooned by the Rocky Burn deluge. When Qwilleran called Hixie Rice, she referred him to Susan Exbridge, who referred him to her ex-husband. From Don Exbridge he learned the surprising information that the Cavendish sisters had lived in southern California and had brought home a fondness for margaritas. When Qwilleran rang their doorbell, he was greeted as a hero and supplied with everything he needed for the drinks.

Wetherby Goode arrived at the promised time and was sequestered in the bedroom, with the door ajar. "Try not to sneeze," Qwilleran told him. The Siamese, glutted with a substantial meal that would slow them down, were shut up in their own apartment with the television turned on, minus audio.

Shortly after two-thirty, the Land Rover pulled up in front of the condo, and Qwilleran greeted his guests with the right mix of solemnity and hospitality. Carter Lee was subdued, but Danielle was her usual giddy self.

"Ooh! Look!" she said, pointing at the display of weaponry on the foyer wall. Her cousin turned away in a silent rebuke.

The cordial host took advantage of the situation. Craftily he said, "Those are Scottish dirks from Gil MacMurchie's collection. He had five, but the best one was stolen during that epidemic of thievery a few weeks ago." He unhooked one from the frame and continued his lecture while ushering them into the living room. "The dirk is longer than a dagger and shorter than a sword — a very useful weapon, I'm sure. It's interesting to know that the grooves in the blade are called blood grooves. This hilt has a thistle design, which is an emblem of Scotland, but the most desirable is a lion rampant." He placed it on the coffee table in its scabbard, hoping that its presence would arouse their guilt. Then, having chafed the subject long enough, he asked, "May I offer you a margarita? I've been told I make a good one."

Both faces brightened. They were sitting on the sofa, facing the windows, and Qwilleran would be able to study their countenances. He wondered if Wetherby Goode was enjoying his performance. He proposed a toast to Lynette's memory, causing the bereaved husband to nod and look down woefully. Danielle pouted and studied the salt on the rim of her glass.

"You're wise to come home and plunge into your commitments," Qwilleran said in his avuncular style. "Work is said to be a great healer."

"It's painful but therapeutic in the long run," Carter Lee agreed. "I know Lynette would want me to carry on. I have dreams of making Pleasant Street a memorial to her, perhaps calling the neighborhood the Duncan Historical Park."

"A beautiful gesture," Qwilleran murmured, feeling hypocritical. He knew that neighboring property-owners, though outwardly friendly, would resent such a designation. "I hope you're aware," he continued, "that this county has enough historic property to keep you busy for a lifetime. There are two projects in which I have a personal interest. A great deal of money is being budgeted for their restoration. First is the historic Pickax Hotel downtown, boarded up since an explosion last year."

"I've seen it," Carter Lee said. "What are the interior spaces?"

"Twenty guestrooms and many public areas, including a ballroom. The other project is the Limburger mansion in Black Creek, slated to operate as a country inn . . . May I freshen your drinks?"

So far, so good, Qwilleran thought as he mixed two more margaritas. The guests were relaxing. They talked easily about the flooding, and Danielle's role in the play, and the future of the gourmet club. They listened receptively to the plans for *Short and Tall Tales* and said, yes, they would like to hear one.

"I like ghost stories," said Danielle, wriggling in anticipation.

They listened to "The Dank Hollow" and called it sensational. As Qwilleran served another round of drinks, he said, "And now I'm going to play one that no one else has heard. It hasn't even a name as yet. I want your opinion."

A hundred years ago, when Moose County was booming and ten mines were in operation, the wealthy mine-owners built mansions in Pickax and lived in grand style on Goodwinter Boulevard. But they had an annoying problem. Their houses were haunted by the restless spirits of dead miners, buried in cave-ins or killed in underground explosions. Ghostly noises kept the families awake at night and terrified the children. A newspaper Down Below went so far as to send a reporter to Pickax by stagecoach; after investigating, he wrote about the moaning and coughing and constant chip-chip-chipping of invisible pickaxes.

Shortly after the story was published, a man by the name of Charles Louis Jones drove into Pickax in a covered wagon, accompanied by a pretty young woman in a sunbonnet, his sister Dora. He said he possessed the gift of conjury and could rid the neighborhood of ghosts. He said he had worked the miracle for many communities Down Below. There was a sizable fee, but the harassed mine-owners were willing to give him anything. To do the job he asked for a pickax, a miner's hat, and several burlap bags filled with sand.

The contracts were signed, and he and his sister went to work — at night, after the families had retired. She carried the pickax and chanted spells, while her brother wore the miner's hat and scattered sand in attics and cellars. After two weeks, clients reported the condition somewhat relieved and signed new contracts at a higher rate.

All the while, the two strangers were treated royally, being a friendly and attractive pair. Charles Louis was particularly charming. No one wanted to see them leave, least of all Lucy Honeycutt. Her father owned Honey Hill mine. Though not the prettiest girl on the boulevard, she had the largest dowry. When Charles Louis asked for her hand in marriage, Mr. Honeycutt was flattered and Lucy was thrilled. With her handsome and gifted husband she would travel far and wide, helping other distressed communities. Dora would teach her the conjuring chants. So the marriage took place — rather hurriedly, the gossips said.

As the tape unreeled in the silent room, with only the sound of the rushing river to distract, Qwilleran observed the visitors. Danielle was enjoying it; her cousin was listening more critically. At the mention of Charles Louis Jones, his eyelids flickered. As the story went on — Lucy's dowry, the gifted husband, the hasty marriage — he uncrossed his knees, set down his glass, glanced at Danielle. He was gradually getting the point, Qwilleran thought. There was more to the tale:

After the wedding the nightly sand rituals

continued; so did the partying and the payments, although there was grumbling about diminishing results. Then, one night, after eating a mullet stew prepared by her sister-in-law, Lucy became ill. The same night, Charles Louis and Dora disappeared in the covered wagon, along with Lucy's dowry and certain silverplate and jewelry from the haunted houses, probably in the burlap bags.

It would be easy to chuckle about this tale of haunted houses, gullible countryfolk, a glib con man, a woman posing as his sister, and a clever swindle — if it were not for the tragic ending. Lucy died, and the cause of death, according to the post mortem, was not mullet stew but arsenic.

Carter Lee's jaw clenched and he stared wordlessly at Qwilleran, who said amiably, "Did you enjoy that? Would you like to hear it again?"

The man on the sofa turned to his companion and thundered, "Go to the car!"

"Why?" she whined, pouting at her unfinished drink.

*"Go and get in the car! Do as I say!"*

Reluctantly she went to the foyer to put on her boots.

*"Forget the boots! Get out of here!"* Then, as the door slammed, he said to Qwilleran, "Very funny! What kind of game are you playing?"

There was a click overhead as the levered door handle of the cats' apartment unlatched. The other door squeaked.

"An old Moose County game known as 'Call the Prosecutor.' "

With one swift movement Carter Lee was on his feet and reaching for the dirk.

Qwilleran jumped out of his chair. "Hold it! There's a witness up there!" He pointed to the balcony. Koko was teetering on the railing. Wetherby was coming out of the bedroom.

In the split second that Carter Lee hesitated, a flying object dropped down on him like an eagle on a rabbit. He screamed as claws gripped his head. Half blinded by trickles of blood, he staggered toward the foyer, falling over furniture, groping for the front door, with Koko still riding on his head and howling. Qwilleran was yelling at him to get down; Yum Yum was shrieking in alarm; Wetherby was bellowing as he pounded down the stairs. It was one minute of chaos until Koko swooped to the floor and Carter Lee made it out the front door.

"Let's follow him!" Qwilleran shouted.

"We'll take my van! It's in the drive!"

They grabbed their jackets and left Koko licking his claws.

The Land Rover splashed down River Lane and turned left to the gatehouse, then left again on Ittibittiwassee with Wetherby's vehicle not far behind.

"Where do they think they're going?" Qwilleran said as he reached for the car phone.

"She's driving. Look at that van weaving!"

On the phone he said, "Qwilleran reporting. Suspected murderer and accomplice headed west on Ittibittiwassee in white and red Land Rover. Male suspect has head injuries. Female driving erratically. Now three miles east of bridge. This report from pursuit car. Over."

The reply was inaudible as their tires whined through floods. Plumes of spray from the car ahead hit their windshield, and the wipers worked frantically to maintain visibility.

Qwilleran shouted above the racket, "If they get across the bridge, they'll run right into the police!"

"I'm gonna hang back a bit, Qwill. This is suicide!"

They covered the next two miles without talking. Then Qwilleran shouted, "It worked! The trick worked!"

"I heard every word."

"Let's hear it for Koko!"

"The bridge is around the next curve," Wetherby said.

"Stop on the hill."

On the crest they pulled over and parked on a muddy shoulder. From there they could see the fugitive vehicle approaching a bridge submerged except for the guard rails. The river was churning and roaring.

"They'll never make it."

"They're gonna try."

As they watched, a surge came downstream — a huge wave bringing tree trunks, a chunk of concrete from a culvert, and timbers from the shattered millwheel. It was the kind of debris that would collect at a crook in the river, then suddenly let loose. The surge hit the bridge like a battering ram as the Land Rover put on speed.

"Stupid!" Wetherby yelled.

The bridge-bed cracked and heaved and pitched the white and red van over the guard rail to be swept along in the turbulent water until it snagged on the branches of a fallen oak. There it hung, trapped between the crotch of the ancient tree and an enormous boulder.

"Can you see them, Joe?"

"No sign of life. I hope their seatbelts were fastened."

The flashing lights of police vehicles came into view across the river, and the far-off sirens of rescue equipment wailed above the crashing tumult. Qwilleran called his newspaper to send a reporter and photographer. Wetherby said it would take a crane to release the trapped van, but the rescue squad could probably reach the passengers with a cherry picker.

Qwilleran said, "Let's go home and see if the surge is doing any damage."

"Yeah . . . and I could use one of those margaritas."

The water was running high past the condos, but there was still no threat to the buildings.

While Wetherby mixed himself a drink, Qwilleran checked in with Polly.

"Qwill! Where have you been?" she asked anxiously. "I've been trying to reach you!"

"I had to go out for a while."

"They just announced that a surge coming downstream from the Rocky Burn was diverted by a cave-in at the Buckshot mine, at least temporarily. That's why we're not flooding."

"Stay tuned," he said. "You may hear some more surprising news."

Wetherby called to him, "Shall I pour you a Squunk water?"

"No, I need something stronger," Qwilleran said. "Open a ginger ale."

## 19

Moose County's last square inch of snow melted at 2:07 P.M. on February 15, an all-time record. The rain stopped falling; the flood waters receded; and soon the farmers would be worrying about a summer drought. On the air the weatherman said, *"Come, gentle spring! ethereal mildness, come!"*

"Lynette would have loved that quotation," Polly said to Qwilleran.

"It sounds familiar. Who wrote it?"

"Coleridge . . . I believe."

Since meeting Wetherby Goode, he had stopped making needling remarks about his literary allusions. The two men now shared a secret. They had agreed not to reveal their role in the entrapment and flight of Carter Lee James. When Brodie questioned him, Qwilleran shrugged it off. "I simply confronted Carter Lee with what I thought was the truth; he threatened me; and Koko chased him out of the house."

Miraculously the fugitives had survived the rough tumble in the raging river but were still hospitalized under police arrest. The man would be charged with murder and twenty counts of fraud; the woman, an admitted kleptomaniac, would turn state's witness against him in exchange for immunity. On the gossip circuit the locals were saying:

"That ain't his real name. Down Below they fake driver's licenses, credit cards, Social Security numbers — everything."

"He looked like such a gentleman! All those monogrammed shirts! I can't believe he'd commit murder!"

"Everybody said she shouldn't have married outside her clan and not so fast. She hardly knew him!"

"Well, she was forty. She didn't have time to waste."

"CLJ must be his real initials, or he'd have to buy a new bunch of shirts every time he changed his ID. That'd cost!"

One evening Qwilleran and Polly met for their weekly dinner of flattened chicken breast. This time the recipe called for shallots, lemon zest, chopped spinach, and blue cheese.

"Hail, noble Brutus!" he said when the erstwhile Bootsie met him at the door. The cat paraded back and forth with tail erect to demonstrate his nobility.

Polly said, "He can hardly wait to meet his little companion. Her name is Catta. She can't leave her mother for another two weeks . . . Qwill, whatever happened to all the cat names your readers were sending you?"

"There were thousands of postcards, and I finally hired Wilfred Sugbury and his girl friend to tabulate them. They turned over to me pages and pages of listings, classified according to number of syllables. One-syllable names are in the minority. Apparently two syllables are more effective in getting a cat's attention."

"Will you write a column on the subject?"

"Or a scientific paper on Feline Nomenclature in Northern Climates. I just happen to have a few notes with me." He drew a folded paper from his pocket:

1. In Moose County, with its large population of barn cats as well as house pets, a large percentage are named after edibles: Pumpkin, Peaches, Sweet Potato, Butterscotch, Jelly Bean, Ginger, Huckleberry, Pepper, Marmalade, Licorice, Strudel, Popcorn, and so on.

2. Names are not always complimentary: Tom Trouble, Stinky, Lazy Bum, Hairball.

3. Cats named for famous personalities, real or fictional, are so named as a compliment to the namesake: Babe Ruth, Socrates, Walter Mitty, Queen Juliana, Maggie and Jiggs, Eleanor Roosevelt, George Washington.

4. Cats in the same family often have names that rhyme: Mingo and Bingo, Cuddles and Puddles, Noodle and Yankee Doodle.

Polly read the notes and asked him to talk on

the subject at the next meeting of the Friends of the Public Library. He said he would consider it.

After dinner he asked, "Do you know anything about the dirk that Lynette used to cut her wedding cake?"

"Yes, it was a gift from Danielle. It had the lion rampant of Scotland on the hilt."

"Well, I happen to know that the light-fingered Danielle stole it from the MacMurchie house when she and Carter Lee were doing their so-called appraisal of the premises. Gil was very much upset. It was the last gift he'd received from his late wife."

"That's terrible!" Polly said. "Lynette would have been mortified if she had known. The MacMurchies were such good neighbors. In a plumbing emergency she could call Gil and he'd rush over with a wrench."

They both fell into silence. Qwilleran was thinking: Did Danielle know she'd get her wedding present back again — after New Orleans? Was she a genuine neurotic with a compulsion to steal? Or was her pilfering intended to focus public attention on minor crimes while Carter Lee committed a major swindle? The latter would explain the "theft" of his own coat, which was not missing for long. As for the heist from the money jar, even a banker's wife could use a couple of thousand. But what did she do with the bag of old clothes from the church's donation box?

Polly broke the silence. "I never suspected either of them. Did you, Qwill?"

"Well . . ." He contemplated what to tell and what not to tell. "Carter Lee's talk about the official registration of historic buildings aroused my curiosity. How does it work? I found that it involves complicated nomination forms, technically and professionally correct, with photographs and documented information about the architecture, materials, workmanship, and history of the building — all of which had to be approved by the state before going to national headquarters. How could he guarantee his clients anything? Yet, twenty families were convinced, and I was only a doubting Thomas . . . When I discovered he was a fraud, it was too late."

Polly sighed deeply. "For Lynette's sake, I wish we could return the dirk to Gil MacMurchie. She would want it that way. You know, Qwill, I have a key to her house. She asked me to keep an eye on the property while they were honeymooning. Do you suppose . . . it would be all right if . . . I went over there and simply —"

"No, it would not be all right!" he interrupted sternly. "That would be stealing — inappropriate conduct for the administrator of the public library. However . . . if you went over there to check up . . . and discovered a leak . . . a mysterious puddle of water under the kitchen sink . . . you could call Gil, and he'd rush over there with his pipe wrench. It's not stealing if you take something that belongs to you."

Another evening, Qwilleran was at home, and his doorbell rang. On his doorstep was a man wearing a respiratory mask and holding a glass jar.

"What — what?" Qwilleran spluttered. From the neck down, the figure was recognizable as Wetherby Goode. "Come in, you screwball! Take that thing off your head! What's in that jar?"

"Horseradish from my great-uncle in Lockmaster. He grows his own and grates it himself. One whiff is enough to kill a rhinoceros."

"I'll take a chance," said Qwilleran, who was a horseradish addict. "How about a bourbon?"

Koko made an appearance, looking regal, and Yum Yum rippled into the room in the flirty way she had.

"Do they ever catch mice?" Wetherby asked.

"It's Yum Yum's secret dream, but Koko is more of a thinking cat. He specializes in thought transference. He's telling me he'd like to move back to the barn. Is this good weather going to hold?"

"Don't ask me about the weather. I'm only a meteorologist. Ask the fuzzy caterpillars."

Qwilleran said, "Polly tells me your listeners send you suggestions for your daily quotes."

"They sure do, and I appreciate it. Polly sends me weather quotes all the time — from Shakespeare and all those other old guys."

"She knows the Bard forward and backward," Qwilleran remarked casually, but he was taken aback. Why had she not told him? True, he concealed his investigations and Koko's collaborations, because she would discourage one and laugh at the other. It came as a surprise, however, that Polly would conceal anything from him.

The garrulous weatherman rambled on. "Fran Brodie is taking over the lead in *Hedda Gabler*, we're all glad to know. The bad news is that Danielle didn't pay her decorating bill before all this happened. Dr. Diane says the two fugitives wouldn't be alive if they hadn't drunk all those margaritas. They were so relaxed, they were like rubber . . . Have you been to Lois's since Lenny was cleared and got his job back?"

"I have! And she was so happy she was handing out free apple pie."

"Everyone in the bridge club thinks it was Danielle who framed Lenny. Did you know Willard very well? I've been wondering if he was in on the scam. He brought Carter Lee up here and was pushing his project."

"That's because his bank wanted to make restoration loans. It's my belief that he didn't know the score. He met Danielle in a nightclub and hadn't known her long before they married. I'd guess that she and Carter Lee had been longtime partners in the con game and everything else, and they thought a rich husband would be a big plus."

Wetherby was watching Koko slap the floor with his tail. "What's he doing?"

"Communicating," Qwilleran said. "I've been trying to read that tail for years!" Then he assumed a confidential tone. "Polly gave me a set of Melville novels for Christmas, and Koko has been obsessed with volume ten. If you want to see something weird, have a look at the title of volume ten."

Wetherby went to the hutch cabinet and looked at the Melville shelf. "It's *The Confidence-Man*! Are you kidding me?"

"Not at all."

"Is that a coincidence — or what?"

"Your guess is as good as mine, Joe."

After the weatherman had taken his gas mask and gone home, Qwilleran watched Koko lashing his tail — right, left, right, left. He was trying to convey something else; he had not told the whole story. More likely, Qwilleran had failed to read it.

"What's bothering you, old boy?" he asked.

Koko stopped the tail business and walked across the room with Siamese poise, stopping on the way to give Qwilleran a stare that could only be described as scornful. He walked to the spot where Yum Yum was sitting contentedly on her brisket and hit her on the head with his paw.

"Stop that!" Qwilleran shouted. "Stop tormenting her!"

Koko looked at him impudently and hit her again, adding a contemptuous "Yow-ow-ow" in Qwilleran's direction.

Qwilleran went immediately to the phone and called Andrew Brodie at home. He heard the passive hello of a televiewer who is watching a good show and resents being interrupted.

He asked, "What's on TV, Andy?"

"Look it up in the paper," Brodie barked.

"Don't go away, Andy. I have information. Remember when Willard Carmichael attended that banking seminar in Detroit? Carter Lee was down there at the same time, on business of his own." Qwilleran pounded his moustache with his fist. "His business, I say, was hiring a hit man to eliminate Willard!"

The successful prosecution of Carter Lee James would last all spring as preliminary arguments addressed change of venue, conflict of interest, selection of jurors, and TV cameras from Down Below. Newsmedia everywhere called it a bizarre case. Only Qwilleran knew how bizarre it really was, and he took pains to conceal Koko's input.

One sunny afternoon he was lounging in his big chair and fantasizing about the "smart cat" in the witness box, biting the defense attorney, yowling in spite of the judge's gavel, flying around the courtroom in a catfit, swinging from the chandelier.

As a matter of fact, both Siamese were busy being ordinary cats — Yum Yum lounging in the sun and Koko prowling, sniffing invisible spots, scratching an ear, grooming a shoulder blade. He was restless. He had lost interest in Herman Melville. He looked at everything and nothing, jerking his head without reason, racing madly, staring into space.

Qwilleran thought, Koko has more whiskers than the average cat and more senses than the average human, but basically he's just a cat. At that moment, Koko leaped four feet in the air, and Qwilleran looked up. He saw a tiny black speck darting around the room in wild swoops and circles.

"Mosca!" he shouted.